THE
EXPERIMENT

A NOVEL BY

HENRY DENKER

SIMON AND SCHUSTER · NEW YORK

Published by Simon and Schuster
A Gulf + Western Company
Rockefeller Center, 630 Fifth Avenue
New York, New York 10020

Manufactured in the United States of America

1 2 3 4 5 6 7 8 9 10

Library of Congress Cataloging in Publication Data

Denker, Henry.
 The experiment: a novel.

 I. Title.
PZ3.D4175Ex   [PS3507.E5475]   813'.5'4   75–45437
ISBN 0–671–22268–6

To Edith, my wife

ACKNOWLEDGMENTS

For the scientific and medical research that serves as a basis for this novel, the author wishes to express his deep appreciation to Professor Chester Southam, Division of Oncology, Jefferson Medical College, Philadelphia; Professor Herbert Buchsbaum, Director, Oncology Service, University of Iowa Hospitals; Dr. Peter Carmel, Department of Neurosurgery, Columbia Presbyterian Medical Center, New York City; and Drs. Lawrence Cone, Chief of Immunology and Infectious Diseases, Craig Fischer, Chief of Pathology, Dwight Oxley, Chief of Nuclear Medicine, and Peter Lake, Director of Education and Research of The Eisenhower Medical Center, Palm Desert, California.

TRASK INSTITUTE OF SCIENCE
TRASK PARK

Office of
OTIS CRUIKSHANK,
Director of Research

January 31, 1977

Edgar Woolsey, Director of Administration
Trask Institute of Science
Trask Park

Dear Edgar:

For painful reasons well known to you, and which do not bear repetition, I hereby tender my resignation as Director of Research, since I no longer feel worthy to serve in that post.

As to Dr. Robert Niles, I strongly urge you not to take any reprisals against him. He had no choice but to act as he did.

I envy him his sense of integrity.

I trust I have not brought such dishonor to Trask that my earlier contributions will be completely forgotten.

With deepest regrets, I remain,

Most sincerely,

OTIS CRUIKSHANK, PH.D.

ONE

September 23, 1976

As the plane circled to make its approach, Dr. Robert Niles could notice the changes that had taken place in the architectural landscape of this Midwestern city in the seven years he had been gone. Sunlight glinted off bright, new polished steel, aluminum and tinted glass. All cities looked the same now.

The No SMOKING sign lit up. The pilot had received permission to land. The jet engines took on new drive. The angle of descent became steeper. In a few moments the craft would be on the ground.

Robert Niles looked forward to it eagerly. Though it was Otis Cruikshank who had given him his first chance to become a research assistant, seeing the old man would be much more than a professional reunion. Cruikshank was the man who had insisted on renewing his term of employment after his first year, though others in the political hierarchy at Trask Institute had argued against it.

Despite them, Otis Cruikshank had maintained, "Research isn't a sprint. It's a marathon. The race isn't to the swift, but to the most persistent. That young man Niles is extremely persistent."

There had been some grumbling over Cruikshank's decision. Bob Niles had been aware of it. In any large research institution such as Trask, gossip, well intended or malicious, had a way of seeping down. He had been tempted to refuse the appointment even after Cruikshank had assured it for him.

"Robert, lad, you do not look a gift horse in the mouth," the lean Scots scientist had chided him. "Unless, of course, you're doing research on the dental difficulties of gift horses."

Then the old man had turned serious. "Continue on the job. And consider yourself lucky. You've learned two lessons for the price of one uncertainty. First, how easy it is to lose your job in the field of research, since you're always at the mercy of others. Second, that you'd be wise not to depend on research alone if you wish to pursue that fickle mistress with any peace of mind."

It was not apparent to Bob Niles that the old man had his larger plan in mind even then. He first revealed it three years later, when Bob had finally won his Doctor of Philosophy with a paper on the immunological possibilities of vaccines for the common cold. On that day, Otis Cruikshank had called him in and closed the door of his private office. Out of the lower desk drawer, Cruikshank took a bottle of twelve-year-old Scotch whiskey.

"Robert, to your future. Which is very bright now that you're leaving here."

The old man's words were calculated to startle him. They did. Cruikshank smiled as he announced, "Robert, you are going to medical school."

The old man waited for that to settle in before continuing. "I sent your curriculum vitae to an old friend of mine at Physicians and Surgeons in New York. Unless you disgrace yourself in your personal interview, you've been accepted on a partial scholarship. That means you'll have to hustle to earn your keep and the rest of your tuition. But you can do that, I'm sure. Working in some lab there. No matter. You are going to become a doctor of medicine."

It had been a simple declaration of fact.

"But I plan to continue in research," Bob had protested.

"It's because you do that you're going to become a physician as well," Cruikshank had insisted quietly.

"*You* never became one, and you're in charge of one of the largest research institutes in the country. Why, four years ago everyone was sure you were going to win a Nobel."

"I didn't receive it, though, did I?" Cruikshank asked.

"But what about my place here? I've worked hard to keep it. This is my home." He had almost added, "And you're my father."

"You have no choice, Robert," Cruikshank said flatly. "Your appointment here will not be renewed!"

Bob Niles was stunned. The old man put down his glass.

"You think I like to turn you out? I don't. But neither do I want you one day to find yourself in the position of so many researchers whose positions are terminated. At least as a physician you will have some independence. It sometimes takes a long time to make a discovery of any consequence.

"Many was the time before my first important discoveries when I wished that I had medical credentials to fall back on. So that if I were untimely terminated I could at least go into practice to support Ellen and the children."

Cruikshank took a moment to indulge in a soft personal aside.

"There were two children then. One a boy. He died at seventeen. Leukemia. That's what started me on the work I've done since.

"Well, what I couldn't have, you're going to have. Whether you like it or not. There is no appropriation in the budget here for your job. But there *is* room for you in New York."

Otis Cruikshank finally smiled. "I don't see that you have any choice, do you?"

That had been the end of the discussion. Though Bob

Niles had resented it at first, his years in New York had gone by swiftly enough. Now he was finally finished, free to return to his first love. He was flattered and delighted that Cruikshank had written saying he would meet him at the airport. It was a testimonial to his personal regard.

Many times during the seven years of school and internship and residency Bob had wanted to return to Trask for a visit. But with his time so limited and money so scarce, the three-thousand-mile round trip was not easy to manage.

Twice he had seen Otis Cruikshank in New York. Both times the professor came to attend research conferences. They had a brief dinner once and drinks the other time. The first time, Cruikshank had been honored by being asked to chair the meeting in his specialty. The second time, he read a new paper on work he'd just completed and that showed promising results. But aside from those two reunions, both shortened by Bob's tight schedule at the hospital, they had not seen each other.

The rasping of the plane's tires shook Bob Niles back to the realization that they were landing. In his eagerness, Bob Niles disobeyed all the stewardess' instructions. He unfastened his seat belt. He slid his bag out from under the seat, then stood up to take his coat from the overhead rack. Because of his penurious life as a student, aside from his books and a pair of skis, all his possessions of any consequence could be packed into one bag small enough to fit under the seat of a plane. His briefcase contained all the notes he'd made during his years away, concerning designs for experiments he planned to propose now that he was resuming research.

Today he would invite the old man and his wife, Ellen, to have dinner with him. Or perhaps they would invite him, though the old man had always preferred to keep his family apart from his professional life as much as possible. In the three years he had worked at Trask, Bob had been invited to the Cruikshank home only a dozen times. And even then, aside from acting as a gracious hostess, Ellen Cruikshank had not seemed much involved with the personnel at the Institute.

Cruikshank had once said, "I have to do enough politicking to get my budgets approved. I don't inflict that on Ellen. My house is my home. Ellen is my wife. I will not have her smiling at people we both dislike."

Bob Niles was at the hatch of the aircraft before the wheeled dragon of a gate lumbered out to make contact.

The stewardess smiled and said, "I hope she's here to meet you."

It didn't dawn on Bob till a moment too late that she attributed his eagerness to a girl. He bolted out of the aircraft and down the corridor to the main terminal. He could hear an insistent loudspeaker paging, "Dr. Robert Niles! Dr. Niles. Please report to the Information Desk."

Surprised for a moment, Bob suddenly feared that the professor might not have been able to meet him after all. Otis Cruikshank was no longer young. Illness might have kept him home. Bob spotted the INFORMATION sign and raced to it, colliding with several people on the way.

When he reached the counter, his fears were confirmed. Otis Cruikshank was not there. Bob pushed past a blond young woman to ask anxiously, "I'm Dr. Niles. You have a message for me?"

"*I* do," the blond girl said.

He turned to face her. She was slender, tall and attractive. Her blond hair fell to her shoulders. It was her blue eyes that gave her away. The same clear blue eyes that distinguished Otis Cruikshank.

"Harriet?" he asked, trying to remember. He hadn't seen Cruikshank's daughter in eight years. She had gone away to college before he left Trask.

"Close," she corrected a bit intolerantly. "Heather."

"Your dad? He's okay, isn't he?"

"Depends," Heather Cruikshank answered. "Healthwise,

15

as they say, he's fine. But professionally, he is right now playing host to an unexpected Site Committee. Hoping for a big grant if all turns out well."

"The battle goes on," Bob commented.

"That's why he couldn't meet you. So you'll have to be satisfied with me," she said, smiling. It emphasized her blue eyes and pretty face.

They were pulling out of the airport when he asked again, "He *is* okay, isn't he?"

"Why do you ask?" she countered without taking her eyes off the heavily trafficked road.

"I have a right to be concerned. He's done a great deal for me."

"I mean, why do you ask in that particular way? As if you knew that he hadn't been fine?"

"The last time we met in New York was two years ago. There were two other men with him, so I didn't ask. But he seemed especially tired," Bob said. "He *is* okay, isn't he?"

"Yes," Heather said, but it was clear that that was not the complete answer.

"But . . ." he prompted.

"You know Dad," she said. "He has a tendency to over-work. A compulsion."

"People say he wasn't that way before Duncan."

"Duncan." She picked up on it at once. "Did you know Duncan?"

"It all happened several years before my time here," Bob said. "But I've heard all about him. It must have been a terrible shock to lose a son of seventeen."

"For a father to bury his own son is the ultimate trag-edy," Heather said. "But with Duncan it was even worse. So handsome. And bright. Brilliant was the word most people used about him. I was only nine at the time and so in love with my own brother I used to daydream about marrying him. Duncan was all any father could have asked for. All his books since then are dedicated to Duncan."

16

"I've noticed."

"In times of stress some men take to drink. Others to different forms of self-pity. Dad took to his lab. He worked so hard trying to obliterate the fact of Duncan's death that he often was exhausted."

"I know. But two years ago he seemed more than just tired. There was something tense and different about him," Bob persisted. "Has something happened that I don't know about?"

"No, of course not," Heather replied quickly.

Too quickly, his trained medical mind observed.

She must have realized her slip, for she attempted to obscure it by explaining, "It's the administrative pressures. He often says it was a mistake to become Director of Research. He's still more at home in a lab than an office. He hates all the meetings. And especially today's chore, entertaining and showing off for a Site Committee."

"National Institutes of Health?"

"Worse. The Carter Foundation," Heather said.

"Oh." It was one of those monosyllabic comments that said a great deal.

Marietta Carter was the nation's single most powerful individual when it involved doling out private funds for research. Third wife and the widow of a wealthy inventor and manufacturer of farm machinery, she had succeeded to his huge fortune. Because Eamon Carter had not been distinguished for philanthropic enterprise during his lifetime, Marietta had determined to make his name famous after his death.

She was not a woman to hire others to administer her charity. She dominated it completely. She made site inspections in person. She passed judgment on the institutions, the men and women, the laboratories, the actual work in progress before she handed out money. But once she was satisfied, her grants exceeded all others in size. It simply took a great deal to satisfy her.

"She's coming to the house for tea," Heather said. "I'm supposed to get you there in time. But if this traffic gets any worse we won't make it."

She applied herself to deftly cutting into and out of the stream of cars. Despite the fact that she was an expert driver, some of her maneuvers made Bob nervous.

"You can stop braking. You're safe," she remarked tartly.

He leaned back and studied her face. She was a pretty girl. No, pretty was a belittling word. She had a strong face. Clean and classic features, which she inherited from her mother. The last time he'd actually seen her was eight years ago, just before she had gone off to college. She must be all of twenty-four or -five now. He found himself wondering what she did, whether she had any commitments.

His speculations were cut short when they reached the Interstate highway off which Trask Institute was located. It would be no more than ten minutes now.

Soon he could see the main buildings of the Park. Trask was one of the new research communities resembling a college campus. All the structures here were of concrete and glass, surrounded by green lawns and tree-shaded walks. On the periphery of the main group of research buildings were the private homes of the staff.

Set within this protected environment, Trask Institute was still only half an hour's run to three of the best metropolitan hospitals in the Midwest. Thus, Trask offered its researchers isolation to concentrate on pure scientific research, with ready access to the world of practical medicine when it was necessary to test out findings.

Otis Cruikshank had been instrumental in choosing this location and moving the Institute from the dingy old buildings it had occupied in what had become a slum area of the city. His reputation had attracted men of standing, and the buildings that Bob Niles could see now were the gradual accretion earned by Otis Cruikshank and his staff through their achievements.

18

Bob speculated that if things went well today, Marietta Carter might be induced to add yet another building to Trask Park, or at least some new and highly expensive piece of nuclear or electronic research equipment.

As they left the highway and climbed a circular road, centered on the street was an impressive house bordered by neatly trimmed hedges that gave way to a modest circular driveway. As Heather pulled in, she was confronted by a line of cars that barely left her room to park.

A huge royal blue Bentley stood by the door, a chauffeur at the wheel. There was no need to guess that this was Marietta Carter's limousine.

"Leave it to her to pretend modesty by owning a Bentley instead of a Rolls," Heather said.

"Then you've met her."

"Not yet. But I've heard enough about her," Heather said. Then she smiled. "Natural ambivalence, I suppose. We resent most those we depend on most. And Dad is surely depending on her now."

At the door they were challenged by an Institute security officer: "Admission is by written invitation only."

"I live here," Heather said, smiling.

"Miss Cruikshank. Of course. Sorry. Only the very top brass are allowed in there today," the guard explained.

"Well," Heather said to Bob, "let's go in and polish some brass. It'll do Dad a lot of good. And it won't do you any harm either."

He gripped her elbow and whispered, "Yes, let's go in. And you be nice to Marietta Carter."

Before she would budge, she turned and said curtly, "Why must the best scientific brains in the country sit up and beg like trained dogs before they can get enough money to carry on their work? I think you're a fool to come back into research!"

Briskly, she pulled her elbow free and preceded Bob Niles into the Cruikshank house.

19

TWO

The room seemed crowded, though there couldn't have been more than thirty people. Ellen Cruikshank had provided great quantities of coffee, tea and pastries. But it was obvious from the tenor of the voices that everyone was having cocktails instead. Why do people tend to talk more loudly while holding a highball glass than a teacup? Bob wondered.

Louder than all the rest, though by no means unpleasant, was the confident, clear voice of a woman who, Bob assumed, must be the famous Marietta. The name Carter had been noted for great wealth ever since Bob could remember, so he was surprised to see a woman who seemed barely forty-five. Her glistening brown hair was fashioned into a striking halo to frame a fine-looking if determined face. Yet she smiled with great warmth and radiance. Her bright brown eyes were sharp and discerning, so that she could talk with Edgar Woolsey, Director of Administration of Trask Institute, and at the same time appraise the rest of the guests without seeming either rude or overly inquisitive.

As Bob Niles and Heather stood in the archway, Cruikshank spied them.

"Robert!" the old man said affectionately. Cruikshank, lean and ruddy-faced, came toward them. He shook Bob's hand, at the same time throwing a welcoming arm across his shoulder. For a person who usually appeared so dour and reserved, Cruikshank was actually a man of deep affections and strong emotions. He led Bob Niles into the room, introducing him proudly to everyone, including those who already knew him. Finally, as if saving the best for last, he brought him to the small group that consisted of Marietta Carter, Edgar Woolsey and Carole Evans, Cruikshank's own assistant.

"Ah, the prodigal returns!" said Woolsey.

His role as the Administrator of an institution that was dependent on charitable grants made it necessary for him to be charming and to try to brighten any conversation in which he was involved. Woolsey listened attentively only to those who possessed great wealth.

He held out his hand to Bob, at the same time turning back to Marietta Carter. "One of our own, returned with his degree in Medicine. Mrs. Carter, I'd like you to meet Dr. Robert Niles."

She extended her hand to Bob, saying. "You're the victim of a very common mistake, Doctor. Everyone assumes that 'prodigal' means wandering. Actually it means wasteful. Which I'm sure you are not."

She smiled. Her brown eyes were mischievous, as if she enjoyed having a joke at Woolsey's expense. Closer to her now, Bob was impressed with her beauty. It was obvious why an old man like Carter would have fallen in love with such a pretty girl. It was equally obvious why a girl so ambitious would have married a man as old and rich as Eamon Carter. Marietta Carter was gracious yet imperious. She had aspired to power all her life.

"Tell me, Doctor, why would a young man like you, equipped to practice medicine, want to come back to this slow, trial-and-error world that we call research?"

"For the same reason you're so generous with your grants. One doctor in one lifetime can treat perhaps ten thousand people, twenty thousand. One single discovery made in a laboratory can save the lives of millions."

21

Edgar Woolsey beamed. Young Niles was not only a very bright researcher; he was a good diplomat besides. Cruikshank, too, was delighted with Bob's response, since it freed him from the burden of flattering Marietta Carter any more than he already had.

Just then his wife, Ellen, came back into the room, and he seized the opportunity to lead Bob away. But as he turned, Mrs. Carter said, "Professor Cruikshank, I hear you have a most promising experiment planned."

Otis turned back to stare first at her, then at Woolsey. He would have preferred not to reveal his projected work at this time. But obviously it had already been mentioned. So he stifled his anger at Woolsey and said, "Until an idea proves out, every protocol is only a researcher's pipe dream. But it seems promising."

Woolsey laughed. "A very extravagant admission from a close-mouthed Scot. For myself, I have a rule. When Otis Cruikshank says something is 'promising' I know it's as good as done."

"All I'll say," volunteered Carole Evans, "is that the first time I read through his protocol I was thrilled. The most exciting experiment we've ever contemplated at Trask."

"And one of the most costly," Woolsey observed dryly.

"When can you expect results?" Mrs. Carter asked Otis Cruikshank directly.

"We might begin to accumulate some data soon," Cruikshank equivocated. He had not definitely decided to proceed at this time. He made another attempt to break away. "Come, Robert, Ellen'll be delighted to see you. . . ."

Marietta Carter refused to be put off. "How soon is soon?"

Cruikshank responded with a puzzled look.

"You said 'soon.' *How* soon? Soon enough for you to chair and address the Section on Immunology at the Carter Foundation Symposium next January?"

Cruikshank was not prepared to answer so direct a question. At the same time, he did not wish to undo all the hard

22

work Woolsey had obviously put in on Mrs. Carter. There were other pressures as well. Only last month the Director of Administration had remarked that it seemed odd to many people that the head of Trask Institute had not been invited to chair any important scientific meeting for almost a year now. Nor had Otis been invited to present the main paper at any convention in some months.

Remembering that conversation, Otis felt pressed to say, "It's conceivable we might be ready to report our results by next January."

Sensing the old man's discomfort, Bob attempted to break up the conversation by saying, "Mrs. Cruikshank is trying to get our attention. . . ."

Marietta Carter cut him off abruptly. "Precisely what area of immunology is your work in, Professor?"

Any other benefactor would have been satisfied with a general description. Otis Cruikshank knew that that did not apply to Marietta Carter. Discerning, demanding, she was never satisfied with less than the total knowledge at the disposal of anyone with whom she dealt. Much as he preferred not to, Cruikshank realized he would have to tell her.

"I'm considering some unprecedented work in the field of transfer factor," he admitted.

"Ah, yes," she responded, indicating she wished to know more.

"Transfer factor," Cruikshank proceeded to explain, "is that element within the white cells of a donor which when given to a patient can stimulate the patient's immune system to fight back and possibly overcome the disease. Any number of diseases."

"And in what specific area will you be working, Professor?"

"Melanoma. Cancer of the skin and other soft tissues."

"Melanoma?" she repeated, seeming a bit disappointed. "There's been some work done on the use of transfer factor in melanoma, hasn't there?"

23

"Yes. But nothing conclusive," Cruikshank said.

"And you expect your work to be conclusive?" she challenged.

"We're using a method quite different from any that has ever been attempted."

"What method?" Marietta Carter asked pointedly.

"Our approach mimics the clinical situation. We want to work with animals under conditions that closely parallel those which confront the practicing physician when he treats a human patient."

Marietta Carter's eyes lit up. "That could completely revolutionize cancer research."

"It's still theory now—a model for an experiment."

"I've always admired your modesty, Professor. I'd rather have your uncertainty than the extravagant predictions I hear from most investigators I meet." She smiled, and tried to force a more positive answer. "What would you say the chances are? Honestly, now."

"I . . . I feel hopeful about it. Very hopeful."

Both Woolsey and Carole Evans smiled with satisfaction.

"Then, Professor," Mrs. Carter said, "I insist you chair the Section on Immunology at our Symposium! I want the Carter Foundation to be first to break the news!"

"You understand it's still only a projected protocol."

"If you feel optimistic, I'm willing to take the chance," she insisted, determined not to lose such publicity.

"Agreed!" Woolsey broke in, sealing a bargain to which the reluctant Otis Cruikshank was forced to become a party.

"Agreed," Cruikshank said, with far less enthusiasm. He was free now to lead Bob over to his wife.

Once they had left the small circle of power, Mrs. Carter turned to Carole Evans. "I'm glad you told me. Else I'd never have had the chance to insist."

"He's so modest," Carole Evans said. "And too cautious for his own good. Small wonder he's announced no valuable discoveries in the last four years."

If Carole was pretending to defend Otis Cruikshank, this comment betrayed her.

"I assume you're familiar with the design for his experiment?" Mrs. Carter asked.

"Oh, yes. Brilliant. Far ahead of anyone else in the field," Carole Evans said.

It was easy to be impressed by her, for she gave every visual evidence of being a highly competent person. Her black hair was braided and arranged in an unflattering way. She diminished her neat sculptured features with black-framed spectacles which gave her a scholarly, scientific appearance that fitted her title, Doctor of Philosophy in Biology. Because of her severe appearance and attitude, those who worked under her at Trask referred to her as "Mother Superior."

It was her ambition to be the first woman in the country to head a research institute as eminent as Trask. In pursuit of that, she had gradually worked her way up to assistant to the eminent Otis Cruikshank, depending on that to gain her offers as Director of Research elsewhere. But in the last four years his department had produced no startling discoveries and she had been forced to watch numerous men offered jobs for which she felt better qualified. That was why she had deliberately revealed the existence of his protocol on melanoma and transfer factor to Marietta Carter.

It was almost an hour later when Edgar Woolsey finally escorted Marietta Carter safely back to her enormous Bentley. Once the car pulled out of the driveway, Woolsey relaxed, yanked the red carnation out of the lapel of his custom-tailored navy blue pinstripe jacket and tossed the wilted flower into the hedge. It was his usual gesture of relief.

Damn them! he said to himself. It was a sweeping condemnation of both the benefactors who supported Trask and the scientists who labored there. The researchers were always demanding more and more equipment and assistants, but were never cooperative enough when it came to entertaining benefactors. The benefactors were always demanding startling and magical discoveries, yet were always so stingy with their grants. Between the two stood Edgar Woolsey—diplomat, salesman, conniver, public relations man and, at times, tyrant.

These days, with the Government becoming so economy-minded, Woolsey's job was all the more difficult, and he had resented it very much that Otis Cruikshank had to be prodded into a situation which might result in a huge donation. Fortunately, Carole Evans had been there. He felt Marietta Carter was now properly hooked.

Yes, Edgar Woolsey said to himself, thank God for Carole Evans.

He chose to blot out the fact that when Otis Cruikshank had first presented his ambitious protocol, Woolsey was the one who had frowned on it as too expensive. Now that Marietta Carter was interested, he would not only approve it, he would insist on it.

He hurried back into the house and went directly to the bar to pour himself a double shot of brandy. The strain of entertaining Marietta Carter always took its toll. He took a large gulp of brandy and then headed across the room toward Carole Evans.

Trying to appear completely professional, he said, "If you're free this evening, perhaps you'd care to help me welcome a group of new candidates."

"Yes, of course. I'd like to."

They walked over to the Cruikshanks to say good-bye.

Ellen was questioning Bob Niles about his years in New York.

"Ellen, it was lovely," Woolsey said. "She went away impressed and delighted. My thanks."

Otis suddenly interrupted, "Woolsey, one moment please," and the two men walked away a few paces.

"You shouldn't have done it," said the professor. "I have only a model for an experiment. No results. No data."

"By the time you have to preside and address the symposium, you will have," Woolsey said confidently.

"I don't like to be rushed when such an involved experimental protocol is at stake!" Cruikshank said, his lean face grim in anger.

"Don't worry about it, Otis. I'll see you have all the facilities you need. And you'll come through. I have every confidence."

"What if I have only failure to report?" asked Cruikshank.

Woolsey smiled. "Then we'll do what you investigators always do. We'll announce that your very failure proves something of enormous scientific consequence."

"It's nothing to joke about!" Cruikshank said angrily.

"What's the trouble, Otis? Afraid you're losing your grip?"

Woolsey had made the ultimate threat—that Otis Cruikshank might have grown too old for his taxing job. The professor stared at Woolsey, unable to respond.

"Otis, I've never known you to propose an experiment with such conviction. And then to have such second thoughts. You can't be wrong. Don't worry about it. If you need more lab assistants to hurry the work, I'll find room in the budget somehow."

"More lab assistants?" Otis challenged. "A few weeks ago you were opposed to the entire project!"

"If you want more assistants, I'll provide them," Woolsey insisted.

"The number of lab assistants won't do it. The concept has to prove out."

"You'll come through. I have every confidence that you will." Then, to close the conversation, he said, "I have to be going. We have a new group of candidates coming in on the night flight. And you do want Trask to make a good impression. After all, three of the new men you want are in the group."

"Yes, of course," Otis said. "Make them comfortable tonight and I'll meet with them first thing in the morning."

The guests were gone. Otis, Bob Niles and Ellen were left alone. From having had to contend with too many people, suddenly Otis Cruikshank found there were too few. His private asides with Woolsey demanded an explanation, but he felt unable to give one. Instead, he excused himself so that he could change from his dark business suit into more comfortable slacks and sweater.

Bob studied Ellen Cruikshank as she watched her husband leave the room. Her concern was obvious.

"Has Otis been ill?" he asked suddenly.

"No. Why do you ask?" she challenged so swiftly that it reminded him of Heather's quick response earlier.

"He seems tense, tired. Not in response to a single difficult day like this, but longtime tired."

"I can assure you, he's not ill," Ellen Cruikshank said. The way she said it, it seemed only half an answer. Yet Bob knew he had no right to probe further.

When Otis returned comfortably attired, Bob invited them to have dinner with him. But Otis pleaded the need to spend the evening on some important data that had just come over from the Institute.

Instead he suggested, "Robert, why don't you take Heather?"

"Otis," Ellen reprimanded.

He smiled. "You think I'm throwing her at him? Have no fear. *I* wouldn't want her to marry a researcher. And *she's* too smart to marry one. I just don't want Robert to spend his first night back alone."

He turned and called up, "Heather! Robert wants to take you out to dinner."

"Otis!" Ellen said. "At least let him ask for himself, if he wants to."

"Of course he wants to," Cruikshank said. "I could tell from the moment I saw them together. Don't you, lad?"

Bob had no choice but to say, "Of course."

Cruikshank turned to Ellen. "There," he said; "I told you," and he went off toward the den to work.

"I understand Dad insists we have dinner together," Heather said, coming into the room. "Where are you going to take me?"

"I don't know any of the newer places around. Wherever you say."

"Once you get west of Chicago all food tastes the same."

She went to her mother to say good night. Ever since Duncan's fatal illness Heather never left the house without kissing her mother. It was a throwback to the day when young Duncan had died and all Heather could do was try to kiss her mother, saying, "You still have me, Mommy. You still have me."

"Drive carefully, dear," Ellen Cruikshank said.

As they came out onto the driveway, Bob joked, "She doesn't trust the way you drive. Should I?"

"Here, if it'll make you feel more masculine and protective." She offered him the keys.

As he took them he thought back to all the things that had passed between them since they had met at the airport. Nothing he could recall would account for her discouraging aloofness. She cloaked it with little jokes, but she obviously resented him.

At dinner Heather seemed to soften a little, asking about his residency and finally saying, "Doesn't the practice of medicine seem preferable now that you've had a taste of both? And don't give me the same noble answer you gave Marietta Carter."

"I still prefer research, but it is possible to combine the two."

"But you'll be working mainly at the Institute," she concluded.

"Yes," Bob said.

29

They were driving back to the Cruikshank house when he asked suddenly, "Do you think I've come back to take Duncan's place?"

Startled, she didn't answer at once. Then she said, quite simply, "I never thought that."

"But you resent my being here."

"I have no feeling at all about your coming back."

"Yet all you've done since we met at the airport was put me down or discourage me from returning to research."

"Did I?" she asked thoughtfully. "Now that you mention it, no, I don't think I do want you here."

"Why?"

"Maybe what you said. You'll want to take Duncan's place. I won't let anyone do that. Nobody will blot out the memory of him."

"When the patient comes up with a glib answer, he's usually lying. To the doctor. Or to himself. A very good analyst in New York told me that, one night when we were on duty in Psychiatric Emergency."

"You think I'm lying to you?" Heather asked.

"No."

"Then you think I'm lying to myself."

"I think there's something wrong with Otis. And you're trying to keep it from me," he said flatly.

"There is nothing wrong with my father, believe me," she said firmly.

"He's not the same. I have the perspective of time on my side."

"That only means he's older. Seven years when a man's in his fifties is a lot longer than when he's twenty."

"The difference between fifty-one and fifty-eight shouldn't be that great in a man with Otis Cruikshank's constitution. Unless he's been sick and no one told me about it, I have to conclude there *is* something wrong."

Heather didn't attempt to answer.

"His color is okay. His hands don't tremble. All outward

signs are good. Yet there's something different," Bob persisted. "Of course, the burden of carrying such a huge institution doesn't get easier." He paused, then said, gently, "Sometimes families make a mistake."

"Mistake?" she asked, tensely.

"I've seen cases at the hospital. A man with a business of his own, or an executive with an important job, gets a minor heart attack or a slight stroke, and the family conspires to keep it secret. That's a very costly kind of deception."

"Meaning?" she countered.

"If that's what happened to Otis, it would be better for everyone if he let it be known. So he can ease off and not overtax himself."

"I assure you," Heather said with great emphasis, "that is not what happened to my father!"

That was the end of all conversation. But it was not the end of Bob Niles's concern. A doctor with a trained diagnostic eye could make certain observations even without a close examination, and Bob determined to study Otis carefully over the next ten days.

CHAPTER
THREE

Bob Niles was assigned a small but efficient suite in the Bradshaw Residence, a building donated to Trask by Carl Bradshaw's heirs in honor of the late automobile pioneer. The Bradshaw was used to temporarily house staff like Bob who came to Trask without provision for permanent quarters. It was also used to impress researchers who were being recruited.

Those potential candidates were quartered at the Bradshaw, where they were wined, dined and enticed with tours of the impressive buildings, laboratories and equipment. If the candidate seemed impressed, the next step in the courtship was to insist that he return and bring his wife. Or if the candidate was a woman who had a small family, then her husband and children were invited. Competition for brain power among all large scientific institutions had turned into a process of elite bribery, which usually began at the Bradshaw.

When Heather Cruikshank dropped Bob off that night, there were three single candidates and two couples checking in. Edgar Woolsey was there to ensure that their accommodations were satisfactory. Then he would host a small late supper for them. His invitation to Bob was a reluctant afterthought.

Woolsey presided over the buffet, ordering the waiters

about, snapping his fingers for more cocktails, being particularly careful to see that the wives had exactly the food and drink they desired. He knew from experience that in the end it was the wife who made the decision. The matter was usually settled on the flight back home.

The wife might say, "I don't think I'd like to live there. Too institutional."

And the entire expedition would end in failure.

Or she might say, "Deedee would be very happy at that school. They have special provision for problem children."

That meant the mission would end in success for the candidate and for Trask.

From his earlier days at the Institute, Bob Niles knew this courting ceremony well. He watched with amusement as Edgar Woolsey wooed the canididates' wives with almost the same elaborate charm he had exerted on Marietta Carter only a few hours before. Bob was nursing a mild bourbon when he heard a familiar voice at his side.

"How does he do it?"

Bob turned to face Carole Evans.

"He's like a master of ceremonies on a cruise ship. He never sleeps," Bob said.

Carole's reaction let him know she interpreted that as a slight against Woolsey, and to correct the impression he said, "You have to give him credit, though. When you realize that one man like him makes it possible for all the rest of us to go on working."

That seemed to ease the crisis. Carole handed him her glass. "Would you? Vermouth on ice. With a twist."

When he returned from the bar, she asked, "How does he look to you?"

"Woolsey?"

"Otis, of course," she said.

"Tired. But otherwise okay." Bob didn't know how safe it was to reveal his concern.

"I keep telling him he works too hard," Carole said. "If only Ellen would do something about it."

"You know Otis. What can she do?"

"Insist they go on a vacation. He's always had a tendency to overwork. But these last two years it's been even worse. He's got to let up."

"How can anyone expect he'll take a vacation now? Especially after the pressure that . . ." Bob had been about to say, "the pressure Woolsey exerted on him today." But sensing how protective Carole was, he said, "Especially after the pressure Marietta Carter exerted on him to make his report at her annual symposium."

"Take my word for it," Carole Evans said firmly, "his protocol is laid out in such elegant detail that the work could go on without his hovering over it day and night like a mother over a sick child."

"Does it look that promising?"

"It's inspired!"

"You mean he might actually find a way to make transfer factor effective in human melanoma?"

"I think he just might. And he's entitled to it. After what he's been through."

"Duncan?"

"Yes, Duncan," Carole Evans agreed. "There'd be something poetically just in Otis Cruikshank making the crucial breakthrough in cancer research. That's why . . ." And she stopped abruptly.

"Why what?" he pursued.

"I can't understand why, having laid out such a brilliant protocol in such detail, he's reluctant about carrying it out now."

Bob didn't comment. Having been away so long, he wasn't sure which way the political winds were blowing. Was Carole Evans really concerned about Otis' health? Or was she intent on furthering her own ambitions? One thing she had said was significant. Otis Cruikshank had never before been reluctant to put an experiment of his into work once he had designed it. To Bob Niles it was another indication that his worry about the old man was justified.

CHAPTER

FOUR

Bob Niles's first days back at Trask were devoted to the discovery of the new laboratory buildings as well as the new equipment that had been added in recent years. But at the same time he also experienced the anxiety involved in waiting out the routine procedure before his suggested protocols for experimentation were acted upon by the Projects Committee. Failing committee approval, his work could not even begin. He tried to make waiting bearable by familiarizing himself with the place, the new people, the research in progress.

The call came while he was touring one of the newer laboratories. Otis Cruikshank's crisp voice asked, "Robert, can you come to my office at once?"

"Yes, sir, of course."

Otis Cruikshank was standing at the window, his back to the door, staring out at Trask Park. He did not turn but only asked, "Robert?"

"Yes, sir."

Cruikshank was silent for a moment. Bob sought to relieve the old man of the distasteful burden by volunteering, "They didn't approve my protocols."

"Your protocols?" Cruikshank echoed vaguely, as if he needed to be reminded. "They haven't even come before the Committee yet."

"I thought . . ." Bob started to say.

But the old man was pursuing his own thoughts. "I've been waiting for your return. I have plans for you. In New York, you did have some training in nuclear medicine, didn't you?"

"Yes, sir."

"Good!" Cruikshank said grimly. "The field is so new, when it comes to relying on men of my own age group, doctors I've worked with most of my career, there aren't any experts." Then Cruikshank asked pointedly, "Body scans? Brain scans? You had much to do with them?"

"Yes. But not enough to be Board certified."

"Can you read a scan? Discuss one with a highly trained nuclearist?"

"Yes, sir, I can."

"Then would you do something for me?"

"Of course," Bob responded quickly.

"It's a personal matter," Cruikshank explained. "There is a man at the University Hospital. Cyril Berger. Bright, young—not yet forty and already chief of Nuclear Medicine there. We've been doing . . . well, doing some work together. Highly confidential work relating to a patient of his."

Though Bob was tremendously curious, he knew that to interrupt with questions would only add to the old man's discomfort.

"Berger reports a finding to me that I would like to have verified. My opinion wouldn't be worth a damn. So I'd like someone else's. Yours."

"I'd be glad to give it. But if Berger's as good a man as you say—"

"He is, he is. It's just that this is a highly unusual situation. Certain decisions I have to make will depend on it. Therefore, I'd like you to do this for me."

"Of course."

"I'll phone ahead and tell Berger you're coming."

36

Bob started for the door. Before he reached it, Otis stopped him. "Robert . . . you understand this is to remain completely confidential. You are not to mention it to anyone. Regardless of any provocation."

"I understand."

"Thank you, Robert."

On the drive into the city, Bob Niles pondered that strange meeting with Otis Cruikshank. Some things about Otis had remained the same. His terseness. His habit of thinking far more than he spoke. But other things had changed. For one, his face seemed not quite so ruddy. There was a layer of gray just beneath the superficial color. And the weariness Otis had exhibited recently was even more pronounced today.

If anything happened to Otis—a breakdown in his health, a prolonged leave of absence—Bob Niles realized that his own feeling toward Trask would change considerably. In the final analysis, his loyalty was not to the Institute, but to Otis Cruikshank. Otis had had a greater influence on Bob's life than any other man, including his own father, who had died when Bob was still quite a young boy.

Dr. Berger, a slightly heavy young man wearing large-framed glasses, immediately took Bob into his office, where a scan was mounted on a viewing box that stretched the length of one wall.

"Before we look at these results, I have to check a patient. Come!" He started swiftly from the room, leaving Bob no choice but to follow.

Two doors down, in the Nuclear Medicine room, a woman patient lay on one of the scanner tables completely covered by a white sheet. Above her body one of the two collimators moved slowly back and forth, much as a typewriter carriage moves, line by line. Except that when it came to the end of a line it moved back slowly along a line slightly below the one it had just traced. In less than an hour the huge round nuclear eye would scan every inch of her body.

Berger spoke in a whisper so soft he was sure not to be heard by the patient.

"She had a shot of gallium 67 three days ago. Most men say forty-eight hours. I like to give the stuff three days to circulate and settle in. And some men prefer a different nuclear medium. But I use gallium."

"That's what we used most of the time in New York," Bob agreed.

"This particular patient had a technetium brain scan five days ago. Malignant. Question now is, was that primary? And how much further has it spread? We'll know soon enough," Berger said fatalistically.

He turned to consult the small dark green oscilloscope alongside the scanning device. On it was gradually emerging in bright green light a miniature outline of the woman's body as the scanner traced it, line by line. It had already sketched in her neck, her shoulders and the upper part of her body. Eventually it would present a complete outline of her entire body including all four extremities.

Berger checked this monitor to assure himself that the scanner was working properly. He would attempt no diagnosis until he had a chance to examine the total body scan which would emerge from the complicated machine in the form of a large x-ray plate, one-fifth the size of the woman's body.

The radioactive gallium 67 in her body was being picked up by the sensitive scanner. The areas where concentrations of gallium were detected would tell the story. If it collected in any but the usual places, that would be a convincing sign that there was a cancerous mass.

Bob Niles glanced at the small-scale instantaneous reading on the green scope. He could already detect two hot spots. Berger had detected them a moment earlier. Even in the semidarkness, their eyes exchanged knowledgeable and concerned opinions. Berger shook his head slightly. Another verdict of impending death he would have to hand down before the day was out.

Bob followed Berger back to his office. The nurse was just setting up the scans that Bob Niles had come to examine. Before Berger turned on the backlights, he asked, "Did Professor Cruikshank brief you on the case?"

"No."

"Well, then," Berger began, "you're in for a most interesting session. Yes, Niles. Interesting and hopeful, this time." Berger could not help referring to the unfortunate patient still under the scanner. "What we have here is a confirmed diagnosis of melanoma."

He turned to the first set of plates. "You will notice here . . . and here . . . and here . . . lymph-node involvement near the primary site, which was on the patient's side just below the armpit. The mass was removed and the close affected nodes were probed. But the distant ones were left intact."

Berger accompanied his explanation by referring to the hot spots on the x-ray plates which showed the course of the original disease.

"Now, this brain scan taken at the same time, as a precaution, showed no brain involvement, as you can see."

Bob studied all four views of the brain which were on a single large x-ray plate. The clean brain scan had been taken more than three years ago.

"However," Berger continued, "almost a year later the patient exhibited symptoms that called for another brain scan. And this time . . . well, there it is."

He pointed to another set of brain scans and indicated the areas where the scanner had picked up concentrations of the radioactive medium. Technetium.

Bob Niles moved in and stared at the plate. Lit from behind, it showed clearly a small light area near the center of the brain. An abnormal intrusion. By all odds, a brain tumor. And, with this patient's history, undoubtedly malignant. Bob grunted sympathetically. He had seen cases like this in New York during his residency, and he knew the sad prognosis only too well.

"You notice the date on this brain scan, Niles?" Berger asked.

"Almost two and a half years ago," Bob said. "I assume the patient is no longer alive."

"Aha!" Berger said, smiling again. "Now for the surprise. Take a look at this! Taken four months later."

He mounted a fresh set of plates in the viewbox. There were three plates. One a four-section brain scan. The other two displaying a full-length view of a human body, on a one-to-five scale. Berger flipped on the light that illuminated that section of glass. The images, which had been dull before, now stood out sharply.

In a dispassionate, detailed professional manner, Berger began to explain.

"Total outline. Anterior view. Posterior view. The radioactive medium was, of course, gallium."

He was studying the films while he talked, concentrating on various dark and shaded areas which were apparent in both the front and rear views.

"Normally, as you know, the radioactive material concentrates in several areas of the body. Here in the liver. And in the spleen. So these areas are hot spots that are quite normal."

"This hot spot here . . ." Bob indicated a point in the lower part of the abdomen. "Could that be significant?"

"Slight increased uptake in the colon. Probably due to stool. Nothing unusual or significant," Berger said confidently. "These scans are most reassuring. Still, melanoma is so unpredictable. It can metastasize anywhere. You can't be too sure. But in this case, due to added evidence, the fact is quite clear. Take a look at this, Doctor!"

He directed Bob's attention to the brain scan. Bob examined all four angles of it, paying special attention to the area that in the previous scan had clearly indicated evidence of a brain tumor. He found no trace. He moved back to study the old scan. There it was. A clear, distinct hot spot, indicating tumor. He moved back to the newer scan. There was no evidence at all.

"Clean," Bob said, amazed. "Absolutely clean."

"Now take a look at this latest brain scan," Berger urged. Bob studied it. It was also clean. Berger invited, "Look at the date on this scan, Doctor."

Bob stared at the date down in the corner. It didn't seem possible. He turned back to Berger.

"That's right, Niles. Taken only three days ago."

Bob studied the fresh scan, remarking, "None of them show any indication of surgical intervention."

"Because there never *was* surgical intervention," Berger pointed out.

Bob Niles stared skeptically at Berger, who smiled.

"Yes, Doctor. You are looking at clear evidence of a case of spontaneous remission of a melanoma, after it had metastasized to the brain. I've heard there have been several reported. But this is the only one I've ever been privileged to see."

Bob Niles turned to stare at the plates again. There could be no doubt.

A sudden thought struck him. Otis was the patient! The toll involved in waiting out each month to see if his remission would fail could account for everything—his tension, his apparent weariness. And to add to all the evidence Bob could assemble in his mind, there was one overriding fact. Otis had asked him to undertake this mission as a personal and private favor. If Otis Cruikshank had had melanoma, surely he would not want it known throughout the research community.

Tempted as Bob was, he resolved not to ask Berger if his suspicion was correct.

Berger, it seemed, had a suspicion of his own. For when Bob completed his examination of the scans, Berger asked quite directly, "Is the old man losing confidence in me?"

"He has the highest regard for you."

"I want to know the truth," Berger insisted.

"What you really mean is, Why did he send me?"

"Exactly," Berger said. "I've always been truthful with him before. And accurate, thank God."

"I give you my word, he doesn't doubt you."

"Then what's changed?"

"If I knew, I'd tell you."

Berger shook hands with him. "Niles, anytime you need my help, let me know. And anytime the old man doubts my word, persuade him to come down here and see the scans for himself."

"Well, Robert?" Otis Cruikshank asked. He stared up from his desk chair, challenging and expectant.

"Both new scans were absolutely clean," Bob Niles reported.

"You're sure? Berger was sure?"

"If you still have any question, he wants you to examine them for yourself."

Otis Cruikshank nodded thoughtfully, but still seemed grim.

Bob felt this might be a moment to confirm his conclusion in a less-than-direct way. "I should think you'd be greatly relieved."

When Otis didn't answer, Bob continued, "Two years of remission isn't long enough to be absolutely positive. But it's an extremely good sign."

Otis Cruikshank remained so thoughtful that Bob wondered if the man had even heard what he said. Perhaps Otis knew the grim statistics of melanoma too well to take even momentary comfort from such a report if he himself were the patient.

Bob Niles had no way of knowing that at the moment Otis Cruikshank was not concerned with that. He was pondering the relevance of Bob's report to the next step he must take as it involved the Cruikshank protocol.

42

"Well, I thank you, Robert." Otis Cruikshank turned his chair to stare out the window at Trask Park.

Bob Niles knew the meeting was at an end. The old man obviously wished to be alone. Before Bob reached the door, Cruikshank called to him, "Robert, some day . . ."

Bob turned to look at Cruikshank. But instead of finishing what he had started to say, Otis ended the meeting with a soft and genuine "Thank you, Robert. That will be all."

Bob Niles left the old man's office sure now that his suspicion was correct. It would account for Otis' reaction, for the fact that he was not nearly pleased enough with the current scan. Knowing more than Bob did about the original illness, the site and size of the primary tumor, Otis might have good reason to be more pessimistic. In melanomas caught early enough and localized enough, as many as 70 percent achieved a five-year survival. Unfortunately, very few were caught early enough.

CHAPTER
FIVE

After Robert Niles left the office, Otis Cruikshank remained seated in his desk chair staring out across the park. The time had come to prove his theory. If all a man had to do was dream up a solution, research would be easy. There were many men with brilliant imaginations. Otis had seen them come and go. When they laid out a protocol for an experiment, it seemed convincing and airtight. But in the laboratory, the only place where any idea could be proved, they failed. But even proof was not enough. The ability to duplicate the proof was even more important. An experiment that worked once proved nothing except that it had worked once. That could mean it was only a freak happening. Not till the investigator himself, and his colleagues in other institutions, could reproduce his experiment with similar results was any discovery accepted.

Otis Cruikshank was terribly aware of this need for confirming data. He was caught in the dilemma of a scientist who knows the truth, who in secret has demonstrated it to his own satisfaction, but has yet to prove it to the world or to his colleagues.

In his case it was more than a dilemma. It was a matter of great personal and professional danger. That was why it would have been a serious mistake to allow anyone, including Bob Niles, to share that secret. Perhaps it should never be revealed.

For what Otis Cruikshank had done would be judged criminal in a court of law.

Perhaps he should never have recorded it in the hidden lab journal in which he had carefully noted each and every step he had taken, as if he were performing a perfectly acceptable and legally approved experiment. At times he was tempted to destroy that book. But he still kept it, locked away, always in contemplation of making it public once he'd proved his thesis in the laboratory.

The benefit to medicine would eventually outweigh his personal risk. Or if he were to die before proving it, the journal would remain extant for other men to use for the good of the human race. By that time Otis Cruikshank's reputation wouldn't matter, and the world would have the benefit of his work.

The fact that Ellen knew, and Heather, was unavoidable under the circumstances. But no one else. Not as long as he was alive, and certainly not as long as he was connected with Trask. It would destroy the reputation of this great and worthy institution.

Otis could well imagine the hysteria that would result if the facts ever came to light. Little secret meetings would be held in every building and the schemers would begin choosing up sides as to who was to succeed him. Corrigan, Smythe, even Carole Evans would be at one another's throats—in nice, subtle ways, of course.

But even a new chief would not quiet the scandal, which would be the worst in decades. No one would ever really try to understand what Otis Cruikshank had done or why he had done it. Yet if he had had to make the decision again, Otis was sure now he would have chosen to do the same thing.

Yes, after Bob Niles's confirmation of those clean scans today, he was positive he would do the same thing.

Otis Cruikshank could remember so well how it all had started. That phone call. He had known from her first

45

word that there was trouble. When a young woman away at college asks to talk to her father, that in itself is a sign of trouble. And the tentative "Dad, Dr. Hopkins suggested . . ." had confirmed his fears.

"Doctor? What's wrong, Heather?" he had asked, startled.

"Wrong? Nothing. Just a cold. But Dr. Hopkins was doing an examination of my chest and back. And, well, she noticed something on my side. A brown spot. She said, 'You ought to have that looked at.' "

"And did you?"

"I thought I'd call you first," Heather had said.

Otis knew well that offhand but significant habit of doctors of suggesting that something "ought to be looked at." They tried to seem casual because they didn't want to alarm the patient, yet they had to be insistent enough to make sure the patient followed their advice and consulted a specialist. Otis hadn't answered Heather at once. He took a moment to consider. Did he want her in the hands of a strange doctor? Or did he want her here at home, where she would receive preferred treatment?

"Heather, darling, get on the first plane tomorrow morning and get back here."

"Tomorrow? But Dad, we're less than four weeks away from end of semester. Can't it wait?" she pleaded.

"It's probably nothing. And you'll be back at school in two or three days. But it should be looked at now," he insisted.

As he hung up the phone, Otis could feel a damp sweat beginning to form on his brow. He wiped it away with his hand. He had two things to do immediately. One was to call Max Slade, a skilled cancer surgeon in whom Otis had great confidence. Whatever Slade would say would be definitive. The other was to tell Ellen as gently as he could, and without causing unnecessary alarm. She had never gotten over Duncan—his illness, his death. She always blamed herself in some way. Mostly for being away so much, for even in those days Otis Cruikshank's reputation was such that he was in constant demand to preside over symposia in other cities.

Fortunately, Ellen was away at the moment, visiting her mother, a dear but senile woman who refused to relinquish her own home though she needed constant care. Otis thought of calling Ellen that night, but decided against it. Before she could return, Heather would be home, tested, and the whole phrase "ought to have that looked at" might turn out to be just as harmless as it was intended to sound. There was no sense in worrying Ellen.

He met Heather at the airport, though he hadn't said he would. She was surprised and guilty to find him there.

"Dad, you didn't have to . . . not with your heavy schedule . . ."

"I wanted to avoid my heavy schedule." He tried to make a joke of it, but he could tell that his very presence had alarmed her.

He had arranged her appointment with Max Slade for early the next afternoon and had offered to drive Heather into the city. But Heather had insisted on driving herself. Actually, there was no reason for her not to. Just that if he were with her, he would not have to contend with this waiting. Otis had stayed in his office, trying to keep his mind off the possibilities of immersing himself in progress reports.

Several hours later that phone call came. As soon as his secretary announced Dr. Slade was calling, Otis became limp with fear. Slade spoke quietly, dispassionately, trying to make the terrible diagnosis sound undramatic.

"We've just done an incisional biopsy. A frozen section."

"Melanoma?"

"Yes."

It took Otis a moment to recover. "How bad?"

"We'll have to stage her to determine that," Slade said.

"It seems to be localized. But of course, we'll have to see."

"Did you tell her?"

"I thought I'd be guided by your advice on that. That's why I'm calling."

Cruikshank was thoughtful for a moment. "Don't tell her. Leave that to me."

"Do it at once, then. Because I want to do a total excisional biopsy as soon as possible. Spread or not, we've got to remove the primary site swiftly."

"Of course," Otis Cruikshank had agreed grimly. "I'll tell her tonight."

He had hung up and started out of his office, ignoring his secretary's attempts to remind him of his schedule of appointments for the rest of the day. He left the building and walked across Trask Park toward the river.

It had been late spring. The new grass was up, fresh and green. He passed colleagues who tried to greet him, but he was unaware of everyone and everything as his mind struggled to recall the dismal statistics on malignant melanoma. An irrational disease. It did not even follow the usual pattern of other malignancies. Whereas others metastasized to predictable parts of the body, melanoma observed no such discipline. It could follow the lymph nodes, or it might show up anywhere. There was no being sure with that wily killer.

Even if he wanted to put the best face on Heather's chances, he wouldn't be able to lie to her convincingly. Members of the Cruikshank family did not lie to one another. He would have to tell Heather the truth. Not only what she had. But what the odds were.

He imagined the scene in many ways. What he would say to open the subject. What she would ask. Otis determined that he would try to avoid the subject of Duncan if it was at all possible, but he knew she would still remember the terrible pain that had tortured him at the end.

By the time he thought to look about, he discovered that

he had walked along the river far beyond the grounds of Trask Park. It would be a full hour's walk back. Heather must be home from Slade's now. He must not keep her waiting. Besides, he would have to call and tell Ellen first.

He had started back at a swift pace. When he was within sight of Trask Park he began to run. By the time he arrived at his own door he was sweating profusely. He stopped, carefully wiped his face dry and took several long, deep breaths. When he felt under control, he opened the door and called out, in as near to his usual tone of voice as he could manage, "Heather?"

No answer. He knew she should be home by now. It was more than two hours since Slade had called.

"Heather!" he demanded, fearful now.

He raced to the living room. No one was there. Hilda, the maid, must have left to go shopping, else she would have answered. He started up the stairs two at a time, to Heather's room. She was not there.

Now the worst thoughts assailed him. She'd guessed the truth and done something drastic. He remembered that Memorial Hospital in New York, where they specialized in cancer, had locks on the windows which could be opened only by a key retained by the floor nurse. This to keep patients from committing rash acts once they discovered the truth of their prognosis.

Though Heather had been a child at the time, Duncan's illness and death had left a deep and abiding scar. For years she had asked questions about it. Was the illness communicable—could one catch it? And the more difficult to answer, Did it run in families? Knowing all she did about cancer, Heather might well have guessed her diagnosis and done almost anything.

Slowly he started down the stairs. He would call Slade's office. He would find out what time Heather had left. Perhaps Slade had detained her for some other tests. By the time he reached the living room he knew he had to call

Ellen. He also knew he should have called her earlier, so that she could have returned home. He made the call, indicated what the trouble might be, but found himself unable to say that there had been a definitive diagnosis. Even so, Ellen said she would catch the night plane.

As he hung up he heard someone at the back door. "Heather?" he called.

Hilda came out of the kitchen still in her coat, asking, "Is Miss Heather back from college?"

"Yes. Yes, she is."

"Oh, nobody told me." Hilda was greatly distressed. "And Mrs. Cruikshank only left instructions for your dinners."

"That's quite all right, Hilda. We'll make do. Just go about your business in the usual way."

Shaking her head, Hilda retreated to the kitchen. Otis sank back down into his chair. Go about your business in the usual way, he had said. From now on nothing in this household would ever again proceed in the usual way. Heather . . . if anything happened to Heather. How would he and Ellen bear that empty house?

When Duncan left them they had consoled themselves with Heather. Otis had always felt a bit guilty about that, realizing that he had not been quite as good a father to Heather as he should have been. Though she had always strived to be a better daughter than he deserved, to make up for Duncan.

And now, before he had the chance to make amends, this had happened. Alone in the dark room, Otis Cruikshank began to weep for the first time since Duncan's death.

Just then a car pulled into the driveway, and he raced to the window. Thank God! It was Heather.

He was tempted to rush to the door, but that would alarm her. He forced himself to wait in the living room until she appeared in the archway carrying two books.

"Dad?" She was surprised to see him home so early. But in a moment she understood. "Dr. Slade called you."

"Yes," he said as simply as he could. "Where have you been?"

"I stopped at the library," Heather said. Otis glanced at the two books she was carrying. They were medical texts. Both contained the word *Oncology* in their titles. The study of *cancer*. He stared at her a moment, and Heather reached out to press his arm.

"Don't, Dad" was all she said.

He embraced her and they held each other a long time. "You didn't plan to keep it from me, did you?" Heather finally asked.

He didn't answer.

"A girl who's going to graduate third in her class at Smith?"

"Have you read it all?" he asked. "About melanoma?"

"There were some terms I didn't understand. But I think I know," she said softly. "We mustn't tell Mother. Not yet, anyhow."

"A girl who was first in her class at Smith?" he chided, trying to smile. Then he said, "I've already called. She's on her way home."

"I can't do this to her!" Heather exclaimed.

He embraced her again. "You're not doing anything to anybody. So don't add guilt to all your other worries. We're a family. It's happening to *us*."

She nodded, trying to accept what he said. "Slade wants to operate."

"Yes, I know," he said, "to remove the primary, and to see if there's lymph-node involvement."

"Involvement," she echoed sardonically. "At school when we talk about 'involvement' and 'being involved' we never think of . . ." She didn't find herself able to say the terrible word.

It was dark in the room. Neither of them had thought to turn on the lights. They sat quietly—he in his usual high-backed leather chair near the fire, Heather on the footstool, resting her head against his leg. He realized sud-

51

denly that she hadn't done that since she was twelve. She was Ellen all over again. The golden hair; the long, graceful body; the face too incisive and intelligent to be merely pretty. Only her eyes were his, her blue eyes. People had always remarked on that. God, he found himself thinking now, what a wife she would have made for some fortunate young man!

He caught himself already consigning her to the past. And they had not yet determined the extent of her illness. He must stop thinking so pessimistically.

"I read where there are sometimes total cures," she said, as if reading his thought. He reached over and began to softly stroke her hair.

Ellen Cruikshank arrived at the airport at nine-fifty. She didn't call, but took a taxi. At ten-twenty, Otis Cruikshank heard the cab pull into their circular driveway. He went to the door and opened it and she was there, her eyes telling him that she knew everything.

"I called Dr. Slade before I left Mother's."

"I should have known," he apologized for not being totally truthful with her earlier.

"Even if I hadn't called, I'd know," she said strangely. "It had to be."

"Why?"

"She's my child," Ellen said with a resoluteness that was resigned as well.

"Ellen? Darling?"

"Don't you see? It's my fault!"

Otis tried to calm her, whispering, "Ellen . . . please. Heather's upstairs—asleep, I hope. I don't want to wake her."

He led Ellen into the living room and sat her down in her chair near the fire. He watched the flames cast their flickering light on her face, which was now not so strong, but seemed possessed.

"Drink?" he asked gently.

"No," she refused, as gently, since her first tensions had exhausted themselves in her earlier outburst. Now when she spoke her voice was so soft she seemed to be talking to herself.

"It began with Duncan. I've heard enough theories discussed in this house between you and your colleagues. That it all comes from some breakdown in the immune system. Isn't that what they say?"

"Many researchers believe that," he admitted.

"If that's true then it's possible Duncan inherited his weakness from me."

"That's ridiculous," Otis said. "No one's ever proved that."

"Someone has. *Me!*" Ellen insisted. Then, because she realized how close to hysteria she was, she begged, "Hold me. Otis, hold me."

He took her in his arms. Eventually her trembling subsided, but it was after midnight when they went upstairs to bed.

Out of deference to Otis Cruikshank, Dr. Max Slade put aside all other appointments to see him first. Slade was straightforward and professional. The follow-up biopsy Slade's pathologist had done after the frozen section had confirmed his original findings.

"Dr. Slade, on the basis of your past experience, do you have a pretty good idea as to what you're going to find when you go in?" Otis asked quite precisely.

"Every surgeon has his hunches. But all of us are wrong from time to time."

"I want to know now—what is your expectation?" Otis urged him to be specific.

"Not encouraging," Slade finally admitted. "I would guess it's treatable but not curable."

"But you do have to do the excision?"

"It would be malpractice not to," Slade said. "Of course, if a patient, knowing all the facts, refuses to submit to surgery, there's nothing the doctor can do."

Otis nodded his head. "What if the patient chose to put limitations on what the surgeon could do?"

"I would expect the patient to sign a consent form, allowing me to use my judgment based on what I find," Slade responded, becoming a bit apprehensive and irritated now. "After all, you can't wake the patient up while the operation is in progress."

"What if there *were* limitations?" Otis Cruikshank responded cautiously.

"Limitations?"

"Limitations agreed upon in advance, as to how far the surgery is permitted to go?"

"I'd have to know exactly what limitations," Slade countered.

"Remove the primary site and limit your exploration to those lymph nodes you can easily reach," Otis said.

Slade controlled his anger as he said, "A good surgeon is paid for his judgment as well as his skill. I'm not used to operating under 'controlled' conditions. Why do you ask that?"

"It's been our experience in the lab that animals whose distant nodes are excised somehow don't do as well as animals in which only the nodes near the primary site are removed," Otis said.

"Nobody's been able to relate animal findings to human beings in cancer. Not with any degree of certainty. Isn't that one of the difficulties you fellows have in research?"

"Yes."

"Then I'll have to use my own judgment," said Slade, as if he had put an end to the argument.

But Otis insisted, "If the melanoma has already reached the distant nodes, you can't affect the outcome. Can you?"

Slade had to shake his head.

"Then why submit the patient to the debilitating ordeal of such extensive surgery?"

"Sometimes I think we do it only as an act of rebellion against a disease that frustrates us all." Then, with great compassion for Otis' feelings, he added softly, "Yes, I can limit the surgery to the primary site. Either we get it all that way or else it doesn't really matter."

"Thank you," said Otis. He paused. "Dr. Slade, have you ever considered trying transfer factor on a melanoma patient?"

Slade looked puzzled.

"Transfer factor," Otis reiterated. "Surely you're aware of it."

"Of course I'm aware of it." Slade resented the implication that he didn't keep up with the latest scientific literature.

"Haven't you ever been tempted to try it?"

"On one of *my* patients?" Slade demanded, outraged.

"There's no harm in it," Otis pointed out. "At least, there are no negative side effects of any consequence."

"Do you realize you're suggesting human experimentation?"

"If there were full disclosure to the patient," Otis pressed, "and if you could get the consent of your Human Experimentation Committee, would you consider it?"

A highly successful surgeon, not used to having his opinions questioned by other physicians, much less men not trained in the medical discipline, Slade tried to control his temper. "Look here, Cruikshank, a medical doctor approaches problems quite differently from you research fellows. I won't deny that after some frustrating cases I consider the possibility of using some new and experimental technique. But I'm dealing with human beings. Not laboratory animals. You can indulge your theories. A surgeon can't."

"But if the patient insisted on it," Otis continued to urge.

"I'd have to go by my own rules," Slade declared firmly. "*First*, I would not try any such experimental procedure on any patient unless I was sure she was terminal! *Second*, it would have to be a patient with a small tumor burden."

"Yes, I know," Otis agreed. "Immunotherapy won't work against a large cancer mass. Not even in the lab."

"Well, then . . ." Slade said, as if he had disposed of Otis' recommendation.

"Once you've done your surgery, the bulk of the mass would have been excised, wouldn't it?" Otis asked.

"Cruikshank!" Slade exploded. "I am not going to try any experimental procedures on any patient of mine! Is that understood?"

Otis finally nodded—an almost imperceptible nod that seemed to admit defeat and frustration.

Slade was moved to say, "I know how you feel. I face the same problem every day. I have days when I'm tempted to try anything. But it would be useless. You can't even make a good case for it before the Human Experimentation Committee. They'd never agree. You know that."

Otis nodded.

"I'll do the best I can during the operation," Slade said. "That's all I can promise. You know how unpredictable melanomas are. She may enjoy a full recovery."

"Yes, I know," Otis Cruikshank agreed. "I'll have Heather here any time you say, Doctor." He rose from his chair and started for the door. Then, as if interrupted by an afterthought, he half-turned to Slade. "Doctor, as a matter of scientific curiosity, I'd like to have some of the tumor tissue you excise. Whatever your pathologist doesn't need for the biopsies, of course."

"What are you going to do with it? Sit in your lab and study the damned thing? Hating it, but helpless. How well I know that feeling. Every time I doubt the pathologist's word I stare through that microscope myself, hoping it will change somehow. It never does. But if you want it, of course."

"If I get it in an unfixed state I can culture it. Maybe even come up with something to help other patients."

"Maybe," Slade agreed halfheartedly. "I'll give my pathologist instructions."

Otis felt considerably relieved. He had secured Slade's cooperation with less difficulty than he'd anticipated and, even more important, without arousing any suspicion.

When Dr. Max Slade had come down from the operating room, he found Otis and Ellen Cruikshank seated on the bench outside his office as silent and grim as the relatives of his patients usually were. Good scientists were no less loving fathers. This time Slade could afford to be more optimistic than usual. As soon as he saw them, Slade smiled and beckoned them into the office. Once the door was closed, Slade said, "Well, it went better than we expected."

"How much better?" Otis demanded.

"I excised the primary mass, which did not involve as much subdermal tissue as I feared. I left safe margins, I'm sure. Then I cleared out the affected nodes in the immediate area," Slade said. "As you requested, I didn't probe any distant nodes. But I think we got it all."

"That doesn't exclude what might be traveling through her bloodstream, does it?" Otis asked.

"With melanoma one never knows," Slade had to admit. "We'll keep checking her. Every three months, if it will make you feel any better, but at this point I believe that girl's as good as new."

The Cruikshanks left happy, but Otis knew that the fear of recurrence would live with them for at least five years. And since it was melanoma, a good deal longer.

CHAPTER
SIX

Heather Cruikshank's life changed in only one way, and at her mother's request. Instead of pursuing work on her Master's degree in Education in Boston as she had planned, Heather lived at home and worked in the city at the Field School. It was a special school for brain-damaged children, where she could experiment with new methods of teaching. On the basis of the results, she would report her findings in a thesis which she hoped would win her her degree.

She undertook her work with great enthusiasm, seeking to immerse herself in it and blot out the memories of her own brush with death. For the time being, at least, it seemed she was one of the fortunate few whose melanoma had been discovered in time.

Otis was delighted with her attitude. Only when checkup time approached did Otis observe renewed tension. At home, they never talked of it directly. But the date was marked on each of their calendars, and each time she went off to be scanned on the third morning following her gallium injection, Ellen said, "Don't forget to call, dear." Meaning, Don't forget to let us know immediately after they tell you the results of the test.

By the time Heather had had her third trimonthly checkup and had come away clean, Otis found himself able to be genuinely relieved. Her illness was no longer his dominant thought during the course of every day. After that third clean scan, he even considered it might be safe to stop culturing those melanoma cells in the petri dishes which he had given a special place in his lab. He had kept them alive in a medium that simulated the nutritive qualities of human blood. And he had mislabeled them, so that no one could even suspect what he was doing. In the end he decided to let them grow, in the event some investigator at Trask decided to do research on melanoma.

It was evening, just two weeks before Heather was due for her fourth checkup and scan. Ellen was off at a meeting of Trask wives, and Otis was in his den working over some data he had brought home from the office. He was deep in the data when his door opened slightly. Heather peered in and sniffed.

"Sorry to break in, Dad. But I couldn't imagine why you'd have a fire going on a mild spring night like this."

"Fire?" Otis repeated, puzzled.

"But then you don't, do you?"

"No, I don't," Otis said pleasantly, and smiled until she had closed the door.

Then he sat a moment, thoughtful, his thumb rubbing the side of his chin. There was special significance to smelling something burning when there was no fire. He couldn't remember precisely what, but he knew that there was. He rose from his chair, turned to the shelves of books that lined the wall behind him and selected a small, fat blue volume, *Merck's Manual*, a comprehensive digest of all diseases: signs, symptoms, treatments and prognoses.

There he confirmed what had only been a disturbing memory.

"The patient smells something burning when no burning exists."

Other symptoms were listed as well. The patient hears noises and music that do not exist. Experiences *déjà vu* flashbacks. Objects appear either too big or too small. Sometimes he has convulsions or sudden, but temporary, paralysis of the side, including face, hand, arm.

Heather had exhibited none of those, thank God. Perhaps even her sudden sensitivity to the smell of burning was a fact, not a hallucination. As casually as he could, Otis made a check of the house, even checking the kitchen to see if Hilda had scorched anything while preparing dinner. He found no hint of smoke in the air.

Otis took a pot of coffee back to his den. He did not resume his work. Instead, he went to the shelf and pulled down another volume more detailed than the Merck manual and spent the next three hours reading up on tumors of the brain. When he was done, he reminded himself that Heather had experienced only one of many symptoms and that there had been times he thought he smelled something burning only to find he had been mistaken.

For the next eleven days, whenever he was home Otis observed her closely. Each evening he questioned her as carefully as he could without alarming her. But nothing of consequence happened.

On the Wednesday afternoon of the second week after the night she had thought she smelled something burning, Heather was walking up the aisle of her small classroom when she felt dizzy. Uncontrollable things were happening to her body. Tremors. Contractions. Then she blacked out.

She came to sometime later, lying on the floor, a book under her head to serve as a pillow. Several children were close by, some of them weeping. Two of her colleagues were hovering over her. Heather stared up at them and heard one say, "He's on his way over."

"What about a doctor?" another teacher asked.

"He's having one meet him here."

Heather stared up, thinking, I wish they didn't make such a thing of it. I'm fine. All I want to do is get up and comfort those poor children. They're terrified. And it's my fault. I've got to tell them I'm fine.

"Children . . ." she intended to call. But nothing came out, and for the first time panic overwhelmed her. She tried to cover her face with her right hand but found she had no control over it at all.

At that moment, Otis and Ellen pushed their way through the group of concerned faces. Otis knelt down beside her, took her hand and pressed it between his own.

"Heather . . ." he whispered as he leaned close. "Heather, darling, can you hear me?"

Heather tried to nod, but couldn't. So she made a sign with the left side of her face, which she did seem able to control.

"The doctor will be here soon," Otis whispered. "Don't worry. Everything is going to be all right."

But all the while there kept going through his mind the symptoms he had memorized: *Tumor involvement in the brain can manifest itself in smells of burning that does not exist. Convulsion followed by partial paralysis, temporary loss of ability to speak or understand.*

He held her hand and rubbed his fingers soothingly along her soft cheek. Tears began to run down the sides of her face. He thought it was fear and tried to reassure her. Actually, she wept for another reason. Her father was touching her as he had done a thousand times before, yet she could not feel him.

The doctor arrived. Carefully and gently he had her moved to the ambulance, then to the hospital. Within twenty-eight hours Heather Cruikshank recovered her ability to speak. By the end of the second day she gradually regained the use of her hand and arm. By the morning of the third day when she searched her hand mirror she saw that her face had returned to normal. She felt relieved enough to bury her face in her pillow and cry.

At the same time, in Dr. Slade's office two floors below,

a consultation was in progress. Slade, Otis and Cyril Berger, the nuclearist, were reviewing what the neurologist had discovered. There seemed no doubt that they were confronted with a classic syndrome of brain involvement. In Heather's case, with her recent history of melanoma, it presented a fairly certain case of metastasis from the primary site to the brain.

The indicated first step was to do a total scan of body and brain. Berger would see to that. Cross, the neurosurgeon, would undoubtedly want to do an angiogram. Depending on all the findings, the decision would be made on any future course of treatment. Till then, Otis had to become adjusted to these new and terrible realities.

Slade suggested, "We might as well keep her here till we do the scans and the angiogram."

"Yes," Berger said. "I can start her on the proper nuclear media today."

Five days later, when Slade had all the results, he called Otis at home.

Within twenty minutes Otis reached the hospital and made his way to the Nuclear Medicine Department. The consultation room was dark except for the glow that emanated from behind the films of Heather's scans. Berger was examining the four-part brain scan. Slade and Dr. Cross, the neurosurgeon, listened as Berger spoke.

"There's no doubt. The uptake here is clear and defined," he said as he pointed to a hot spot on the film.

Cross stated that his angiogram agreed with the scans and delineated the location of the tumor near the angular gyrus in the temporal lobe.

"I've read where a blood clot can present symptoms and readings similar to a brain tumor," Otis said, refusing to admit the worst of all possibilities.

"It could also be a focal encephalitis," Cross suggested. But he put it forth as a remote possibility, not a probability.

"And if it *is* a clot it could clear up by itself," Otis insisted.

"Yes," Cross agreed. "*If* it's a clot."

Otis slipped weakly into a chair. All three doctors sought something comforting to say. "Her body scan is absolutely clean," Berger declared.

"Otis," said Cross, "if you were simply a layman this would be easier for us."

"And if I were a layman?" Otis challenged.

"I would insist that we do exploratory brain surgery at once. If it's a clot we can remove it. If it's a tumor, it would be best out too."

"Or as much of it as you can take out," Otis responded bitterly.

"In neurosurgery we don't make any promises," Cross said. "We do the best we can with what we find. Fortunately, it's not a large mass. We might catch it in time."

Otis Cruikshank nodded his head slightly.

"Do I have your permission to talk to your daughter and get her consent to operate?" Cross asked.

Otis Cruikshank didn't answer.

"Otis, would it make it easier if I talked to her first?" Slade suggested.

Cruikshank was silent for a time, then said, "Thank you, gentlemen. But I shall talk to my daughter myself."

He started toward the door, then stopped. "If you do operate, and it turns out to be melanoma, what would her chances be?"

None of the doctors answered quickly, so Otis continued, "Ten percent? Or less?"

Cross had to be truthful. "Less."

Otis nodded thoughtfully. But he did not commit himself to any course of action. Instead he said, "Gentlemen, there is a request I have to make of all three of you. I wish to be sure that no matter what the decision, this case will remain absolutely confidential. I do not wish it known that my daughter is seriously ill. I do not wish any disclosure as to the nature of her illness."

"Otis, you don't have to caution us about confidentiality," Max Slade reminded. "After all, we're physicians."

"And I know how some of you are prone to talk. The last time . . . with my son . . . we were inundated by concerned friends and colleagues. Private grief is difficult enough. But when one has to contend with constant inquiries, and later with profuse condolences, it is just too much to bear."

"Of course, Otis, we understand," Max Slade assured him. "We'll respect your wishes completely. Meantime, let us know about the surgery."

"Yes, yes, of course."

Otis did not try to talk to Heather until he had driven her home and settled her in bed.

"They didn't like my scans, did they?" she asked before he could begin.

"The body scan is clean," he said, hating himself for doing precisely what the doctors had done, trying to put a good face on the situation.

"And my brain scan?" Heather asked without any show of emotion.

"There's something there. They're not sure what it is."

"So they want to operate," Heather concluded.

"They suspect it might be a blood clot."

"Or an encephalitis?" she asked.

She had indeed done her research well, and evidently more of it than she had ever let on.

"Yes," he answered gently. "They can only discover what it is by 'going in,' as they like to call it."

"And if they 'go in' and find more than a blood clot or encephalitis, they'll remove what they find."

"That's the purpose of it," Otis said.

"And possibly part of my brain too?" Heather asked.

He couldn't refute her.

"Dad, did they say what part of the brain it was in?" she asked finally.

"The temporal lobe."

"What *part* of the temporal lobe?" she persisted.

"Why, what difference—"

She interrupted. "Just tell me what part."

"Near the angular gyrus, Cross said. Why? What difference—"

"I won't let them do it!" she said suddenly and strongly. "I won't let them." She was silent for a moment and then said, "Dad, my children . . . my brain-damaged children . . . who have such trouble speaking. That's exactly where they have their lesions. I've researched it as part of my thesis. I could end up unable to speak, or read or understand. I could be worse than most of my pupils. I won't let them do that to me. I won't!"

"Heather, darling, listen to me. It might do some good. The mass is still small. There is a chance—"

"Don't quote me statistics," she interrupted; "they're in every oncology textbook. And they're not hopeful enough for the risk involved!"

He hadn't the heart to argue with her.

Later, Otis Cruikshank made his way across the misty campus to his lab. There, in seclusion, he studied Heather's melanoma cells which he had cultured for so long. With delicate forceps he put bits of the deadly tissue on a slide and inserted it under his microscope. They were still active, alive and reproducing. Reassured, he returned home prepared to reveal his plan to Heather.

She was still awake when he entered her room.

"Heather, there is one possibility I have not discussed with anyone, but it is something I think we should try. You know there have been experiments that give us reason to believe that a deficient immune system can be 'educated' to function properly."

"Dad, what are you talking about?"

"Just listen carefully. And don't interrupt. There is a substance that at times does have some effect on small tumors. It is called transfer factor. It is derived from the white-cell antibodies of healthy immune animals. When it

65

is injected into sick animals, they become more resistant to certain diseases.

"Animals, Dad? What about human beings?"

"It hasn't been tried very much on humans with cancer. A handful of cases. It's still highly experimental."

"And the results?"

"The percentages are not good," Otis admitted. "There've been a few temporary regressions reported. That's all. But there's a reason for that. And I don't intend to let that happen to you."

"What reason?"

"Physicians. Their fear of being accused of human experimentation. So their first rule is, never try anything new on a cancer patient until they are certain the patient is terminal. Well, good God, how can they expect anything new to work on a patient who they themselves say is sure to die!"

He realized that in his anger he had uttered the word "die" for the first time since the onset of Heather's illness.

"I am not going to let that happen to you, my darling," he promised. "I am not going to sit by patiently watching you grow worse from day to day. They'll not do that to you. They'll not do to you what they did to Duncan. I won't let them!"

"But if it's already spread to my brain . . ."

"It's small! Still small! That's important. Transfer factor hasn't been known to work against large masses of tumor, so time is important. That's why I have to get your consent, *now*."

He took her hand. "Heather?"

"What happens? What does the doctor do?" she asked.

Otis hesitated, then said, "The doctor doesn't do anything. The doctor doesn't even know."

Heather glanced at him, her puzzled face demanding an explanation.

"*I* will do it," he said.

"But Dad, that's . . . that's practicing medicine, isn't it?"

He nodded.

"You're not allowed. If it ever came out . . ."

"It needn't come out. Only you, your mother and I will know."

"I'm not going to let you do that for me!" Heather declared firmly.

"Heather! Listen to me! A medical doctor wouldn't be allowed to do it either until it was approved by committees of other doctors. By that time it might be too late. If it's going to work, we have to start quickly."

Heather hesitated.

"There's no more risk that way than leaving things as they are," he argued.

"I was thinking of the risk to you, Dad," Heather said softly.

"No one must ever know," Otis said in a hoarse whisper.

After a minute, Heather nodded.

CHAPTER
SEVEN

Otis Cruikshank had long ago established a procedure at Trask that would serve him well now.

In order to prevent release of the sort of disastrous and deliberately false findings that had emanated from other respectable research organizations, no paper bearing the endorsement of Trask Institute was allowed to be given public exposure unless the method and the results of the experiment were duplicated by a researcher senior to the investigator involved. Otis had set down the rule and had adhered to it firmly. Now, by saying he was checking the work of one of the assistant professors, he managed to explain hours of late-night lab work to his colleagues without attracting attention or arousing any suspicion.

He began his procedure by taking some of Heather's cultivated melanoma cells and forcing them through a fine stainless steel strainer. It was the first step toward deactivating them and keeping them from multiplying. Because they would still retain their antigenic ability once he had sensitized his system to them, any future injection of those cells into his bloodstream should cause his body to manufacture quantities of white cells from which the vital transfer factor could be extracted. Yes, he would use his own body to cultivate the precious material with which he hoped to save Heather's life. He would be the human key to the experiment.

Carefully he added some phosphate-buffered saline solution to the ground-up cells. Then he froze the mix in a test tube to 20 degrees below zero centigrade. After five minutes he inserted the test tube into a 37-degree solution, where he left it until it had thawed. He continued to repeat the process. Freeze to 20 below zero, thaw, then freeze again, thaw again. He carried out the procedure seven times.

That done, he selected a small-bore needle and a hypodermic barrel. Slowly he drew a minute amount of the solution into it. Then he slipped his left arm out of his lab coat, rolled up his shirt sleeve, dabbed some alcohol on his inner forearm and injected the substance under the skin. This first small dose should sensitize and alert his system to the foreign cells.

In a few days he would be ready for the next step in the procedure.

Four nights later, Otis Cruikshank gave himself a huge injection of processed melanoma cells. If his immune system responded properly, in a matter of a day or two he should exhibit a large red blotchy reaction in the area of that massive injection. That was the crucial sign. If it did not appear, then his experiment had failed at the start.

For two days he exhibited no reaction. It was not until the morning of the third day that Otis was wakened early by a distinct soreness in his left arm. He eased out of bed, went hastily to the bathroom, closed the door, flicked on the light and looked. There it was—a large blotchy, angry red reaction. He couldn't have been happier or more relieved. At that moment, the door behind him opened quietly.

"Otis," Ellen asked softly, "aren't you well?"

He pulled down his pajama sleeve so hastily that instead of avoiding her suspicion he invited it. She pushed back his sleeve and saw the rash.

"Otis?" was all she asked.

"For the patient to receive injections of transfer factor there has to be a donor," he explained simply.

"The way they use horses and cows to breed vaccines?" she asked.

"Fortunately, Heather and I are both the same blood type. That eliminates some very difficult problems."

"Otis, Otis" was all she could whisper.

"Didn't Heather do as much for me once?"

"When?" Ellen asked, puzzled.

"Years ago in Vienna. When I contracted that damned strep infection and needed transfusions. Her blood saved me."

"Did it?" Ellen asked, smiling.

It had been a sentimental joke between the two of them that a child of eleven should insist on giving blood to save her father when physicians could take so little from her. But they hadn't been able to talk her out of it. So to please her the doctor actually did transfuse a small amount of her blood into Otis.

"Well, at least it helped *her*," Otis said. "That was one time when the donor benefited more than the patient."

Ellen smiled and kissed him again. Staring at the rash on his arm, she asked, "What now?"

"This rash means that my body is producing white cells, lymphocytes, to fight off her cancer cells. Hidden in my white cells is the transfer factor that's going to teach Heather's immune system to fight her melanoma!"

Before Ellen could mount any false hopes, he added truthfully, "It hasn't been proved. But then, no one's tried it at so early a stage of the disease, while the patient is still strong. We have to pray it works."

"It'll work," she said to reassure him.

Because they were both extremely doubtful.

A week later, when he felt his body had had time to build up a strong white-cell response, Otis Cruikshank began to verify his first step in the experiment. Late at night, he locked himself in his lab, drew a full pint of his own blood and submitted a sample of it to the electronic Coulter counter. His white-cell count proved to be very high—as high as he had hoped. He was ready to proceed.

Before Otis could begin, a knock on the door interrupted him. To his relief, it turned out to be only a cleaning woman, who came and left quickly. Otis Cruikshank turned back to the intricate procedure of processing his own blood—separating the white cells from the red in the centrifuge, processing the white cells and finally isolating the transfer factor which he hoped would save Heather's life.

When he was done, he set out a fresh white lab towel and placed in it a new hypodermic barrel and needle and a sealed test tube containing the transfer factor in solution. He folded the towel neatly, slipped it into his coat pocket and left.

At dawn he arrived home and gave Heather her first injection, just under her left shoulder so that it would not show or hinder her right hand's mobility.

He repeated this process every two weeks. The strain on his system began to show and gave rise to comments by his colleagues about how pale and thin he looked. So now, after he drew his blood, Otis reinfused his own red cells to restore his strength. Soon there were no more comments on his appearance.

Four months later, after Heather had received regular injections of transfer factor and had undergone her periodic body and brain scans, Otis Cruikshank was suddenly summoned to the hospital for a consultation with Slade, Berger and Cross.

They were waiting for him in Berger's office, where sets of scans were mounted in the viewing box.

Slade began. "Otis, these are the scans we took of Heather this week. You'll notice there is something extremely strange about them." He turned to Berger. "Doctor?"

Berger indicated another set of scans. "These were taken four months ago, the time we detected brain involvement.

Notice the hot spot here that caused Dr. Cross to recommend brain surgery. Well, that hot spot does *not* appear in her brain scan this week." Berger pointed to the clean, fresh brain scan.

Otis Cruikshank felt a surge of exhilaration and relief. But caution made him ask, "Meaning, Doctor?"

"Meaning, Otis, that we are coming to the optimistic conclusion that your daughter has had a marked regression, if not a complete remission. This is rare, but there are cases on record of spontaneous remission of melanoma."

Otis Cruikshank stared at the lights and shadows on the films that confronted him. So it worked! Keeping his exultation in check, he said calmly, "I see."

"Of course, we'll continue to check her out every three months for at least five years," Slade went on. "But the evidence is there. Spontaneous remission!"

Otis thought, She's saved! Call it spontaneous remission or anything you wanted, from now on he had two important duties in his life: to continue giving Heather her periodic injections to prevent retrogression, and to duplicate his own results officially in the lab so that the world could benefit from his startling discovery.

EIGHT

For days after Slade and Berger had revealed Heather's surprising cure, Otis Cruikshank closeted himself in his office at the Institute.

When administrative pressures urgently demanded his attention, his secretary explained that he was deep in a new concept and could not be interrupted, not even for Edgar Woolsey. Frantic at any development he could not control, Woolsey called Carole Evans. She was as mystified as everyone else by Otis' sudden seclusion, but she was able to allay some of Woolsey's more neurotic suspicions.

She remembered that when she had first come to Trask, Otis had acted in exactly that same manner. And some weeks thereafter he had emerged with a protocol which, when it finally proved out, brought tremendous acclaim to the Institute. She reminded Edgar of that time and suggested that Otis be left alone. No administrative problem was so pressing that it should be permitted to interfere. Between them, Edgar Woolsey and Carole Evans made all the decisions that could not be delayed.

Laying out a protocol for an experiment was an art in itself. One had to have a clear view of the problem and the desired result. One had to know laboratory procedure intimately, to know what instruments, techniques and facilities were available. One had to have a detective's un-erring sense of how to arrange the clues and how to pro-vide for the proper number and variety of controls so that all possible questions were anticipated and all doubts elimi-nated.

A protocol also had to provide for the procedure to be done over and over again so that other men in other labora-tories could duplicate the experiment and achieve the same result. Many times scientists had announced significant findings only to have them challenged by other researchers who could not duplicate the experiment with the same degree of success. But in this case Otis was not worried. Before he started, he *knew* that he had proved his premise. Not *in vitro*, in the test tube, where many results seemed so clearly defined, only to fail to prove out when applied *in vivo*. Otis Cruikshank had proved his thesis in a living human being. It should be possible—not necessarily easy, but absolutely possible—to reproduce that result in the laboratory. The fact that he had defied one of the most basic rules of scientific research by experimenting on a patient was a fact he firmly refused to consider. With Bob Niles's help he would prove his theory in the lab and then tell a few key scientists his results with his daughter. For the time being he would concentrate on the protocol and block out all other thoughts.

But before Otis first revealed his protocol to any of his colleagues, Ellen voiced his fear.

"Your model is so complete. It follows what you did so closely. Won't they suspect?"

"As nearly as possible I've made it read like any other protocol I've ever designed," Otis assured her.

"The similarities are so striking."

"Only to the three of us who know."

"Otis, I've this terrible feeling that someone will discover what you did."

"It's a risk I'll have to take. The work is too important

to bury," he said. "Besides, I've already arranged the meeting."

"Meeting?"

"Instead of circulating my protocol in the usual way to members of the Projects Committee, I've called a meeting in the conference room tomorrow."

"Be careful, Otis; be very careful," she pleaded.

Edgar Woolsey, Carole Evans, Wolfam, Corrigan and the other department heads at Trask all attended, curious as to what Otis had devised while locked away from them. He entered the room carrying under his arm a dozen copies of his protocol. He took his place and stared down the long polished table to where Edgar Woolsey had seated himself, as was his practice. Though Woolsey controlled the purse strings, and thus the heartbeat, of the Trask Institute, he made it a point to present the image of a self-effacing man when in the company of his scientists. It was a bit of Christian modesty that he trusted did not escape the notice of his staff.

Edgar Woolsey had before him a fresh yellow pad and a sharp pencil. While scientists spoke of aims, ambitions, purposes, Edgar Woolsey made notes about prices of animals, costs of feeding and tending, laboratory personnel, evaluating committees, man-hours, operating rooms, necropsy rooms and all the other costly items required to carry out the elaborate schemes the scientists devised. Scientists and their ambitions were like children and their fantasies. Someone had to concentrate on the dollars-and-cents reality, and that was Woolsey's job.

Otis Cruikshank opened the meeting without any preliminaries.

"It is time for science to take a marked stride forward in research into malignant tumors. No matter how much work we do in the laboratory, we are never in a position to duplicate the physician's clinical experience.

"*Till now!*" Otis announced, pointedly.

There was a stir about the table, and a number of the men suddenly worried that their chief might have evolved a totally impractical protocol.

"In the laboratory we've done thousands—I suppose in all, tens of thousands—of experiments with animals in which we build up their resistance to cancer cells by treating them in advance. Then we inoculate them with cancer and watch them resist it or completely fight it off. From this we derive certain bits of helpful knowledge.

"But what good does it do to build up an animal's resistance to accepting cancer cells when the experience of the human patient is the complete opposite?

"My protocol proposes to re-create in the laboratory the actual clinical conditions that prevail with human cancer patients. And to do so on a scale vast enough to shorten our ultimate goal by many years."

Otis' colleagues continued to listen attentively to his daring proposal, but Edgar Woolsey was stopped by the phrase "on a scale vast enough to make some significant discoveries." With grants already cut down due to economic conditions, Trask's budget had been stretched beyond the point of safe fiscal management. He had just reviewed the figures this morning. It was quite evident that either Trask Institute must find new money sources or else he would have to eat into capital to see the year through. The Trustees would not welcome that. Nevertheless, for the moment Woolsey said nothing, allowing the scientist to continue.

"In the clinical situation, cancer is rarely discovered by the doctor until it has become a detectable mass. It is then treated by various established means. Primarily by surgery, which means that the mass of tumor is greatly reduced. At least temporarily. Then, in many cases, it reappears either at the original site or some distant site within the body. The human cancer patient thus has had a lengthy and debilitating exposure to the disease before any treatment. The reverse of what we do in our labs. Therefore the animal studies that we do now are inadequate for research in transfer factor."

At the term "transfer factor" several of the scientists looked down. They had expected something more startling. Transfer factor had been worked on in many laboratories, and while it always seemed promising, there had been little real evidence produced that it would accomplish a regression of the disease on any acceptable scale.

"What I propose is a laboratory model that will mirror in every way what happens to the human patient in the clinical situation. To do this will require an enormous number of albino New Zealand rabbits.

"And not only a great number of animals, but daily care and testing of those animals, extensive implants of human tissue, both benign and cancerous, considerable surgery, blood tests, biopsies and nuclear body scans."

Woolsey stared down at his yellow pad and began to doodle. After this list of expensive procedures, which would require much staff, lab and other fees, he had just closed his mind to the entire experiment. All he needed now was some argument with which to attack it.

Carole Evans watched him draw a series of zeros, which meant that he had already begun to assemble the figures that would justify his veto.

Otis was just winding up. "First we must breed and select two hundred rabbits which are tolerant of human melanoma cells. One hundred of those will become our "patients." The second hundred tolerant rabbits will become our first control group, which will receive melanoma cells but no transfer. A second control group will receive only transfer factor. A third control group of one hundred rabbits will receive neither melanoma nor transfer factor. And, of course, our final group of one hundred rabbits will be treated and used as donors of the transfer factor.

"Once we've established our groups, we will treat the first two groups precisely the way human melanoma patients are treated. We will allow them to develop tumors until there is a detectable mass, just as in humans. Then we will perform surgery on them. Once they have been treated surgically, we will keep scanning them until the moment of reappearance of the tumor somewhere in the body. From that point on we shall make a key distinction in treatment between the two groups. One group, our patients, will receive transfer factor from our donor group on a regular basis, and we shall observe whether the tumor regresses or if remission occurs. The second group, our control animals with melanoma, will not be given any but the standard surgery and chemotherapy.

"At the same time, the control group without cancer will be given only transfer factor, so that if there is anything wrong with our preparation of transfer factor it will show up in them. Of course, the rabbits that receive no tumor and no treatment will serve as controls for the entire group. Thus we shall have eliminated all factors of chance.

"When the results are in, we shall have a very clear idea of the clinical effectiveness of transfer factor when used *in time*."

There were numerous scientific questions to which Otis supplied the answers. But the meeting was not closed with his replies. All the department heads sensed that the real battle would be between the scope of the experiment and the budget that Woolsey had to work with. They were not disappointed. For Woolsey spoke up finally, trying to sound ingenuous and self-effacing.

"Otis, one thing I didn't quite understand. The part where you mentioned the need to, I believe your phrase was, 'breed and select two hundred rabbits with a tolerance for human melanoma cells.' Precisely what did you mean?"

"I know you're aware of the phenomenon of rejection in human-to-human transplants. Well, a xenograft, that is a graft across species lines, human-to-animal or animal-to-human, has even less chance of taking. But it is possible to breed and inoculate newborn rabbits with human tissue and eventually make them tolerant. However, I must be truthful and admit that the percentage of success is very low."

"So," Woolsey countered, "we're really not discussing hundreds of New Zealand albino rabbits, but possibly a few thousand."

"Probably more than that," Otis Cruikshank was quick to admit. Then he explained, "To produce one rabbit tolerant of human melanoma cells we might have to go through as many as twenty or thirty. And to select only the best and most productive rabbits for our donor group we may have to discard five for every one we finally use."

Woolsey nodded, not in agreement, but with a sense of foreboding. "Then, Otis, are you saying that we might be involved with the purchase, care and feeding of five or six thousand New Zealand rabbits?"

"If we're lucky, we'll get by with that number," Otis granted.

Edgar Woolsey's mathematical mind was spinning in a frenzy now. To purchase five thousand New Zealand rabbits would cost a minimum of twenty-five to thirty thousand dollars in today's market. But that was only the beginning. It cost fifty cents a day to feed and care for each animal. Even if the average group of rabbits on hand at any time were half that number that expense alone would run to almost ten thousand dollars a week during the months of the experiment. Added onto that were the other items Otis had glibly mentioned—implants, surgery, blood tests, biopsies, nuclear scans, and, of course, a staff large enough to accomplish all this.

Finally Woolsey spoke up, "Otis, do you realize that you're proposing an experiment that will run into the hundreds of thousands of dollars?"

"I said it would have to be done on a vast scale," Otis admitted frankly. "But the results will justify it, I'm sure!"

"I see," Edgar Woolsey said thoughtfully, trying to give the impression that he still had an open mind. But for himself he had found the basis on which to disapprove the entire protocol.

Later, after the meeting, Edgar Woolsey received a strange and surprising call from Otis Cruikshank.

"Edgar," Otis began, "one thing I forgot to mention."

"Yes?" Woolsey responded cautiously, expecting some disclosure that would increase costs still more.

"This is only a *proposed* plan. I do not intend to implement it at once. I myself want time to think it over. Even if you approve it."

Woolsey had been caught off guard. No scientist who had exhibited such a burning desire to proceed with an experiment had ever asked for the right to change his mind once approval had been granted. It was a strange and unsettling development. Otis Cruikshank would bear watching, Woolsey decided.

He applied himself with special concentration to reading the Cruikshank protocol. When he had finished, he glanced at his wristwatch. Just before three o'clock. Carole Evans must be back from lunch by now.

He dialed her private line. He never called her through the switchboard if it could be avoided.

"Carole?" he asked cautiously.

"Yes," she responded coolly, since there were two laboratory assistants in her office.

"Could you get away this afternoon? Say about four?"

"I think my schedule would allow that," she responded, making every pretense of being both professional and casual.

"Good."

There was no need to agree on a place. It was always the same. The Lakeview. A motel far enough from Trask not to be frequented by the personnel of the Institute.

CHAPTER

NINE

Edgar Woolsey was a man for whom the only proper description was distinguished-looking. Tall, muscular, he had once been a second-string halfback at Princeton, and still carried himself well. His hair, which had been blond, was sandy gray now. His features were regular, and under his trim nose there was a thin graying mustache which he felt lent him a certain British air. Edgar Woolsey had graduated from Princeton with an academic degree that qualified him for nothing in particular. With no special professional field in mind, he went off to New York, where, aided by an alumnus who was a vice-president in a large agency, Woolsey had entered advertising.

Early on, he developed the art of sitting in meetings and appearing interested, thoughtful and creative while scrawling notes on a large yellow pad. Later he would be seen pecking away at a typewriter, ostensibly working on his notes, but actually making sure that the partners saw him through his open door as they left for the day.

Gradually he caught the eye of Bruce Britten, president of the agency, whose daughter was finishing at Wellesley without impressive scholarship and with a social life that was nothing short of disaster. She was a plain-looking girl who had assumed that the way to social success in Boston academic circles was promiscuity. But she proved a failure even at that, and only won herself a reputation as an easy lay.

Under the constant nagging of his wife to produce a husband for Lorna from among all the young men he employed, Bruce Britten decided on Edgar Woolsey. Woolsey was handsome, seemed reasonably intelligent and might conceivably succeed him as head of the agency one day. So he invited him for a weekend of tennis and swimming at the club. For a young man with no specific ambition except success, Edgar Woolsey recognized the opportunity and began his courtship of Lorna Britten. It went swiftly and well, aided by Mrs. Britten's urging. Within four months there was a wedding, and the following Christmas, Edgar Woolsey was advanced to assistant account executive on Britten's part of the General Motors account. He did very well at the job, since his main function was to entertain GM executives when they came to New York or to accompany them to California when GM commercials were being filmed on the wide expanses of California desert and mountains.

During the day he watched the shooting with an intent and seemingly expert eye, but never made any suggestions. At night, he provided the GM brass with a variety of sexual diversions from his little blue book which contained an endless supply of names and phone numbers for Los Angeles, New York and Chicago. GM executives did not screw around in Detroit. Not for fear of their wives, but because it was against company policy.

Edgar Woolsey would have pretended to engage in those activities because it was good for business. But actually, he was a man of insatiable sexual desire, with a flair for exotic and adventurous experimentation in bed. His wife, who had never really enjoyed sex even while she was being promiscuous, was revolted by some of his practices and had limited their sexual life to what she considered acceptable sex, leaving Edgar free to satisfy his desires with young women who were handy, convenient and pliant. When he was entertaining clients, the agency paid for his sex. When he was on his own, he had a weakness for young, busty girls who wore miniskirts around the office and flaunted long, enticing thighs and legs.

Since advertising men's hours are notoriously irregular, Lorna Woolsey never thought to question Edgar. She was actually relieved when he came home late and didn't make any sexual demands on her. They had made one try at having a child, but it ended in a miscarriage and from that time on she had felt little responsibility for either sex or childbearing. If she suspected Edgar's affairs, she never reproached him. When her father asked how things were going, she pretended to be happy. Actually, she contemplated suicide several times, and once had taken an overdose of barbiturates, though not sufficiently large to cause anything but a diagnosis of an inadvertent act.

Edgar Woolsey's current affair in the office had been going on for five months. One day the girl, who had now been advanced from the mail room to the stenographic pool, came to his office while his secretary was away from her desk. She closed the door softly, sat down in a large leather chair usually graced only by other company executives and said simply, "Edgar, we have to do something."

"Do something? About what?" he asked.

"Remember that night you wanted to do it straight," she said, "but without a safety? You said you liked it better that way. Remember?"

Edgar Woolsey said, "Oh . . ." in a guarded, tentative way that admitted very little.

"Well, I think I'm pregnant. I've missed two periods already."

Since it was in the days before legalized abortion, Edgar Woolsey had now to consider one of two courses. Either make contact with one of the secret abortionists that he knew, or else disclaim responsibility.

He remained as controlled as possible, though inwardly raging. This girl threatened his career, his entire way of life. What would happen if that old straitlaced bastard Britten discovered that his son-in-law had knocked up one of his office girls? And if fired, what else could he do that would pay him so well, allow him so many tax-free expense-account privileges, for being no more than convivial and charming? Edgar Woolsey had no choice. He had to disown this girl and anything to do with her.

"How do I know it was me? I only see you on Tuesdays and Thursdays. And not at all when I'm out of town. And I'm out of town a lot. It could have been any one of a hundred other men. I'm not taking responsibility for that! Oh, no!" he declared.

At that the girl's face began to crumble. She started to weep.

"That won't help," he warned, more fearful than forbidding.

The girl sniffled and recovered. "I thought you loved me. At least had some feeling for me." She rose and started for the door, saying softly but making sure it was distinct enough to be heard clearly, "That's what she said you'd say."

"She?" Edgar Woolsey asked with new interest and much greater concern.

"My roommate."

"What does she know about this? I thought she was off at school every Tuesday and Thursday night!" Woolsey countered.

"She dropped out weeks ago. So on Tuesdays and Thursdays when you come over, she disappears. Goes off on a date. Or to a movie. We kind of have an arrangement. I do the same for her. She's even seen you twice when you were leaving. She thinks you're very handsome."

Edgar Woolsey didn't know if he was being set up or if the girl was telling the truth. One thing he did know. He couldn't afford to find out. Before the day was over, he made several calls and arranged for the girl to have an abortion over in Jersey City. Unfortunately, there had been complications, and the girl had to be admitted to Lenox Hill. Edgar Woolsey paid all the costs, channeling the money through the girl's roommate. Once the girl was out of the hospital, he was free of the whole dangerous and sordid episode, since it was understood that she would not return to the agency.

It was the closest brush with disaster Edgar Woolsey had ever had. The one time before that he'd knocked up a girl, at a weekend party back at Princeton, her family had taken care of everything, and kept it secret as well, so he was in the clear.

He was in the clear again. So he thought. Until the girl applied for unemployment insurance. Unaware of the facts, the controller of Britten, Ward and Osman disputed her claim, since a girl who had been ill and who had resigned on her own was not entitled to such payments. The girl's lawyer contended that since her illness had been induced by an executive of the company, hers was a work-related illness that entitled her not only to unemployment insurance but probably workmen's compensation as well.

The case and her claim were so unique that a reporter on a New York tabloid picked it up, and it became an amusing scandal. It was not amusing to Edgar Woolsey. And much less so to Bruce Britten. When word of it reached him, he immediately summoned Edgar back from Detroit, even though the agency was making a most important presentation of a new campaign to the GM hierarchy.

Britten sat Edgar down in his office.

"You dirty sonofabitch! You fucking whoremaster!" This was strong language from Britten, who liked to pose as a religious Christian churchman. "You prick! I have put up with your screwing around from the day you married my daughter. Well, screw all you want on the outside! But not in my office! I thought we had a gentlemen's agreement. You live your own life. I won't tell my daughter. But keep it within bounds. But no, you can't resist a young piece of ass, can you? You are a sucker for tits and legs. I can see it in your eyes whenever some young pair of knockers comes bouncing down the hallway. But this is the end. This whole damn scandal can ruin me unless I do something about it.

"Well, I am going to do something about it. You are fired, son-in-law. Clear out your desk! And haul ass out of here! Today! By the time I get back from lunch! Is that clear?"

Edgar Woolsey sat there stunned, until Bruce Britten commanded, "Move!"

Edgar Woolsey had withdrawn to the solitude of his own home. For days he sat there, silent and alone, brooding over the destruction he had brought upon himself. After several weeks he tried making calls to old schoolmates and associates he had known at Britten, Ward and Osman who had moved on to other agencies. But few of his calls were accepted and none of his messages were returned. Suddenly he had no present, and worse, no future. He grew depressed to such a degree that his wife interceded with her mother. And her mother with Bruce Britten.

Finally Britten relented. Using some of his extensive contacts, he was able to secure for Edgar Woolsey a position as assistant to the administrator of a small research foundation on the West Coast. That satisfied Britten on two counts. His daughter would be provided for. His son-in-law would be removed from New York.

Edgar Woolsey worked at his new employment with the same degree of charm he had exerted in his old. He came to be known as a nice, willing young man. Handsome and presentable, chastened by his shocking loss of the sinecure he had expected would see him through his life, he applied himself to this new work with great intensity and energy. The experience in New York had taught him two things. To be eminently circumspect and careful in the manner in which he conducted his sexual life. And not to permit anything, or anyone, ever again to threaten his career. His new attitude won him a reputation for being a young man with most conservative habits and outlook. It served him well in his new work, since trustees of foundations were usually conservative people.

To avoid scandal, he limited his sexual life to his own wife, except when business took him out of town. Then he was exceedingly careful. Eventually the whole distasteful episode in New York was forgotten by everyone save Lorna and himself. She hardly dared mention it, for he went into uncontrollable rages, accusing her of trying to destroy his career. He carried the experience around like a hair shirt. It made him paranoid to the degree that he suspected everyone. Which prepared him perfectly for institutional politics.

Thus, when his boss retired, Edgar Woolsey took over his job without any opposition. After he had occupied the position for six years, building up contacts among foundations and families given to charitable works, he was ready to move up to a larger institution.

When the job at Trask opened he applied, and with some additional help from Bruce Britten, Edgar Woolsey was appointed Administrator.

He came to Trask well trained for the work. In middle age he had the sort of looks that qualified a man to play a physician in television commercials. Despite his outward appearance of mature confidence, two things had never changed in Edgar Woolsey: his basic insecurity, which gave him a tendency to panic, and his eye for a good-looking, sexually promising woman. He was better able now to curb his desires, but they were as strong as ever. Since his work called for him to travel a great deal, he had much sexual freedom and opportunity. At home, within the confines of Trask, he was much more careful, but no less predatory.

It was only natural that he would discover Carole Evans.

They always arrived at The Lakeview in separate cars. Since Carole Evans was the second to arrive this afternoon, she deliberately drove past Edgar Woolsey's Mercedes to park at the far end of the grounds. Even a chance observer who might recognize their cars would not be inclined to mark the coincidence. Woolsey always registered in a room on the side of the motel away from the road, facing the nearby woods. In accordance with their ritual, he brought along a bottle of Scotch in his attaché case and had collected a bucket of cubes from the icemaker. By the time there would be a discreet knock on the door, he would have arranged everything as usual. Then Carole would arrive. He would admit her and carefully lock and latch the door. First he would kiss her—a long, open-mouthed, devouring kiss. Then he would ceremoniously remove her black-framed glasses. To him, that was one of the most sensuous moments in their affair. To remove her glasses was to strip her more totally than to divest her of her last bit of clothing. The transformation that took place never ceased to arouse him.

With her glasses went every vestige of the cool reserve she steadfastly exhibited at Trask. She was no longer the staid Mother Superior but a sensuous woman. There were many times during meetings of staff when Edgar Woolsey secretly admired the totally different impression that she was able to project in the stainless steel and glass, computerized world in which she practiced her profession. Her glasses, her severe hairstyle, her white lab coat all conspired to conceal both her voluptuous body and her enormous sexual hunger. If she weren't so ambitious she would have made some man a fine wife or an even more fascinating mistress.

Only occasionally, when her lab coat came open, did one

detect her marvelous breasts—full, round, beautifully separated. She was feminine enough never to wear pants in the lab, a habit that many women researchers and technicians had fallen into of late, much to Woolsey's dismay. He had always admired a good pair of legs. Carole Evans had good legs.

Edgar Woolsey and Carole Evans had discovered their mutual desire for each other at a scientific meeting in Boston. She had gone there to deliver an important paper. He went along to solicit funds from two wealthy trusts which he hoped would be impressed by Carole's paper. Her presentation went brilliantly and was extremely well received. As a result, Woolsey had spent dinner and the evening with family members of both trusts. He came away with the assurance of important financial support. He had returned to the Ritz late that night and called Carole from the lobby, asking permission to drop up and congratulate her.

He had been stunned when she opened the door. She wore no glasses. In place of the starched white lab coat or the severe gray suits she affected at conventions, she wore a red negligee. Her black hair hung loosely and provocatively over her shoulders. Her breasts protruded promisingly above the red lace trim of her gown.

In that moment Edgar Woolsey felt an uncontrollable surge of arousal and excitation that reminded him of his early youth. Sexual adventurer though he was, it had been years since he'd been so instantly and irresistibly determined to seduce any woman. He would never discover that the most subtle and effective part of Carole Evans' sexual aura was to allow the man to consider himself the aggressor, the victor. In the end it was she who always had her way.

His profuse congratulations became a form of wooing. He made love to her that night and the succeeding two nights they were in Boston. When they returned to Trask, she had every intention of breaking off the relationship. It would have to become another chance affair—brief, unplanned, impetuous, under circumstances that would not be re-created.

But Edgar Woolsey would not allow it. She had become part of him and he would not let her go. He offered to divorce his wife for her. She forbade it. Carole Evans had her own life plan, and marriage and children were not part of it. She had her work, her ambitions. If their affair were to interfere with them, then it was the affair which must end. She wanted to be renowned for her professional achievements. Not to be remembered as "Oh, yes, she's the woman who was involved with Edgar Woolsey."

Carole Evans had made several important contributions in the field of microbiology. She intended to make a great many more. She also intended, though she did not announce it publicly, to be the first woman Director of Research at a large and important institute.

That passionate part of her which hungered for a man could be served only so long as it was consistent with her ambitions. Twice during the last three years she had broken off with Edgar. Not because she was tired of him or wished to end the affair, but she was testing herself, making sure that she could end it when that became desirable. When she was sure she could control the situation completely, she felt free to resume their secret meetings.

Today Carole came to The Lakeview relaxed and happy. It had been some time since they'd made love, and she was eager for him. From the moment she let him remove her glasses, let him take the pins out of her lustrous hair, she was excited.

They took each other with the familiarity of practiced lovers. They wooed each other with every part of themselves. When it was over, and they lay spent, he rested his cheek against her warm breasts and was at peace.

It was usually in precisely those moments of warm, moist intimacy that Edgar Woolsey offered to divorce Lorna and marry her. Carole always listened, indulging him, and wondering if it was his way of repaying her. Possibly guilt made him pursue her that way. Or else her constant refusals enabled him to make such proposals in perfect safety. Either way, she didn't mind. It amused her.

Today when he lay there, cheek against her breast, he mentioned neither divorce nor marriage. He had more urgent matters in mind.

"Darling, have you talked with Otis recently?"

"Has anybody?" she asked. "He's been locked in by himself for days now."

"He never discussed his protocol with you before the meeting today?"

"Not a word," she said, tracing the lines of his profile from his forehead down his short, handsome nose.

"He had no right to hold that goddamned meeting!" Woolsey exploded suddenly.

"Edgar!" She was surprised by his vehemence.

"No right!" he repeated. He turned and looked up at her. "He did it deliberately to embarrass me."

"Come now, Edgar, it had nothing to do with you."

"Oh, didn't it?" he challenged. "Just think! He admitted that it was one of the costliest experiments he'd ever proposed. He knows we don't have that kind of money. So he thought he'd put me on the spot by asking me in front of all the department heads. And damn it, I have to refuse! There just isn't that kind of money!"

"Edgar, please, calm down and listen," she tried to interrupt.

"That man hates me. He always has. He thinks he owns this place. Because he's been chief here, because he designed Trask Park, he thinks it belongs to him. He's resented me from the first day I came here."

"I've never heard him say that."

"Of course not! He's too damn shrewd to say it openly. But sometimes I think he spies on me!"

Carole laughed.

"It isn't funny! He wants to destroy me," he raged, then realized his voice might be heard beyond the walls of their own room.

"Edgar, Otis Cruikshank isn't the kind of man who would like to destroy anyone. Every time he has to tell even an incompetent researcher that he's fired, it's like an amputation."

"This may all be amusing to you. But not to me!" Woolsey said.

His mind was already plotting strategies that involved all kinds of vengeance against Otis Cruikshank.

Suddenly he exploded again. "Did you read that damned protocol?"

"Of course. I skipped lunch to read it."

"Me too," Woolsey had to admit. "Well?"

"Theoretically, it's unchallengeable. He's gone at it with his usual perception and insight."

"I don't mean that," Woolsey exploded intolerantly. *"Can it work?"*

"Edgar, my dear, if we were sure in advance that experiments would work, we could just sit around and spin our daydreams into scientific facts."

"What I mean is, do you think it has a chance?" Woolsey demanded.

"We never know till it's over, do we?"

Frustrated, Edgar Woolsey rose from their warm and fragrant bed and crossed the room and mixed them fresh drinks. As he returned, Carole laughed. Embarrassed, he asked, "Something wrong?"

"I was just thinking. What would Otis say if he could see you now—naked, limp from making love and discussing his protocol at the same time?"

In his present mood Edgar refused to smile. Instead he let his lips move across her neck and her soft shoulders to dwell on her nipples. Then he moved down across her soft curving belly till he lost himself between her thighs. She never resisted him when he did that. She didn't this time either. He evoked her most passionate and ecstatic moments that way. When he had brought her to the point of orgasm not once but several times, he felt almost as satisfied as she.

With passion spent, his paranoia seemed to recede. They were both quiet, sipping their drinks, contented, until Carole asked, "Are you going to see that he gets the money?"

"I wouldn't know where to get it!" he exclaimed, hating to be reminded of the subject when he felt so relaxed and warm.

"You always have before," she reminded him.

"Damn it, things are not the same. You may not have noticed but there's a recession! Trusts and foundations are earning less than half what they used to. Even if things get better economically, it'll be a year or more before dividends catch up with the recovery! Or doesn't Otis Cruikshank take things like that into account?"

Woolsey jumped out of bed and began to pace. "You know, sometimes I think he does it intentionally!"

"Does what?"

"Comes up with these costly experiments! To see if I *can* raise the money! Or else he wants to get rid of me. Suppose I approve this protocol of his, and by some miracle find the money, and it fails? Who gets called on the carpet in Chicago? Otis Cruikshank? Not on your life! He's a noble scientist. I'll be the one who gets the blame! Why didn't I evaluate the chances of success before squandering all that money?"

He looked to her for sympathy but found none and began to pout like a small boy. "You don't know what I go through up there, Carole. You don't."

Instead of extending sympathy, Carole Evans asked, "You think he'll resign if he doesn't get the funds?"

"That's what he's banking on, the bastard! If I give him the money and he fails, I'll get hell. If I don't give him the money and he quits, the trustees will want to know why I bungled it. After all, he's still a powerful name." He paused, calming himself. "You've worked with him as long as anyone. What do you think?"

"I don't know," Carole was forced to admit. "I've never seen him so personally involved. He's usually cold as ice about his work. I just don't know."

"My God," Woolsey exclaimed suddenly, "you don't think he's suffering a personality change?"

"Paranoia isn't contagious," Carole said, laughing.

He turned on her. "That's right, make fun of me! Carole, I want you to do something for me. Watch that man. If you observe anything peculiar, let me know at once!"

"You mean you want me to spy on him," she corrected.

"*Observe!* I didn't say anything about spying!" he said, adding somewhat frantically, "Oh, darling, what do I do?"

"Whatever you have to do to keep a man as valuable as Otis Cruikshank from resigning," Carole said finally, getting out of bed.

That was how things stood until Marietta Carter's enthusiastic response to the project took the decision out of Edgar Woolsey's hands.

Now it was no longer a question of whether Trask Institute could afford the enormous cost. Edgar Woolsey would find the money somehow. It was a matter of making sure that Otis Cruikshank delivered, that his protocol proved out.

His success could ensure Trask's future over the next decade . . . to say nothing of Edgar Woolsey's.

CHAPTER

TEN

It was nearly a week later that Otis and Ellen invited Bob for dinner. Heather was present, but quiet and withdrawn. She sipped her chilled white wine and listened politely, but Bob could detect a definite reserve in her frank blue eyes.

The meal proceeded pleasantly, involving no discussions of consequence. Bob noticed that Heather was becoming even more silent. He remembered their conversation about replacing Duncan in Otis' affections and wondered if that was what was troubling her now.

Ellen Cruikshank must have noticed, for she tried to introduce a more personal note.

"And have you found a permanent place to live, Bob?"

"An apartment at Trask House. Good view of the river. And just small enough for a man to take care of by himself."

For the first time, Heather spoke up. "I hear it's a place for swinging singles. Practically every unmarried man and woman at Trask lives there."

"I wouldn't know. I've been so busy," he said. "Furnishing an apartment takes time."

"Perhaps I could help," Ellen volunteered. "And Heather, too. She's very good at that sort of thing."

Instead of taking up her mother's suggestion, Heather resumed eating.

Dinner over, Otis invited Bob into his den. Hilda had

brought in the coffee tray, and Otis closed the door. It was clear now that the entire evening had only been a prelude.

"Robert," Otis began, "I've studied your protocols. All three of them. So has the committee. A majority has voted to approve them. In fact, Dr. Evans thinks they should be put into work at the first possible moment. Which, I need not tell you, is a research euphemism for whenever we can get a grant."

Bob smiled stiffly, and Otis continued.

"However, I am going to ask you to forgo them in favor of another project. You don't have to accept what I offer," Otis said. "But I do wish you to consider it before you make your choice."

"What's the other project?"

"I assume you've heard about the Cruikshank protocol?"

"I've heard it mentioned," Bob admitted.

"Do you know the nature of it?"

"Only that it has to do with melanoma research," Bob said, aware of the scans he'd seen in Berger's office and hoping to detect some reaction in Otis that might confirm his suspicion as to who the patient was.

But Otis gave no sign; he merely asked, "Is that all you know about it?"

"It's going to be very costly. There are all kinds of rumors about other projects that'll be delayed or cut off if it goes through," Bob said.

"True, unfortunately," Otis agreed. "There'll be resentment because they all think that I've bulled it through by the sheer power of my position. The truth is, once Marietta Carter picked up the idea I was the last one to agree to proceed with my protocol, and I am still uncomfortable at being forced to move this quickly. That's why I will only delegate this experiment to someone I totally trust. When the data start to accumulate I want to be absolutely certain they can be relied upon. For that reason I'm asking you to put aside your own protocols to take on the execution of mine."

Bob felt flattered, yet deprived. He'd worked for two whole years on his own projected experiments. Otis sensed his hesitancy.

"If this succeeds, Bob, you'll benefit tremendously. Having your name on this paper could be the making of your career. Put you miles ahead of any of your contemporaries."

Otis was not exaggerating. For Bob Niles to have his name linked with Otis Cruikshank's on such an important scientific paper was a great honor.

"But I don't want you to agree without being totally familiar with the project. Take a copy with you. Study it for a few days. Then I want your opinion, impersonal and dispassionate.

"The one thing I do not want is for you to agree because it's I who am asking you to do it."

Otis drew a large envelope out of the top drawer of his desk.

"Read this. Question it. And when you're ready, let's discuss it."

On the way out, Bob stopped by the living room to thank Ellen for dinner. He found her hooking a design for a pillow cover. He admired it, and she offered, "Let me know your color scheme and I'll do one for your new apartment."

"Thanks, I'd like that," he said.

Impulsively, he kissed her on the cheek. She was touched and embarrassed. He left, but not without noticing that Heather had already disappeared upstairs. He was sure now that her resentment toward him was real and highly personal.

He returned to his small apartment at Trask House, kicked off his loafers, undid his tie, opened his collar, took a can of icy beer from the refrigerator and settled down to read Otis Cruikshank's protocol.

He read carefully, visualizing each step of the procedure. When he finished, he leaned back and closed his eyes. He fully understood Marietta Carter's excitement. The experiment was of major importance. If the transfer factor worked in the animals, a major step in the treatment of cancer in humans would be realized.

Bob forced himself to moderate his excitement and read the paper again with a colder, more critical eye. This time he questioned every step, every assumption.

By the time he was done it was dawn. He was exhausted. He went to the window, intending to draw the shades and darken the room so that he could get a few hours' sleep. Instead, he stared out at the river, where the mist was rising. He watched until the first rays of the sun began to dispel the mist and paint the river a pale pink. He was no longer tired. He was imbued with the feeling that he was entering on a great scientific adventure. Such a chance might never come his way again.

Bob Niles was crossing the lobby of Trask House when a familiar voice greeted him. "Ah, good morning. I didn't know you were one of us."

He turned to confront Carole Evans.

"You'll lose your reputation," she said, smiling. "We're supposed to be the swingers of Trask Institute here."

When he stared at the forbidding combination presented by her efficiently braided hair and her thick black-rimmed glasses, he was strongly inclined to doubt it. She was not only unattainable; she seemed unapproachable.

"So far no one's knocked down my door," he said.

"Well, I'll start by crossing the campus with you."

On pleasant days, Institute personnel who lived at Trask House walked along the river and then across the green to their various buildings.

Carole Evans walked in precisely the same manner as she worked. Brisk, efficient, with no waste of time. Her conversation was the same.

"Has he shown it to you yet?"

"What?"

"Otis. His protocol."

Institute politics being what it was, Bob hesitated, wondering how much to admit. But before he could answer, Carole anticipated him.

"Of course he did. If he hadn't, you'd have said so at once," she said, smiling in a self-assured way. "What do you think?"

"It's terrific," he said.

"Terrific?" she challenged. "It's one of the most ambitious protocols I've ever seen! Only Otis Cruikshank could have come up with it. You're going to do it, aren't you?"

"I wouldn't pass it up for the world."

"I'm glad," Carole said. "It'll take a medical doctor and a man with clinical experience to carry out the technical end. If there's anything I can do to help, don't fail to call on me."

"Thanks," he said, and meant it. She didn't seem quite so aloof and forbidding anymore.

Bob called Otis' secretary at once to arrange a meeting, but was informed that four o'clock would be the earliest time. That gave him the chance to do two things he had planned. He would set down the practical demands of the protocol. And he would call Heather Cruikshank.

He called the Field School and found that she was in class and could not be disturbed. He left a message asking if she could have lunch with him at any place convenient to her. Then he started to make detailed notes on the equipment he would need to carry out the protocol. He was still pondering how many of the New Zealand rabbits would accept the human cells as against how many thousand would not and thus would prove costly and useless to the experiment, when his phone rang. The operator told him a young woman had called, left no name, but designated a restaurant in the city, and a time.

Heather was waiting for him at the small table in the corner of the quaint restaurant when he arrived.

"I'm sorry," she explained, "but this tearoom was the only convenient place. I hope you're not hungry. The sandwiches are as thin as bookmarks. And they trim the crusts."

She was making an obvious effort to be lighthearted. But she finally abandoned that tack and got right to the point. "You called me. What about?"

"Last night," Bob said.

"If I was rude, I'm sorry. But I was preoccupied. One of my pupils is having a problem at home. His parents have decided to get a divorce, and he's sure he's the cause. I have to figure out a way to help him through the crisis."

"It wasn't just you," Bob continued. "It was the entire family. You. Otis. Your mother. The Cruikshank home used to be a warm, relaxed place. Last night your mother tried to be as open and friendly as ever, but I had a suspicion she wasn't really feeling that way. And you sat at that table as if you were standing guard and warning off all trespassers. Am I a trespasser? And if I am, on what am I trespassing?"

Heather didn't answer but stared straight ahead, not looking at him. She seemed relieved when the waitress came to take their order.

"Is it what I said that day, about trying to take Duncan's place?" Bob continued after the waitress had gone. "I don't think so. Duncan was too long ago. I think it has to do with *now, today*. And I think I know what it is. I don't know everything, but I think I know enough."

"Such as?" she asked.

"Your father recently asked me to go to the University Hospital and view some body scans. Of a patient who had melanoma, and then showed a remarkable spontaneous remission. There is no doubt that the body scans were those of a mature adult."

"And?"

"Last night I read your father's protocol on melanoma. It's fascinating, ambitious and could be most significant."

For a moment she seemed to tense. "Do you believe it can work?" she asked.

"I think it might. It's certainly convincing on paper." Bob was determined not to let the conversation drift off into speculation. "The point is, that doesn't release me from my suspicions," he said. "There is something I have to find out. I'm hoping you'll give me a truthful answer."

Heather waited, silent.

"That protocol could only have come from a man who experienced a close contact with melanoma recently," Bob said. He studied her eyes. Against her will, they seemed to confirm what he had suspected. There was nothing to do but ask point-blank, "Tell me, Heather, has Otis had melanoma?"

"No, of course not!" she replied quickly. "If that's what this lunch is all about, you can go away assured that my father is perfectly healthy. The only thing he's likely to suffer from is overwork."

"You're sure?"

"Yes, of course," she insisted. "We're a close family. And we're truthful with each other. If anything were wrong, I would know." Then she turned her attention to her food. It was clear she did not want to continue this particular conversation.

They finished their lunch in silence and had gone to the parking lot when Bob said, "Promise me one thing. If Otis shows any symptoms, looks unusually pale or seems to have lost weight, if he evidences any unusual pain, you'll let me know?"

"I told you there is nothing wrong with him, but if you insist, yes, of course." She paused. One thing Bob Niles had said vibrated in her mind. She had to ask. "Suppose my father did have melanoma, and then had a complete remission—why are you still so worried about him?"

"Because remissions don't always last," Bob said. "Sometime, anytime, without warning, they can reverse themselves. Especially in melanoma."

Heather remained still and breathless for an instant as if frozen in time, her mind full of further questions she dared not ask. Finally, she said only, "See you" and turned to go. She was tall, as slender as her mother and graceful too. The kind of woman a man could easily fall in love with, Bob thought as she walked away.

At four o'clock Bob Niles appeared in the waiting room of Otis Cruikshank's office suite, but Dr. Cruikshank was tied up in an unexpected meeting. Twenty minutes later, Edgar Woolsey emerged and passed by, oblivious of Bob, muttering under his breath. It was obvious the meeting had run into hard questions and sharp answers.

Otis Cruikshank was standing with his back to the door, staring out at the grounds of Trask Park, when Bob entered. He neither turned nor acknowledged Bob's presence. Finally Otis exploded, "Oh, yes, they want results! Proof! Cures! At bargain prices! Well, damn it, it can't be done!

"First he opposes the experiment. Then because Marietta Carter is intrigued and he can smell big money, he supports it. Now he wants it done on a cut-down scale. . . ."

Finally, Otis turned to Bob. "I'm sorry you had to catch the brunt of my temper. On a project like this, with so much at stake, you'd think he'd be reasonable. But no! To press his point, Woolsey read me a list of the projects that are going to be jeopardized by putting my experiment into the works. He said several men have already threatened to quit. Pity is, I know exactly how they feel."

Otis Cruikshank was silent for a moment. Then he admitted, "I guess we all have to compromise. So I have too. I agreed to cut my protocol in half. Instead of one hundred animals in each group we'll only have fifty. At that it'll cost several hundred thousand dollars. But at least we'll be able to do it. We'll have to be even more careful; we'll have to . . ." Otis left the sentence suspended in midair.

He took a sharp look at Bob. "Here I am, speaking to you as if it's two of us, and you haven't even told me if you want to undertake the work."

"Of course I want to," Bob said. "It's the most fascinating experiment I've ever come across!"

"Then you don't mind putting aside your own protocols?"

"For something as important as this? I've already started to list the physical requirements. Space. Personnel. Equipment."

Otis was pleased. He smiled proudly. "I'll try not to keep looking over your shoulder, Robert. But I'll be mighty curious. I consider this the most important work of my life. And it will succeed! I *know* it!"

Thinking back on it, Bob Niles could never remember a time when Otis Cruikshank had been so positive about future results. It was his usual manner to urge caution, to remind the younger researchers that a good scientist was a man with an open mind, not one with preconceived convictions. This sudden change in temperament gave Bob further cause to worry.

Late that same night when most of the laboratories of Trask Institute were closed, Otis Cruikshank returned to his workroom. He inserted a needle into his arm and drew a pint of his own blood. He set the centrifuge at fifteen hundred revolutions per minute and placed the blood bag in it. When the machine had spun the blood for ten minutes, Otis turned it off. Through the clear plastic bag he could see that the blood had separated perfectly. Red cells on the bottom. White on top. First, for his own health and safety, he must reinfuse the red cells into his own bloodstream. Then he had to continue to process the white cells in order to isolate a fresh supply of transfer factor.

By now, the process had become routine. Still, Otis worked carefully, recording each step in the green canvasbacked journal he had kept faithfully since the first eventful night more than two years ago. With Bob Niles's decision to work on his protocol, the moment when Otis could reveal the journal and its startling contents became suddenly closer. How many times he had locked it away in his safe, worrying about what might happen if it were ever discovered!

Otis worked cheerfully, washing the white cells in a PBS saline solution to rid them of any plasma and then, to be safe, subjecting them to the centrifuge once more. Next he began the tedious process of freeze-thawing the white-cell lymphocytes seven times. This not only opened up the cells to allow them to easily release the transfer factor; at the same time it would insure against an adverse reaction when Heather received her injection. A soft, thick mass of white matter remained. He diluted this with the enzyme DNase and, finally, stoppered the test tube.

Then Otis Cruikshank carefully arranged the lab to indicate he had done other work. He selected a sterile injection kit, wrapped both the test tube of TF and the kit in a white lab towel and shoved them into his coat pocket.

Nothing had interrupted him, and no one had seen him except the usual cleaning woman and the uniformed security guard at the door. Otis walked home, gave Heather her regular biweekly injection and went to bed content that his secret was still safe.

He did not know that early the next morning the security man reported his late-night departure to Edgar Woolsey, who added a note to the file he had begun some time ago concerning Otis Cruikshank's habits.

Once it had been decided to proceed with the costly Cruikshank protocol, Edgar Woolsey began to prepare his own defenses in the event that it failed.

He knew that in any showdown between a Director of Research and a Director of Administration, trustees would always decide in favor of the Research chief. Unless there were extenuating circumstances. Edgar Woolsey did not intend to be caught unprepared if that time ever came.

ELEVEN

The tiny white-and-pink newborn New Zealand rabbit lay in Bob Niles's hand, its little heart beating furiously. This was the first of the new generation of rabbits his lab assistants had bred to serve as potential patients in the Cruikshank protocol. The chief lab assistant, Rosa Gregory, handed him the first hypodermic. To predispose them, each infant rabbit would receive two million normal human cells treated with 2,000 units of radiation to minimize the possibility of rejection. Bob injected the minute dose into the soft pink ear of the animal and handed it to Ania Sokolov, his second assistant, who returned it to its cage to be fed and watered. Every day that followed, it would be examined to determine whether or not it reacted to the human cells. Evidence of rejection would take the form of red rashes or lumpy areas on the rabbit's ear.

Bob Niles injected two hundred rabbits that day, hoping that at least one hundred rabbits would prove tolerant and provide fifty melanoma patients and fifty melanoma controls.

In the first two days there were several cases of marked rejection. After days three, four and five, more than 90 percent exhibited such signs, and had to be eliminated from consideration. He injected three hundred more newborns and then an additional hundred. And two hundred beyond that.

By the time Bob Niles had injected and observed several thousand rabbits, one hundred and sixty-seven had proved tolerant to human tissue, a number sufficient to permit him to proceed.

A third lab assistant, Charles Sanders, joined them for step two. Sanders carefully shaved the bellies of the young tolerant rabbits, using a No. 10 head in the electric clippers to remove most of the hair, and passed the animal to Ania Sokolov, who finished the job with the finer No. 40 head. Finally Rosa vacuumed the area so that no loose hair could get into the wound.

Bob placed the first shaved rabbit onto a layer of ether-saturated cotton on the bottom of a large glass jar. Within two minutes the animal was sufficiently anesthetized, and it was then placed on the stainless steel table where the operation would take place.

Using a scalpel, Bob carefully sliced off a thin layer of pink belly skin. He lifted a corresponding layer of human skin from a sterile dish and laid it over the area, making sure to place the human skin crosswise to the grain of the skin of the animal so that later he would be able to judge whether the graft had taken. He sutured the human skin in place with tiny, precise stitches, packed the area with Vaseline gauze and covered it with a protective bandage.

He would have to repeat this same procedure in exactly the same way for all one hundred and sixty-seven apparently tolerant animals.

By midafternoon Rosa Gregory suggested they take a break. They had worked straight through lunch.

"Good idea," Bob agreed. "Let's send out for some coffee."

"We're going out for it," she said with a tone of authority. When he looked at her a bit resentfully, Rosa smiled and said, "I'm old enough to be your mother. And if you haven't the sense to quit when you should, it's my duty to remind you."

He smiled in turn. "All right, then," he said; "where shall we go?"

Sitting in a booth in a nearby coffee shop, Bob felt free to talk. Talking to Rosa was easy somehow. She *was* like a mother, and he hadn't had one for a long time. He talked about his past, about the time he was a young boy.

He had been only ten years old when they sent him off to school. A fine boarding school in Massachusetts. One of the best, everyone said. From there, boys had an excellent chance to make it into Harvard. Perhaps he had been too young to leave home, because after that Robby Niles began to feel shunted aside.

Finally, after the initial feeling of being isolated and lonely receded, Robby enjoyed the school. His teachers liked him because he exhibited the degree of curiosity that marked the exceptional student. By the time he had finished the lower school and was ready to be graduated into the upper, he had collected honors in two courses, science and history. He looked forward to the day his parents would arrive to see him accept his prizes.

That day he donned his cap and gown and, like all the other boys who were graduating, went down to the tall old iron gates to await the arrival of his parents. Gradually parents came and claimed their sons and went off, until the graduates at the gates grew fewer and fewer. There was still no sign of Robby Niles's parents. Finally he was left, last and alone. They hadn't come. Despite their promises in letters and on the phone, they hadn't come.

Robby turned away from the gate, fighting tears, determined to take his honors despite them. But the messenger from the Headmaster's office stopped him. He was wanted. At once.

Controlling his tears, Robby went. When he entered the Headmaster's office there was a state trooper there in a gray uniform and with a broad-brimmed gray felt hat in his hands. Both men looked uneasy.

"Robert," the Headmaster asked, "who are your closest relatives?"

"My mother and father, of course."

"Aside from them?" the Headmaster asked gently.

"Uncle Fred. Fred Atkinson. My mother's brother. Why?"

"Where does he live, Robby?"

"South Orange." Robby started to explain, then asked, "Sir, please, what is it?"

The Headmaster signaled the trooper to leave them alone.

"Yes, sir," the trooper said. "We'll make contact by teletype."

When they were alone, the Headmaster said simply, "Robby, on the way here, your father had an automobile accident. A very bad accident. Your mother was with him."

"Both of them?"

"Yes, I'm afraid, both of them, Robby," the Headmaster said.

The tears of disappointment he had fought back at the gate burst forth as tears of grief. The Headmaster reached out, took him by the hand and embraced him.

In time, Uncle Fred came and took him to South Orange, New Jersey. His aunt made the proper speech about this being Robby's home now and that they would try to be like a mother and father to him. But no one could ever take the place of his real mother and father. Robby became determined that as soon as he was capable he would leave his uncle's home and strike out on his own.

He was working his way through college when he discovered the laboratory. His chemistry professor had taken a liking to him and arranged a job as a handyman. He had worked his way up to lab assistant. By the time he was graduated with his B.S. in Chemistry, Robby knew that he'd found his chosen field. Once he attained his Master's he felt qualified to apply to Trask, for he had been an avid admirer of the work of Dr. Otis Cruikshank.

Sitting across the table in the coffee shop, Bob Niles confessed to Rosa Gregory, "In my wildest dreams I never expected that he'd take me on. But I had a personal interview with him and he did."

"He was still searching for someone to take Duncan's place," Rosa said.

"It was several years after Duncan," Bob said softly.

"How well I know. I'll never forget the day Duncan died," Rosa said. "I could see Otis walking down there by the river. So alone. It was cold, a strong wind blowing. He had no coat or hat on. Just walking alone. With his hands behind his back. You know the way he stands sometimes."

Bob knew that characteristic pose of Otis Cruikshank's.

"Finally, one of the men went out and brought him in. I was in the hallway when they came by. He looked at me but never saw me. It wasn't only Duncan who'd died. His whole world had died. Yes, he needed you when you finally came along."

"I guess we needed each other," Bob said thoughtfully.

He had finished his last transplant of the day and was packing up to leave when Otis Cruikshank walked in, curious about the course of the experiment. Bob explained there would be a three- to four-day wait before they would know how many of the grafts were successful.

"All we can do is hope enough of the animals are tolerant enough to give us fifty patients and fifty controls," he said.

He was about to leave when Bob suggested they might walk out together. Take in some fresh air. His conversation with Rosa had brought home to him what a solitary life he was living, and he would have enjoyed the company. Otis hesitated, seeming preoccupied and uneasy as he said, "Thanks, but I've a few things to clear up here tonight."

When he arrived home, Bob decided he'd call someone and go out. Immediately he thought of Heather, but then

he reconsidered. She had been so aloof. He did not understand why, but he hesitated to press the point. Perhaps he
should just stay in and catch up on some of those scientific
journals that had been piling up for the last few weeks.
First, though, he decided to go out for dinner, even if he
had to go alone. He shaved and showered and took the
elevator down to the lobby. As he approached the front
desk, Carole Evans was standing there.

"Hi," he greeted. "Just coming in?"

"Uh huh," she answered.

"Had dinner?"

"Taking a survey? Or issuing an invitation?"

"A survey. On the effect of red meat on the feminist
revolution. How about a steak?" he said.

"If you can wait long enough for me to change," she
replied.

Bob sipped a bourbon and soda while Carole showered
and dressed. He let the events of the day and all thoughts
of the experiment slip from his mind. Dinner with Carole
was a perfect opportunity to get to know her better. Perhaps he could get beyond her laboratory efficiency and
begin to consider her a friend. He had almost finished his
drink when she came back into the living room looking
quite different from the way she had before.

She was wearing a pink knit dress that clung to her body,
outlining it in a way that no starched lab coat ever had.
More startling, she no longer wore her black-framed glasses.

"Contact lenses," she explained, noting his reaction. "I
wear them sometimes."

Dressed this way, wearing a light fragrance, her dark eyes
now bright and sparkling, Carole Evans was no longer a
colleague but a very attractive woman. And, suddenly, a
challenge.

"Mind if I say something?" Bob ventured.

"Should I?"

"You might."

"Take a chance," she invited.

"Quite frankly, dressed like this and without your glasses, your whole image is totally different. You startled me at first."

"Did I? Why? Like all other women in the world, I like a beautiful dress. And I love perfume. Especially after a day in those air-conditioned laboratories where the same stale acrid air is recirculated forever. I douse myself all over with perfume. Between my breasts too. Surprised?"

Bob laughed and took her arm. "Come on, 'Doctor,' let's go."

Over dinner, Bob learned more about Carole. She had come from a small town in Connecticut, where her father had been the only and devoted physician for all of his professional life. He spent more than ten hours a day in his office practice and made house calls besides. His one complaint was that science didn't know enough. Carole remembered him always complaining, "Damn it, we are given a responsibility but we're too ignorant to fulfill it. What we need is fewer men trying to practice medicine and more men seeking answers."

"I think my ambition to become a researcher started with his grumbling," she said, laughing. "Oh, I went through all the phases girls do. I was going to be a nurse. And then a movie star, or possibly an airline stewardess. But by the time I got to college, I knew it was going to be science."

She laughed—a small, light, regretful laugh. "The irony was, my father never approved. He was sure women had no place in medicine. Or research."

Carole asked about Bob's early life, and he answered freely. He described how Otis Cruikshank had virtually forced him to go to medical school, and how happy he was to have followed Otis' advice.

Now he felt committed to bridging the gap between pure research and clinical medicine. The Cruikshank protocol was one step in that direction.

Carole's apartment at Trask House was the penthouse. She had expected Bob Niles would get off the elevator before she did, but instead of pressing the button for his floor, he pressed only hers.

"Isn't your apartment on two?" she asked.

"When I take a lady out, I always see her safely back home," he said.

Carole did not protest, but when they reached her door and Bob took her in his arms to kiss her, she avoided him.

"That wouldn't be wise," she said. "It's been a pleasant evening. Let's not spoil it."

She was obviously uncomfortable in this sudden confrontation.

"Sure. Sorry," Bob said. "It was nice not having to eat alone for a change. Can we do it again sometime?"

"We'll see," she said evasively, and quickly opened her apartment door.

Inside, Carole Evans poured herself a cognac and sat down to consider the entire evening. She was not surprised by Bob's advances. She had made herself look especially attractive tonight. She had wanted to entice him. Yet when she'd succeeded she couldn't deal with it.

She'd done as much with Edgar Woolsey but had gone through with it. Before Woolsey, she had been involved in one other long and intense affair, also with an older man, a married man. But Bob Niles was young and not married. So he posed a danger. She would have to avoid him from now on. She must not jeopardize everything she had worked for. Not this late in the game. Certainly not when Edgar Woolsey had just begun to consider her as a future candidate for Director of Research.

The next morning Edgar Woolsey received another report to add to his file on Otis Cruikshank. Again Cruikshank had remained late, working in his lab. And there was one new fact. The security guard had noticed an edge of white lab toweling protruding from Dr. Cruikshank's top-coat pocket when he left.

Edgar Woolsey studied the file before him. There seemed nothing of great significance in it, yet it tantalized him. He had placed it back in the file drawer of his desk when a sudden thought provoked him to consult it again.

Flipping it open, he studied the dates against his calendar. What he had only suspected turned out to be true. There was a regularity to Cruikshank's night work. Every two weeks, Otis stayed in the lab until just before midnight. A clear pattern had been established. But why?

Whatever the reason, Otis Cruikshank's activities would bear continued investigation. If the Cruikshank protocol failed, Edgar Woolsey would need a defense before the Trustees.

TWELVE

Bob Niles stared down at the twitching white animal, warm, furry, pulsating. He turned it over, gently removed the protective coating from its pink belly and examined the area of the human-skin graft. There was no undue redness. After four days the animal had tolerated the graft.

"Rosa, mark this one as a patient," he said.

He reached into the next cage. On this animal he discovered a patchy redness. He ran his finger over the area of the graft. There was definite induration.

"This one is out."

By late afternoon he totaled up the score. Animals exhibiting tolerance to the human-skin graft: one hundred twenty-one. Though the revised protocol called for only fifty controls and fifty patients, to be safe Bob decided to use all hundred and twenty-one. Sixty-one patients. Sixty controls. There would likely be some dropouts along the way.

From now on the experiment would proceed along several parallel lines.

The tolerant patients and controls would now begin to receive injections of live human melanoma cells that had been breeding in petri dishes in Otis' lab. At the same time, Rosa would be in charge of sensitizing their potential donors by inoculating each with a tiny dose of devitalized melanoma cells. Since these rabbits had never been treated to make them tolerant of human tissue, they should prove sensitive to it. After that a second, much stronger dose should induce in them the production of antimelanoma lymphocytes and the precious transfer factor.

Days would be required to allow them to mount the desired reaction to the antigen, so Rosa began her work by freeze-thawing live melanoma cells seven times until they were no longer dangerous and then inoculating each potential donor.

Simultaneously, Bob and Ania Sokolov injected each of the one hundred twenty-one tolerant rabbits with a massive dose of live active cells. The size of the dose was one of the key points provided for in Otis' protocol.

In previous experiments, animals had always been given doses so infinitesimal they were virtually undetectable. But if the experiment was to duplicate actual clinical experience, each animal would have to receive one billion live melanoma cells.

As Otis had said to Bob at the outset, "A patient never shows up in a doctor's office and complains of symptoms with an undetectable mass. Let our lab patients be the same."

Ania measured out the live dosage while Bob worked in the operating room. He carefully inserted the needle of the hypodermic under the animal's skin but parallel, thereby depositing the deadly cells near to the surface, where melanoma usually thrived. The proper note was recorded on the animal's chart, and the animal was returned to its cage. Then the second patient was handed to Bob for the same treatment.

Bob was injecting his forty-third patient when Otis Cruikshank stopped by.

"How's it going?"

"Billion-cell dose should do it."

Bob handed the patient back to Ania, and as he began to examine the next one he asked casually, "These melanoma cells—where did they come from?"

For an instant Otis was taken aback. "The Cleveland Clinic," he answered quickly. "Then I cultured them, of course."

Otis seemed to grow uneasy. He remembered some urgent business and said, "Got to rush. Have a meeting with Woolsey. You know what that means." And he was gone.

Bob Niles hadn't considered questioning Otis Cruikshank's word on the source of the live cells. He had no reason to suspect they had originated with Heather Cruikshank. But he had to note the source in his final data, just as he had noted the strain of the animals, their weight, their special genetic characteristics. All materials, the specific cells and the medium in which they were cultured—no detail was inconsequential if other scientists were to repeat the experiment. Bob would have to contact the Cleveland Clinic for the precise strain.

In the next several days, Rosa's donor rabbits received all the necessary injections, and Bob's patients should have had sufficient time to produce symptoms of human melanoma if the live cells had taken.

He placed the first patient on its back, brought the light close and stared down at its pink belly. Surrounding the inoculation was a small nondescript brown spot, hopefully an early stage of melanoma. Bob calipered the spot and dictated to Ania the precise size of the affected area for the chart. It would be measured every two days from now on to track its growth.

The next rabbit seemed more advanced. It presented a black spot, surrounded by slight inflammation. They would have to get back to this one sooner than the first. It would be a candidate for early surgery.

The third rabbit presented no sign of the cancer and had to be eliminated.

The examination continued all afternoon and well into the next evening. Each blemish was calipered and its size noted.

Bob leaned back against the examining table after the last patient had been studied and returned to its cage. Then he made a final inspection of the animal rooms, making sure the animals had sufficient water and feed. Finally he hung up his lab coat and headed home.

The air was crisp, and he breathed in deeply as he walked across Trask Park, flushing the weariness out of his body. Relaxing. Then suddenly he remembered. It was Thursday. The Cruikshanks were entertaining Marietta Carter at seven-thirty and Ellen had invited him. Less than an hour from now!

He started to run.

Marietta Carter was escorted by an especially attentive young male secretary. Edgar Woolsey, Carole Evans, Wolfam, Smythe and several other department heads rounded out the guest list. From all outward indications the evening had no special significance. Marietta Carter just happened to be in this part of the country en route to a symposium in Dallas. So she had had her private jet make a stopover.

Cocktails passed pleasantly enough. Since Mrs. Carter dominated all conversation, Bob had only to be politely attentive. But at dinner the atmosphere changed. Sitting on Otis' right, Marietta Carter began to ask pointed questions about the way the experiment was proceeding.

Otis answered casually and was reserved about his expectations.

But Edgar Woolsey interrupted. "Dr. Niles is actually carrying on the work. I'm sure he'd be glad to tell you whatever he can."

Mrs. Carter peered down the table at Bob.

"Dr. Niles, don't I remember something rather special about you? Oh, yes," she reminded herself; "the last time I was here you'd just returned. You and that very pretty blond girl."

"Heather," Bob said. "Heather Cruikshank."

"Oh, sorry," she apologized, turning to Ellen. "I meet so many people. I was struck by the fact that they made such a nice couple. I just took it for granted they were together."

Ellen smiled politely. "Heather had other plans tonight," she explained.

Mrs. Carter focused on Bob Niles again.

"Well, Doctor, how *is* the work going?"

"So far, according to plan. There've been no developments that lead us to question the method of the experiment."

"And the results?" Mrs. Carter pressed.

"It's still too early. Until now and for weeks to come, it'll be all input."

"If you had to define how the work stood right this minute, what would you say?" she persisted.

Bob glanced at Otis, whose face was growing quite flushed. The older scientist detested this interrogation, but was powerless to stop it.

"Come, Niles," Woolsey spoke up, "there's no harm in giving us a brief status report."

As simply as he could, Bob related the progress of the work, stressing, "As yet we have no evidence from which to draw any conclusions."

"But there've been no reverses so far?" Mrs. Carter tried to pin him down.

"Everything is proceeding as planned."

Mrs. Carter nodded, her brown eyes intent and glistening. She turned to Otis.

"When can we expect an abstract of your lecture? We're preparing our literature on the Symposium."

She turned to her male secretary. "Tony, what's our deadline at the printer's on those announcements?"

"The twenty-second," he replied promptly.

"The twenty-second," Mrs. Carter remarked. "Well, that hardly gives us any time at all, does it? So we do need your abstract, Otis."

"Yes, of course," Otis agreed with no noticeable enthusiasm.

It was quite clear now that Marietta Carter had come here expressly to check up on the progress of the Cruikshank protocol. And to pin down Otis. He *would* chair her Symposium and he *would* report on his work. Now that she had succeeded in that, the rest of the evening held no real interest for her. She turned away from Otis and Bob Niles and began exchanging bits of gossip with Edgar Woolsey, who beamed under her attention.

Finally, she said, "Come, Tony." And she was gone, her male secretary trailing after her.

"Thank God that's over!" Woolsey said, turning back from closing the door.

"Damn it!" Otis exploded. "I don't like being made to dance at the end of a string because that woman happens to have more money than almost anyone else in this country!"

"I know many an institute where they'd be delighted to get that kind of pressure from Marietta Carter," Woolsey reminded him.

"We may not be ready!" Otis protested. "We're on a breakneck schedule now. There's no room for error. No time to go back and correct mistakes."

"*And*," Woolsey reminded him, "no mistakes. You were right when you picked Niles. Scuttlebutt around the labs confirms it. His assistants respect him. They work their heads off for him, even Rosa Gregory. You don't fool an old hand like Rosa. She recognizes ability. So everything points to excellent results. I don't know why you're so nervous."

"We should have some leeway," Otis continued, "at least another year!"

"Another year?" Woolsey shot back. "Who knows what economic conditions will be in another year?" He paused. "Besides, she's drooling over the possibilities. I couldn't say no to her when she asked to drop by."

Otis turned on him fiercely. "Damn you," he shouted, "you knew precisely why she was coming. You could have at least prepared me!"

Even Ellen Cruikshank stared at her husband in amazement. It was unlike Otis to lose his temper in this way.

Woolsey grew red in the face. "Would it have made any difference?"

Otis was too furious to answer, but he knew he would have to send Marietta a brief abstract. Of course he knew that if the protocol didn't prove out it was always possible to withdraw his abstract. Recently some papers issued from Harvard had been withdrawn because some of the data were less than accurate. But damn it, he thought, he had never been forced to suffer such a professional indignity. Let others overestimate their results; he always preferred to underestimate and be sure!

The evening ended abruptly when Edgar Woolsey pleaded that his wife was not feeling well and he had to get home. In turn, the others began to say their good-byes.

"May I walk you home?" Bob asked Carole at the door.

"Since we're both going to exactly the same place by exactly the same route," she answered coolly, "I suppose that's unavoidable."

They were out the door when Otis called after them, "Robert, come see me in my office first thing tomorrow, won't you?"

"Yes, sir," Bob said. "First thing."

They stepped into the elevator at Trask House. Carole Evans pressed the penthouse button, and before Bob could press "2," she asked, "Care for a nightcap?"

He glanced at her, surprised. "Fine."

Once they were inside her apartment she shed her tailored wool jacket, flinging it onto the couch.

"Brandy?" she asked.

"Okay."

Bob watched her fix the drinks. He admired the way she filled the orange satin blouse, which was open at her throat and for a good way down. As she bent over to hand him his glass he couldn't resist staring. He looked up quickly, and for a moment his eyes met Carole's. He searched for something to say.

"You didn't ask me up just for a drink. Something on your mind?"

"I want to ask you about Otis," she said.

"Otis?"

"I think we should compare notes. I've never seen him react as vehemently as he did tonight," she said. "He seemed to be on edge, and has been for a while now."

"A job like his has unusual pressures—you know that," Bob said. "He had good reason to blow up at Woolsey."

"I know. Still, Otis is usually completely in control. I was wondering if he might be under some personal pressure."

"How would I know that?"

"You're closer to him than anyone else," she said. "Ellen likes you. I assume Heather does, too."

He didn't attempt to correct her assumption, even though she betrayed just a touch of jealousy. All he said was "No, I haven't noticed anything unusual." He did not feel free to reveal his earlier suspicion that Otis might have had melanoma. Heather had denied that. He would accept her word. But Carole's observations now revived his own concern.

"You were here during that whole episode with Duncan, weren't you?" he asked suddenly.

"Yes. It was quite terrible. Researchers from all over the country sending advice and experimental drugs. And Otis forcing the doctors to try them all, knowing it wouldn't help. I remember him being so helpless. And desperate. Ellen blaming herself. And he blaming himself.

"Blaming himself? Why?"

"I don't know. Maybe because when science failed Duncan, Otis felt he had failed him too," she replied.

A silence fell between them. Then Carole said, "Can I fix you another drink?"

"I could use it," he said, handing back his glass.

As she reached for it, their fingers touched. Once again his eyes fixed on hers. She made an effort to turn away, but that momentary contact had betrayed her desire. He embraced her. She didn't resist. He held her tightly. Her body pressed against him. He kissed her, and she kissed back with sudden passion. She pressed her face against him, whispering softly, "Oh God, oh God." She knew she should resist, but she could not.

She reached up and pulled the pins from her hair. It cascaded over her shoulders. He reached to open her satin blouse and she did not forbid him.

He made love to her with a fury, and she gave herself without reservation. When he rested upon her body, spent and breathing hard, she kept him locked in her embrace as if never intending to let him go. Her hands played across Bob's biceps and his back, feeling his young, strong muscles. When he wanted her again, she was as desirous as he was.

Finally, she lay back, apart from him. "It can't be allowed to happen again," she said.

"You did enjoy it."

"It must never happen again! You're not to speak of it. Not even to me. And certainly never at the Institute, even when we're alone. It simply did not happen."

"But you enjoyed it . . . as much as I," Bob protested.

"I won't discuss it," she said, ending the conversation.

He stared at her in the dim glow of the table lamp.

"Did you know there's something very sensuous about your eyes once you take those glasses off?"

She laughed. Poor Edgar, she thought suddenly. God, what a glorious thing youth is! Then, to drive Woolsey from her mind, she said, "I seem to remember long ago I offered you another drink and you accepted. I'll get it for you."

She started to slip away from him, but he caught her

hand and drew her back. He pressed his face against her full breasts, reached up and felt her silken hair. He brought her face close to his and kissed her again. She drew him to her. Every part of her seemed to embrace him and need him as if in desperation born of the knowledge that this was to be their final time.

It was past two o'clock in the morning. She was in her dressing gown.

"You're smiling," he said, staring at her over his fresh drink.

"That'll have to stop, too."

"Why?"

"You know how strict Trask is about personal involvements."

"I know. No two members of the same family can work there. But we're not the same family."

"If we became involved, the effect would be the same," she said.

"We *are* involved," he pointed out.

"*Not anymore.*" Then, as if to close the subject for good, she said, "I hope you will tell me if you notice anything unusual about Otis."

"Yes," Bob said, "I will."

"Good. Now you'd better go."

He rose, putting his empty glass down on the coffee table.

"It isn't just me," she said. "I don't want anything to distract you from your work. A great deal depends on Otis' protocol. The results could affect us all."

"Of course, Dr. Evans," he said with mock formality.

"Damn it," she exploded, "I know what's best. For both of us!"

"They're beginning to close in on me," Otis said the next morning, as soon as Bob Niles had seated himself in the chair opposite the imposing desk. "It's become a race, a competition. Science was never meant to be conducted like the Olympics."

He gestured toward a shelf of leather-bound volumes, representing a lifetime of his work.

"I didn't accumulate those by making promises. I asked questions and followed them to the ultimate answers. Favorable or not. Nothing can be guaranteed."

He rose from his creaking swivel chair and began to pace.

"Robert, I will send in my abstract for the Carter Foundation Symposium. I may even indicate the work is promising, if you tell me now that it is."

"We do have a sufficient number of patients and controls who are tolerating the melanoma. We'll know within a week or ten days if our donors are reacting properly. I've no reason to doubt that they will."

"Doubt! That's the word." Otis seized on it. "I want you to think of yourself not only as carrying out my protocol but as my adversary. Question my methods. Challenge the results. At the first moment there is any doubt, I wish to exercise my privilege of withdrawing from the Carter Symposium. I would rather face the embarrassment of doing that than commit the crime of presenting unverified or misleading results."

"Of course," Bob agreed.

"Mind you, Robert, I've never been so confident about an experiment in my entire career. Which is the very reason I need someone to resist me, to oppose my conviction."

Two days later, instead of going to lunch, Bob hurried over to the library. He wanted to consult a paper by the Hellstroms on immunoresponse in osteosarcoma.

The library was a large room with row after row of floor-to-ceiling shelves full of scientific and medical journals and bulletins from all over the world. White-coated scientists sat at long library tables with books in front of them, reading and making notes on long yellow pads. The room was absolutely still.

As he looked around for a librarian who might direct him to the stack he wanted, he noticed Carole Evans. Alone, in her starched white lab coat and thick-framed glasses, her glistening black hair efficiently braided. She was engrossed in the paper she was reading, so that when he reached her table she did not acknowledge his presence.

"Mind?" he asked finally.

She looked up and said quite impersonally, "Sit down, if you wish." She resumed reading, saying only, "Crosswell at Harvard. On immunological responses. You might find it pertinent to the Cruikshank work."

He stared at her. She stared back, giving not the slightest hint that only nights ago they had been lovers—intense, passionate lovers.

"Is that all?" he said. "You are a very remarkable lady."

Her face flushed faintly, but she did not reply.

"What about Evans at Trask on sexual responses?" Bob demanded in any angry whisper.

He had no way of knowing that twice in the past two days Edgar Woolsey had tried to cajole her into meeting him. But she had refused. Something about the night with Bob Niles had diminished her need for Edgar Woolsey. And this was a most disturbing change. Until now, she had been sure she had the sexual part of her life well under control. Everything had been carefully arranged and had proceeded as she dictated. Until Bob Niles came along.

"I told you that night. That was not the beginning of anything. It was the end. A stupid indiscretion which I have no desire to repeat. No desire whatsoever," she whispered back.

Her only safety lay in severing the relationship at once. She remained silent, concentrating on the scientific paper she was reading, until Bob Niles got up. As he walked away, she realized, with considerable pain and regret, that she had succeeded in accomplishing just that.

CHAPTER

THIRTEEN

Heather Cruikshank arose at her usual time. She examined herself in the mirror as she had done every day since her lunch with Bob Niles. Her face seemed no thinner. She stepped on the low, flat scales. This morning, as on all other mornings so far, she was within a pound and a half of her normal one hundred and twenty-three.

Because of all the publicity in recent times about the President's wife and the Vice President's wife, she carefully examined her breasts. Most women of her young age would not have been so meticulous about such an examination, but with her medical history Heather could not afford to take any risks. When she had finished she stood back from her mirror and examined the totality of herself.

She was not vain, but she knew she had a good face, a combination of strength she had inherited from her father and the softness and beauty that were her mother's. Until the discovery of her illness, she had led an active social life at Smith. But since her return home she had become cut off from old friends and had been hesitant to make new ones. At first, she had been conscious of the need for secrecy concerning her cure. But now, after two years of remission, Heather knew there was another reason for her self-imposed isolation.

Although she had been only nine at the time of Duncan's death, Heather still remembered her mother's terrible fear that Duncan had inherited the fatal weakness from her. Heather had since done considerable reading on the subject, and while no one had ever substantiated Ellen's fear, there had been sufficient scientific speculation to give it some credibility.

What science had been unable to verify seemed to have been proved that day by the discovery of the small molelike spot just under Heather's right armpit. Today there was only a thin, nearly invisible white scar, but its significance burned in her mind. She had survived because of her father's unorthodox sacrifice, but nothing could remove her fear of passing along the illness to her sons and daughters. If she dared have any.

So Heather Cruikshank had studiously avoided all serious relationships with men. She had such dedication to her work with the brain-damaged children that her time was full, and she had felt satisfied.

It was not until the return of Bob Niles that she had had reason to question the life she had chosen for herself. She had held herself back from him, despite her attraction. Soon, she knew, she would have to make a decision she had been avoiding. But first she had to find out one more fact about her remission.

Unfortunately, since her cure was unprecedented, only her father could speculate intelligently. Or Bob Niles. He was deeply involved in the actual experiment, and he was a medical doctor besides.

She thought about it for several days and finally evolved a plan. She would take the children to visit Trask.

Heather dressed with care, selecting a gray flannel skirt and her favorite red cashmere sweater. She arranged her hair simply but most attractively. She believed she was dressing for the children, who loved to touch her soft sweaters and to play with her silky blond hair.

But she would also be seeing Bob Niles.

Bob had just finished examining the last of his donors when he heard a familiar voice.

"I hope you are all remembering the rules we made up for this visit."

Heather Cruikshank was shepherding a group of her youngsters down the hall toward his lab. They were between eight and eleven years old, and they clung to Heather's skirt and held her hands as they walked toward Bob Niles's lab.

Delighted to see her, Bob went down the hall to meet Heather halfway. She introduced him, and he shook hands with each child.

"Come to inspect our labs?" he asked.

"They've heard me talk about Trask Park and Dad. They were curious, so we had a planning session and organized a trip." She turned to the children. "And what did we decide?"

Several children started to answer at once. In their eagerness, they did not succeed. Pleasantly but firmly, Heather cautioned, "We think what we want to say. Then we speak up clearly. And we do it very proudly."

The children tried again, speaking to Bob, while at the same time looking toward Heather for encouragement and approval.

"We came to see the animals," one boy managed.

"Miss Cruikshank said they have rabbits here. And monkeys," the youngest boy said.

"Miss Cruikshank said they do science here," said a little girl. "Do you do science?" she asked.

Bob knelt down. "Yes, I do," he said. He started to lift her up, but Heather shook her head.

"Want to come in and see the animals?" All the children began cheering and jumping up and down in anticipation. "Okay," Bob said, "follow me!"

As they reached the animal rooms, the sound of the excited young voices summoned Rosa Gregory from the lab. She was delighted. She embraced several of the children and then, taking two by the hand, she said, "Let me show them around. Nobody knows how to spoil children like a grandmother!"

She took them into the room where the healthy control animals were kept. Soon each child had a rabbit to cuddle and stroke. Damaged children or not, their laughter was the laughter of youngsters who were happy.

Heather beamed. Bob enjoyed the glow in her blue eyes. "I'm glad you brought them," he said. "The change'll do us all good."

"Mainly the children, I hope," she said. "Parents have a tendency to hide them. I like to get them out. They live in this world and they have to learn to cope. They have a lot to contribute. The intelligence of some of these youngsters would surprise you. Who knows—some of them might wind up doing research someday."

Bob admired her devotion and confidence. She caught him staring. To cover his embarrassment, Bob quickly asked, "Care to see our work?"

"Yes. I've been curious. Dad doesn't like to discuss work in progress."

Bob showed her through the animal rooms, explaining the functions of his various groups, and then he brought her back to his office and described the rest of the experiment, including what he expected the final outcome to be, if it worked.

The look in his eyes when he spoke of the importance of his work to humanity made her know the kind of scientist he was, and the kind of man. Her problem had suddenly grown not less difficult, but more.

She felt compelled to ask her questions.

"And if it all does prove out?"

"Then we may be able to do similar work on human patients. That's the real purpose of the whole protocol."

"No, I mean the animals. What happens to those who are cured?"

"They're sacrificed, of course."

"Sacrificed?"

"At regular stages. As we achieve cures, we have to euthanize them in order to do autopsies. So we have our proof in demonstrable pathological form," he explained.

"I see," she said. His unexpected answer created new doubts for her. "Won't any of them be allowed to survive?"

"What for?"

"To see how long they live. To see if they have any recurrences later. To see if, despite their cures, they pass on their defect to future generations."

She had asked all her questions. Now she waited tensely for the answers.

"I'm afraid those questions will have to wait for other, much more complicated experiments," Bob explained. "We'll have done enough if we prove out your father's theory by achieving some complete remissions."

His last answer had robbed her of any reassurance she might have gained from his earlier explanations. She knew one thing now that she hadn't known before. She no longer had the choice of falling in love. She had already done so. The guilt she felt about concealing her illness from him made that painfully clear. To escape the thought, she changed the subject.

"Fascinating," she said.

"No, some stages of the experiment are pure drudgery. Nothing glamorous about that."

"I meant it's fascinating that a man who is so observant about scientific things can fail to notice what goes on right under his nose."

"Such as?" he challenged.

"I saw you leave our house the other evening. With Carole Evans. You're wasting your time on her. She has a controlled, cool way about her, but I can always tell when she's interested in a man. Edgar Woolsey, for example. I'll bet there's something going on there."

"Come to think of it, she is pretty defensive about him.

I bet you're right. She ignores him so skillfully no one would ever guess."

"You mean *you'd* never guess. A woman would know. Instinct, feminine radar. Infallible," she said, laughing.

Bob cut her short by asking, "What about you? You're so great with children, I should think you'd want to have some of your own."

"First I've got to get my doctorate. After that I'll have plenty of time to think about marriage and children," she said evasively.

"Someday you're going to discover there's not enough time to live life in sequence. Things have to happen simultaneously. And maybe you'll even learn how important a man is, *one* man, and your *own* children."

He helped her board the children back onto the school bus. Rosa and Bob kept waving until they were out of sight. The children waved back. But Heather did not. She was silent all the way to the school. The children noticed and were affected by it. Eventually, instead of the usual bustle and excitement that were typical of trips away from the classroom, they became as quiet and sober as their teacher.

Three of the children had been given rabbits to take back for class pets. Rosa had seen to that. They petted them and passed them from one to another. But when they wanted to give one to Heather, she couldn't accept it. Instead she turned away and studied her face reflected in the bus window. There was something disturbing about the soft white fluffy creatures. As if in some way her life were dependent on the results of the protocol that her father had created and that the man she resisted loving had been charged with carrying out.

The entire venture had been a mistake—a serious, disheartening mistake. Her strategy had failed. Far from giving her the reassurance she sought, it had only intensified her dilemma.

That evening, earlier than usual, Bob Niles made his regular last-minute check of the animal rooms. Then he strode down the corridor and out of the building. It was the earliest he had left the lab in days. He had no plans. He only knew he felt lonely. More this evening than ever. And he had only one thing on his mind. Heather.

He wanted to see her again. Soon. Her visit to the lab encouraged him. Perhaps she was finally accepting his presence, maybe even growing to like him. He decided to call her for dinner.

But Heather had anticipated this, and had already prepared an excuse. She said she was busy. He tried to coax her into changing her mind. But she would not. Finally, just as he was about to hang up, he heard her say, shyly, "But what about Wednesday? I've got two tickets to the play."

In order to compensate its staff for having to live far away from a large cultural center, Trask Institute arranged for touring plays to come to the campus on Wednesday nights. Otis had a season ticket, but on this particular night he had to work late, and since Ellen had no desire to go, Heather and Bob had their tickets.

Bob found that he enjoyed being with Heather more than he enjoyed the play. In college she had developed an enduring love of theater, traveling into New York sometimes as often as every weekend to see Broadway shows. Bob loved her intense involvement; the way she laughed; her blue eyes, which had become even brighter, more alive than usual.

Her excitement endured all the way back across the campus from the Williston Auditorium to the Cruikshank home. She relived the play as they walked, picking out moments that delighted her, lines of dialogue she had laughed at or admired. Then she confessed she once had contemplated dropping out of Smith to become an actress. But in the end, she had decided on education, especially education of the handicapped.

When Bob asked why, she answered, "Because so few people care about those children. Society avoids them. Someone has to break down that wall and get them out into the light."

"And that someone is you?"

"Yes," she replied with great conviction. "That someone is me!"

Bob Niles admired her passion. And her commitment. She was truly a dedicated girl. No, not girl, woman. A mature, dedicated, unusual—and beautiful—woman.

They had reached the Cruikshank driveway. She would have liked to ask him in, but on this night unfortunately she couldn't. He looked down at her lovely face and said, "Is that how you're going to spend the rest of your life? Is your work enough?"

"My children need me" was her simple answer. "They take all my time."

"The time will come when you'll have to live your own life, too."

"This is my life," she said, defensively.

The night was not so cool, but she trembled slightly, and he embraced her to keep her warm. She welcomed his embrace. But when he tried to kiss her she said softly, "I think that should wait."

Bob didn't pursue it. "I'll call you. Okay?"

"Okay," she said, but she sounded rather tentative.

He released her and waited until she was inside and the door had closed. Then he turned away and started back across campus to Trask House.

Heather went across the foyer toward the stairs.

"Heather, dear?" her father called from the living room. "Have a good evening?"

"Yes. Very nice."

"Good. You know what night tonight is. I've got the things boiling out in the kitchen."

Otis started toward the kitchen door, but she stopped him.

133

"Dad, will it work forever? Or at least for a long time? Years?"

"It's been two years now, hasn't it?" Otis asked. She nodded. "Well, we've no reason to think it won't work for many years more. Do we?"

"No. But it would help to know for certain," she said sadly.

FOURTEEN

The first animal Bob examined showed a marked increase in size of the malignancy. He made a note and moved on to the next cage. By the end of the day he had marked forty-one patients ready for surgery.

At seven-thirty the following morning Bob Niles, Rosa Gregory, Ania Sokolov and Charlie Sanders arrived to begin the operations. Rosa would assist Bob during the surgery. Ania and Charles were to maintain a constant supply of sterile instruments—scalpels, hemostats, forceps, sutures. Sanders would return used instruments to the auto-clave to be resterilized.

By seven forty-five, Rose Gregory had placed the first patient in the ether jar. When the animal was completely anesthetized, she handed it to Bob. Applying an Allis clamp, he fixed the tiny patient to the stainless steel operating table with its belly completely exposed. Using forceps, Rosa dipped a wad of cotton into an antiseptic solution and handed it to Bob, who cleaned the entire shaved area around the melanoma. He held out his hand. Rosa slapped a scalpel into it. The operation had begun.

There was little conversation during the procedure, except when Bob dictated notes he considered important for his final data. He removed the diseased tissue and passed it to Ania, who placed it in a solution that would preserve it for later study. He made sure there were safe margins around the wound and probed the lymph nodes that gave evidence of being involved. But he did not go beyond those close to primary site. Otis Cruikshank's model called for leaving all distant nodes intact.

More than six hours later they had finished only the first twenty-two patients. They took a much-needed coffee break and returned in time to receive the pathologist's preliminary report: each excised tumor presented melanoma of the human strain with which the animals had been injected. His reports were noted on the charts and incorporated into the data.

They worked until shortly after eight in the evening and resumed the next morning at seven-thirty, breaking only for a short lunch.

Otis Cruikshank caught sight of them in the Trask cafeteria and stopped briefly at their table.

"I've been intending to look in. How's it going?"

"Very well. But it's tedious. Takes time," Bob said.

"What about the donors?"

"I'm having their blood drawn as soon as the surgery is done. Based on macroscopic observation, we've got some beauties."

"Good, good!" Otis encouraged, and he was off to meet someone at another table, probably a scientist he was trying to entice to come to Trask.

Bob and Rosa went back to the operating room and worked late into the evening.

By the afternoon of the fifth day they had completed the last operation. All one hundred and twenty-one patients and melanoma controls had been excised, probed, sutured, bandaged and returned to their cages to recuperate.

Bob Niles peeled off his O.R. uniform, took a hot shower to get rid of the lingering smell of ether and slipped into his street clothes. He walked down by the riverbank, breathing deeply, feeling the tiredness gradually go out of his bones. He was going to call Heather for dinner, but he had at least an hour to wait before she would be home. He stared across the river at the growing dusk. The trees on the other side were beginning to go bare. Under his feet dry leaves crackled, and some spun away in the wind. Winter coming soon. It could be a lonely time. . . .

He walked on until it was nearly dark. Then he headed for Trask House to call Heather.

He picked her up at seven. They drove out to an old 1868 farmhouse that had been converted into a restaurant and was supposed to serve extremely good food.

The place was crowded, and despite their reservation they had to wait awhile for a table to become available.

Over dinner they spoke of little events from their pasts. They mentioned friends they'd had. Places they'd been. Teachers they'd loved. Teachers they'd hated. Exams. Vacations. They were sharing their lives through their memories. They enjoyed the food and the vintage wine. And they laughed.

Bob realized how much he liked to see her smile. It did nice, warm, friendly things to her eyes. He recalled she had smiled like that when she had met him at the airport. He had liked it then, and he liked it even more now. Tonight she seemed free of whatever burden had caused her earlier aloofness. She seemed natural, relaxed. Happy.

Until they reached Trask Park on their way home. Then suddenly her silence returned, as if she were no longer free to laugh.

The light was on in Otis' den when Heather came in to say good night. "Have a pleasant evening, dear?" he asked.
"Yes."

"Nice lad, Robert," Otis said. "Did he say anything about how the work is going?"

"He completed surgery today. Evidently it's exhausting work."

"It is. And he's too conscientious to delegate it to anyone else," Otis said, returning to the sheets of data spread out on his desk.

Heather was tempted to linger, to ask him certain questions. But what was the use? There seemed to be only one solution to her growing dilemma. She must not see Bob Niles again. And certainly not alone.

FIFTEEN

When Edgar Woolsey appeared in the operating room where Bob Niles was drawing blood from his potential donors, all work stopped.

"Yes?" Bob asked.

"Don't mean to interrupt. I was just passing through the building and I thought I'd look in," he said, striving to seem completely casual.

"Please do. Come in."

Bob went back to work. He inserted the needle into the vein of the animal.

"Donors?" Woolsey asked, edging closer to the stainless steel table until he was directly across from Bob Niles.

"We'll know in a matter of hours."

"What's your guess?"

"Based on their macroscopic reactions to the melanoma antigens, I'd say eighty percent of them should be good donors. Of that eighty, we'll use the blood of the best half."

"Have you been able to project a tentative outcome yet?"

"We know two things quite definitely," Bob said.

"Oh, yes?" Woolsey sparked, delighted.

"We know we can finally give melanoma to a rabbit, and that we can create a strong reaction in other rabbits with treated melanoma cells."

"I see," Woolsey invited, obviously expecting more information.

"Beyond that I'd be a damn fool to make any projections. And you'd be a bigger fool to believe them."

Woolsey flushed angrily and, after a moment of hesitation, stormed out the door.

The procedure continued throughout the day. The blood of each potential donor was given a white-cell count, and those that revealed the highest titer level were approved for the next step. Then samples of the selected blood were separated in the centrifuge and the white-cell lymphocytes were extracted. These were added to live melanoma cells growing on a layer of nutrient in a petri dish. The next few days would reveal if those white cells possessed the specific qualities necessary for them to yield the precious transfer factor.

As Bob slipped off his lab coat, the day's work done, he noticed someone had placed a message in the corner of his desk pad:

From the office of
EDGAR WOOLSEY,
Director of Administration

Would you be good enough to stop and see me before you leave.   E.W.

Edgar Woolsey was sitting at his desk, leaning on his elbows, his fingers drumming against each other impatiently.

"Come in, Niles!"

As Bob entered, he saw that Carole Evans was sitting on the couch across the room from Woolsey's desk. Evidently she too had been summoned for this meeting.

Woolsey gestured toward a chair, but Bob chose to remain standing.

"Now, then," Woolsey began, "we'd better have an understanding as to our respective positions and responsibilities. I know how very 'in' and fashionable it is for ardent searchers after truth in science to look down upon those of us who are charged with the mundane duty of administering institutions such as Trask. We are bureaucrats. Moneygrubbers. A necessary evil. To be scorned and joked about.

"Well, I wish to point out to you that without us there would be no labs, no equipment, no computers—nothing!"

Woolsey began to pace angrily back and forth.

"Now, we do not expect your love. Or your admiration. We do not even expect your gratitude. But we *do* expect decent, courteous treatment! We do expect that we will not be given insulting answers to perfectly natural questions."

Bob could feel his own anger well up. He glanced at Carole Evans, but she betrayed no emotion.

"You've had a very special and protected place here at Trask. Because you're Otis Cruikshank's protégé. But do not think that that permits you to insult me to my face. Nor does it make you exempt from reporting on your progress in the usual manner."

"I report to Dr. Cruikshank regularly."

"From now on you will follow the rule that applies to *all* investigators in Immunology. You will report to Dr. Evans at least once a week. You will keep her informed of *all* developments. Is that understood?" Woolsey demanded.

"Has this been cleared with Dr. Cruikshank?"

"There's no reason to clear it with him," Woolsey snapped. "We're not creating an exception. We're abolishing one."

"You understand that I'll have to tell him."

"You may use your own judgment about that!"

"Is that all you wanted to tell me?" Bob asked, moving toward the door.

"No, that is not all!" Woolsey said. "I've just spent two days in Chicago with our Board of Trustees. Because of costs, it was suggested we postpone the Cruikshank protocol. I finally convinced the Trustees that if the experiment worked, a flood of new financial support would follow.

"That's why I'm so concerned about your work. The entire future of Trask may depend on the outcome of the Cruikshank protocol. When Otis Cruikshank goes to New York in January he must be armed with results that will justify the money we have lavished on this project. I can't make it any clearer than that. Can I?" Woolsey demanded.

"You understand we're searching for answers, not guaranteeing results."

"I understand," Woolsey said brusquely. "Thank you for dropping by."

Carole Evans waited until Bob was down the hall, out of hearing distance, before saying, "You were pretty rough on him."

"Not nearly so rough as I felt," Woolsey said. "After that battle in Chicago, I don't need his insolence."

He crossed the room and lifted her to her feet. He slipped his hand inside her lab coat, cupped her breasts and tried to kiss her. But she turned her face away.

"I told you. Never here!"

"But we're alone. And tonight I need you very much," he pleaded.

"I'm sorry, Edgar."

"Later? Eight? Eight-thirty?"

She considered it for a moment. "All right, eight-thirty."

He reached to remove her glasses, but she brushed his hand aside. "Eight-thirty."

"I wanted you to know before I reported to Dr. Evans."

"I've nothing against your reporting to her. She has a good, dispassionate mind," Otis said.

"But what I do not like," he continued, "is the pressure. It's not healthy for science to be conducted in such an atmosphere."

Otis Cruikshank was thoughtful for a moment, then said, "I shall talk to him about it."

As soon as Bob left the office, Otis Cruikshank dialed Edgar Woolsey's extension. Woolsey was out, so Otis left a message asking him to call back. When he did not, Otis called a second time and then a third.

Edgar Woolsey deliberately remained inaccessible. He refrained from calling Otis that day and the next. According to his calendar, in two nights Dr. Cruikshank should engage in one of his biweekly late-night work sessions. Woolsey would speak to him then. In person.

Bob Niles had time for only one observation before his eleven-o'clock meeting with Dr. Evans. He was looking through a microscope at a sample of melanoma plus the donor lymphocytes he had cultured.

It was a beautiful sight. The white cells had left a trail of dead and damaged melanoma cells and were attacking the rest. They were melanoma-specific. Precisely the assurance he needed to begin processing the transfer factor.

If Rosa, Sanders and Ania began right now, by the time he returned from his meeting they should have extracted enough transfer factor to enable him to take the next step in the protocol.

Dr. Carole Evans was studying data. She held up her hand, as if to stop his entrance until she had finished reading. Bob sat down anyway.

After a few minutes she leaned back in her desk chair and glanced at him with a vague look, as if she didn't understand the purpose of his visit.

Acidly, Bob reminded her, "You must remember . . . Woolsey suggested we meet this morning."

"Yes, of course. Where shall we begin?"

Bob thought, Oh, the cool, cool bitch. But he had to admire the way she carried it off.

Aloud he said, "Everything has proceeded according to plan so far. We do have our tumor-specific donors. The transfer factor is being processed right now."

"And the patients?" Carole asked briskly.

"Since I excised the primaries they've been under constant observation to see if any metastases occur. As soon as we detect the slightest evidence of that, we'll start injecting transfer factor."

"So you're really approaching the make-or-break point now," Carole remarked.

"How effective will the TF be if administered before another large mass develops? That's the crux of it."

"And if it works, and can then be translated into effective use on humans . . ."

She didn't dare speculate beyond that. Too many cancer researchers had futilely pursued that kind of wishful projection. Not everything that worked on experimental animals worked on humans. But one persevered in the hope that one day it might.

She nodded thoughtfully. "I think I can reassure Mr. Woolsey."

She readjusted her black-framed glasses so they sat properly on the bridge of her neatly proportioned nose. It was a gesture Bob knew usually preceded a pronouncement of some importance.

"You know, Niles, it wouldn't hurt your career if you adopted a more friendly attitude toward the Administrator. There isn't any field in which a person is more at the mercy of his superiors. There's no real tenure in research. All they have to do is cut off funds for your project, and you're out. Of course, in your case that might not be a great threat. You have a medical degree. And you know what we scientists say: 'Our failures become rich, successful doctors.' "

"I've heard that," Bob said, determined not to become involved in any additional administrative disputes.

"One further word," Carole said. "If you don't have any concern about your own future here, please think about Dr. Cruikshank."

"What about Dr. Cruikshank?"

"There were many pressures exerted on Mr. Woolsey in that Trustees' meeting in Chicago. One of which was to reconsider some of the staff here."

"Otis Cruikshank?" Bob asked, disbelieving.

"They're very conscious of the fact that he hasn't been invited to chair any important symposium in more than a year now."

"He'll chair the Carter Symposium. You can't do better than that!"

"That's the future. Our shortage of funds exists today. If Trask had received its fair share of publicity in the last two years, there'd be Federal money and other grants. We wouldn't be in the fix we're in now," she pointed out.

"You've worked with Otis. You know he doesn't like to announce results until they're beyond dispute," Bob protested.

"That may make for high standards in scientific research. But it's not a very practical approach to the basic question: where does the money come from?"

She had been speaking harshly, but now she recovered and said in a softer, confidential tone. "I receive offers from other research institutions rather continuously. Only two weeks ago at a symposium in La Jolla, I was approached by UCLA's Nobel Prize winner, Max Koestler. He wants me to join him as his assistant, with the opportunity to step up to his present position when he becomes Emeritus. He suggested Otis has lost his touch, could not supply the inspiration of new and exciting thought. He asked me: 'What has Cruikshank produced recently?' "

She concluded sadly, "That is the same point the Trustees made to Mr. Woolsey. The significant word is 'recently.' "

She paused, then went on.

"It's important to realize that you have to protect Otis Cruikshank, just as I do. I told Koestler not to underestimate Otis Cruikshank. 'If he's been quiet for a long time you can be sure it's because he's got a blockbuster on the way.' Of course, all that is just politicking, talk. The

145

work you're doing will be the real answer. Keep me informed."

He nodded.

Carole Evans picked up another set of data and began to read. The meeting was at an end.

Before Bob could introduce the transfer factor into his patients, he had to submit both the sixty-one patients and the sixty melanoma controls to the nuclear scanner. For this, he had enlisted the cooperation of Cyril Berger, the nuclearist. Berger had supplied Bob with the necessary gallium, and Bob had injected it into his animals three days in advance of the test.

Berger improvised a contraption under the nuclear table so that the bands of the Allis clamps could be attached and the restless little patients kept immobile while the collimator did its work. Since it was after normal hospital hours he had both tables available, and still it would take several hours to scan the first twenty animals.

The scanning began. Slowly the huge round collimator moved back and forth across the small furry bodies, line by line. Alongside each table the small green oscilloscope recorded what the moving nuclear eye detected. The bright line of green light, contrasting with the dark green screen, gradually formed the outlines of the animals' bodies.

Bob studied the screens, though Berger would have to make the definitive reading. After four double scans were complete, Berger said, "Now, then, let's see what we have."

He mounted the films in the frosted-glass viewing boxes and flipped on the switches. The glass lit up, showing very clearly the outlines of sixteen rabbits.

Berger moved down the line, examining each scan.

"Hot spot. Here. And here. Definitely positive," Berger said. He passed on to the next one. "A beauty, this one. Look at that concentration. Positive. Positive. This one looks questionable. But I bet we get a different result a week from now. Something's brewing here, I'm sure of it."

By the time Berger had examined all eight scans, two more were completed. They continued on until all twenty patients had been diagnosed. Of the twenty, two exhibited very pronounced hot spots on the scans. Possibly too far along. The other eighteen were precisely what Bob had been searching for: patients with a recurrence of the cancer, but not advanced enough to be invulnerable to the TF.

Within two days, all one hundred twenty-one animals had been scanned. All showed some evidence of melanoma, seven so advanced they were untreatable. Bob named them his "Unlucky Seven." That loss reduced Bob's sixty-one patients to fifty-four. Two more would die soon of unrelated diseases, leaving him with fifty-two patients.

Bob reported the new data to Carole Evans verbally. But he took his charts to Otis Cruikshank.

Otis reviewed Bob's report and studied each chart intently. When he came to the seven that were untreatable, he asked, "And what do you intend to do about these, Robert?"

"They're too advanced to be part of the protocol. But it would be interesting to see if the TF has any effect at all on them. I'd like to treat three of them and see how they fare as compared with the other four."

Otis nodded. He was pleased with Bob's work. But the only outcome that would have any scientific significance would result from the use of TF. That was crucial to Otis Cruikshank and to Trask Institute.

Otis ended the meeting by saying, "Well, Robert, now we'll begin to see."

"Yes, sir."

When Bob returned to his office, he remembered something he should have done some time ago. He dictated a letter to the Cleveland Clinic asking for the precise strain of those melanoma cells which he believed were the basis of the experiment.

SIXTEEN

The next morning Bob Niles assembled his team in the operating room. The transfer factor, which had been stored in frozen form, was thawed and mixed with the DNase to depolymerize it and dilute it enough to inject. Precise dosages had been prepared, and as each patient was injected, that dosage, along with the date and time of the injection, was recorded on the chart.

It went on through the morning. A steady flow of patients; shaved, swabbed with antiseptic, injected with a massive dose of TF; chart noted; patient returned to its cage.

Later that day Bob injected his TF controls. These fifty rabbits had been part of the experiment from the first day, but they had never been inoculated with melanoma cells. They were to receive only transfer factor to test its purity. If they did not react adversely, it would be clear that part of the experiment was working properly.

Next Bob examined the control patients that had received melanoma cells and surgery but no TF. He could feel new, discernible masses in most. He would have a good un-treated group of patients to compare with his TF patients. If the TF patients recovered or survived considerably longer than this group of untreated controls, the Cruik-shank experiment could be considered a success.

By nightfall, Bob headed home. Judging from the temperature and the dark late-fall sky, the next storm would be snow, not rain. Soon the experiment would be largely a matter of waiting. He would have free time, time to ski. Perhaps he ought to find out where.

It was an opportunity to call Heather Cruikshank and invite her out to dinner. But she begged off, saying she had work to do on her thesis. Couldn't she make an exception, he asked, since he needed her help? Well, if he needed help, yes—yes, she could.

They had nearly finished dinner before the subject of skiing came up. Heather had to ask.

"You said you needed help," she reminded him.

"Help?" he asked. "Oh, yes. My work's letting up. I'll have to wait until the animals react. In the meantime I'd like to plan a few ski trips. In fact, if there's any snow before Thanksgiving, that might be a good weekend."

Heather tensed a bit. He realized his prelude to asking for information sounded like an invitation.

"I wanted to know where the best skiing is around here. I figured you'd know. You *do* ski?"

"Yes," she answered guardedly.

"Then you'd know the best places."

"And you should too. Before you went off to medical school you spent several years here. You're not exactly a stranger in town."

"Those days before I left here, I didn't ski," he explained. "I learned how in the Berkshires and Vermont."

"Oh," she said softly, and then grew quiet. Perhaps she had misjudged his intentions.

"When I talked about a weekend, what did you think?" Bob pursued.

"That you were asking me to go with you."

"And if I were?"

"I'd say we don't know each other well enough yet."

"What if we did know each other well enough?"

"I think I'd better get back to my studying," she said evasively. And she rose to go.

Bob knew by now that Heather would not be pressured. So he said nothing, just followed her to the car.

They pulled into the circular driveway of the Cruikshank house. She let him kiss her, but her own response was even more guarded than usual. Evidently his invitation had upset her more than he had thought. As she slid out of the car he noticed a few flakes of snow in the air.

"Look!"

She stood in the driveway, staring up at the overcast sky and then back at Bob.

"We don't have much time to get to know each other," he said. "Do we?"

Otis Cruikshank had just drawn a pint of his own blood and placed it in the centrifuge when there was a knock on the door. He turned, annoyed. Probably the cleaning woman again, having forgotten a rag or a can of cleanser. He turned on the machine. It began slowly and built up a steady high-pitched sound that reflected its furious revolutions. There was a second knock.

Damn it. He would have to make it clear she could not interrupt like this! He could hardly remember a night when she did not return for something. He unlocked the door and threw it open, an angry, authoritative expression on his face.

"Otis? I hope I'm not intruding." It was Edgar Woolsey.

"Why, no. No, of course not. Come in, Edgar."

He stood aside to allow the Administrator to enter. Woolsey was pleased. His timing had been perfect.

"Sorry, Otis. I didn't mean to intrude while you're at work. But I do have a note that you wanted to speak to me. I've been so rushed at the office that I called you at home.

You weren't there. So I took a chance that you might be here tonight."

The centrifuge would run a cycle of ten minutes, Otis was thinking. He would have to get rid of Woolsey as quickly as possible. "What can I do for you?" he asked.

"Do for *me*? I thought it was the other way around. After all, you did call me a few days ago. You left word for me to get back to you right away."

"Did I?" Otis could think of nothing except getting back to his work. For, once the centrifuge stopped, he must have complete privacy for his next step.

"Here. I received this message." Woolsey handed Otis a slip which read: *Dr. Cruikshank called. Urgent. Please call back.*

While Otis stared at the slip, Woolsey quickly scanned the lab table. There were a severed plastic tube with a needle attached, a small bottle of a solution which he could not identify from this distance, an empty test tube with a rubber stopper in it and in the corner of the lab table a folded white lab towel which obviously contained some instruments. Possibly a syringe and a hypodermic needle, but he was not certain.

There was one other object in Woolsey's line of vision. A green canvas-covered lab log.

Finally Otis said, "I remember calling, but I no longer remember what about. It couldn't have been important; must have resolved itself. Thank you for stopping by." There was less then seven minutes remaining in the centrifuge cycle.

But Edgar Woolsey did not move.

"If I recall correctly, it was the morning after I had that distasteful run-in with Niles," he said. "I hope you didn't object to my ordering him to report to Dr. Evans?"

"Not at all," Otis said, hoping to close the conversation. "We're coming to the stage of things where opinions will be needed. Is that all?"

The centrifuge cycle would end soon, and unless Otis reinfused his own red cells at once, hemolysis would set in, depriving the cells of their hemoglobin and making them useless to restore him.

But Edgar Woolsey did not intend to be hurried. The longer he stayed the more he might find out. He especially wanted a look at that lab journal.

"You know, Otis, there *is* something I've been meaning to discuss with you."

"Can't it wait?"

"It's no secret I opposed your protocol at first. And even though I support it now, there's talk around that you still resent it."

Woolsey interrupted himself to refer to the centrifuge. "You're sure I'm not holding up anything?"

"Go on!" Otis snapped.

"Well, there's still talk around the Institute about it. And it doesn't make for harmonious work conditions if the Administrator and the Director of Research are considered to be at loggerheads."

"Well, you can assure everyone that as far as I'm concerned there are no hard feelings, no recriminations."

The centrifuge stopped just then, with a warning buzz. Otis turned instinctively to glance at it. Woolsey studied him, waiting for his next move.

"Go ahead," he urged. "I didn't mean to interrupt your work."

But Otis had decided to ignore the machine. He was determined that Woolsey not witness any part of the procedure. "That's quite all right. It can wait," he said.

"I was hoping we might be able to give the staff some demonstration of unity." Woolsey had moved closer to the lab journal. "By the way, what are you working on? Checking on Niles?"

Otis flipped through the reports that lay on the lab table. "Smythe's data."

Edgar Woolsey had moved farther and farther along the stainless steel table. He was now close enough to casually open the green lab log which contained Otis' notes on his treatment of Heather.

"We ought to think of some way to demonstrate our cooperation," Woolsey continued. "Do you have any suggestions?"

"Yes!" Otis exploded. "Why don't we have our pictures taken carving the traditional Thanksgiving turkey?" Then, as if to express his anger, Otis slapped down the pages of data so that they completely covered the lab log.

Woolsey's face fell, but then he drew himself up and said, "Well, I'm sorry, Otis. It's become impossible for me to discuss anything with you these days without bringing on a crisis of some kind. And although I hate to mention it, I'm not the only one who has noticed a marked personality change. You're edgy. Is anything wrong? Trouble at home?"

Otis turned on him in rage. "Damn it, Edgar! Nothing is wrong here or at home. And I might add I would appreciate your getting out of here!"

Woolsey was positive now that he had caught Otis in some kind of secret activity about which the old man felt guilty. But he had no pretext for staying on. "Well, if that's the way you feel . . ." He started for the door, then stopped. "I'm sorry, Otis, very sorry."

One day soon, Woolsey knew, he would have good use for the file that reposed in his bottom desk drawer.

When he was gone, Otis went to the centrifuge and drew out the blood bag. The cells were no longer completely separated. He could run it through the centrifuge again, but he did not know what the hemolyzed red cells might do to the white cells. Too risky. Though it would greatly weaken him, he would have to draw another pint of his own blood and start the procedure over again from the beginning.

When Otis finally left, more than an hour later, the security guard made his usual note to report to Mr. Woolsey in the morning.

Heather was waiting up for Otis. Without any ceremony or discussion they carried out what was routine for them now.

Just as they finished, she said softly, "Dad . . ."

Her voice sounded as apprehensive as it had when she had called from school two and a half years ago when all this began. That alarmed Otis. He was always afraid that one day she might report to him some sign that indicated a return of the disease. He waited tensely.

"Dad, tonight Bob Niles asked me to go on a skiing weekend with him. I don't know if I should go."

He did not know what she meant. She was too old to ask permission. Her private life was her own. He and Ellen had always been respectful of that.

"Dad . . . I think I love him. If I go away with him I might find out I do love him. And if I do, it might be too late."

He took her gently by the shoulders so that they were close. He lifted her chin and looked into her blue eyes which were so like his own.

"You'd like to tell him, is that it?"

"If you love someone, the least you owe them is the truth."

Otis recognized his own words. He had taught her truth in relationships. But now he had to dissuade her.

"If you told him, you'd only jeopardize his career. As a doctor, once he knew, he might be deemed an accessory. It isn't fair to put him in that position."

"No, it isn't fair," Heather agreed, and was about to leave the kitchen when she added, "I could tell him about me, my illness. I couldn't let him fall in love with me unless he knew that."

"How will you tell him that without also telling how you were cured? Don't you see, my dear, how impossible it is?"

Suddenly she blurted out, "Dad, I have to know. How *cured* am I? Is it permanent? Or will I have it in me always? Will my children have it? I have to know. Before it's too late."

Otis took her in his arms.

"It's too late already, isn't it?" he asked. She buried her face in his shoulder. "We may know something very soon, Heather—very soon."

Two days later, Bob received a letter from the Cleveland Clinic. According to its records, it had never sent any live melanoma cells to Trask Institute. But if the clinic's records were incorrect and the cells had been shipped, the letter specified the strain of melanoma it would have had to be. Bob noted the strain of cells in his data and put a large question mark in red pencil in the margin. With so many pressures, so many important questions to be concerned with, Otis couldn't be expected to remember every detail. Perhaps the cells had come from UCLA, the only other likely source. He decided to go and ask Otis.

Otis was poring over some papers when Bob entered.

"Damn fools," he muttered. "They don't realize there's no such thing as an unimportant detail. It is not enough to say the skin graft was reversed. Did they or did they not reverse the skin graft a full hundred and eighty degrees? Details, damn it! Details!"

"Sir . . ."

Otis looked up. "Yes?"

"We received a peculiar letter from the Cleveland Clinic."

"Cleveland Clinic?"

"They have no record of sending us any live melanoma cells."

"Cleveland Clinic . . . Cleveland Clinic . . ." Otis repeated, trying to remember. "Oh, yes. The melanoma cells. Well, they must be mistaken."

"You're sure they didn't come from UCLA?"

"Of course I'm sure," Otis said quickly. "There must be a record somewhere." And he went back to the data.

Bob waited. But Otis did not look up.

SEVENTEEN

Bob's fifty-two remaining patients had already been given four weekly injections of transfer factor produced from the white cells of his most potent donors. If they did not evidence some improvement by now, the entire protocol might have to be aborted.

With growing anticipation Bob awaited the day when Berger would scan the animals again. He found himself waking in the early hours of morning, reliving each step of the protocol, reassuring himself that every procedure had been carried out strictly in accordance with Otis Cruikshank's model. He arrived at the lab earlier and earlier each day and left later and later.

About the only thing that he had yet to do was write again to the Cleveland Clinic. He did this and then he continued to wait.

Edgar Woolsey and Carole Evans began to drop by the lab frequently, trying to appear casual but unable to conceal their concern. As for Otis, he would arrive before eight each morning to receive any reports as early as possible.

Finally, the animals, including the Unlucky Seven, were given their shots of gallium 67, and three days later they were taken back to Berger's nuclear lab.

Otis Cruikshank, Carole Evans and Edgar Woolsey stood

by anxiously awaiting the results of the new scans. In fact, all of Trask waited.

Dr. Berger had suspended all nuclear activities at the hospital for the day, in order to concentrate on the Cruikshank protocol. He took the Unlucky Seven first, since they were the smallest group.

Two at a time, they were strapped to the scanning table. Slowly and precisely the collimator did its work, tracing the animal bodies line by line.

Minutes later, the scans were brought into the reading room and mounted side by side with the first scans, taken weeks ago. One animal had received TF and the other had not. Perhaps there would be some noticeable difference.

Berger studied the plates.

"Hot spots are larger. And some new ones have appeared. In both cases. I'd have to say the treatment made no difference whatsoever."

"It wasn't to be expected," Bob said; "the masses were too large." But he was disappointed. He hoped these results were not an indication of what was to come.

They began scanning the patients, those which had been treated with the TF.

The first two completed scans were mounted as before, the new one next to the old. Bob leaned in close over Berger's shoulder as he studied them. They were both silent for a long time.

"One thing is sure," Berger said finally; "there's no evidence of an increase. The hot spots here and here, which also appear on the earlier scan, definitely indicate decreased gallium positivity."

Bob studied the scans. He refused to allow himself to become too optimistic, but the longer he stared the more apparent it was. What Berger said was true. There *had* been a decrease.

"Of course, this is only the first," Berger cautioned.

They examined the second pair of scans. The concentrations in the liver were constant in both the old and the new scans. But the other hot spots had diminished.

"Look at this, Niles!" Berger suddenly pointed to one area.

Bob looked, referred to the old scan, then stared at the new one again. "Gone!" he said softly.

"Yes. Maybe now it *is* time to indulge in a little optimism," Berger said.

"Not yet, not yet."

Bob wanted *all* the evidence first. He did not want to be misled by one result that might be a statistical aberration. A scientist had to remain objective until the sheer weight of the evidence forced a specific conclusion.

They went back to work and worked all day. Each new pair of scans confirmed their early results. The transfer factor seemed to have had a clear and measurable effect. All tumors gave evidence of having been arrested. Many had shrunk in size. A few had completely disappeared.

Bob Niles and Cyril Berger were elated. They shook hands heartily and clapped each other on the back.

"Extremely encouraging!" Berger said. "Extremely!"

Bob returned to find several messages on his desk. Carole Evans and Edgar Woolsey both wanted to see him. And the Cleveland Clinic had called. There was no message from Otis Cruikshank.

He dialed the Cleveland Clinic first. It had made an extensive search of its records, he was told, and there was no request for melanoma cells from Trask Institute and no record of shipment. The error must be at Trask. But in the face of today's results, the matter seemed inconsequential. Bob decided he would straighten it out later.

Carole Evans and Woolsey could wait too. He was on his way to see Otis Cruikshank.

He found the old man sitting at his desk, waiting with dour expectancy.

As Bob spoke, Otis remained thoughtful. Occasionally

the old man nodded, as he absorbed each fact. But the expression on his face did not change. When Bob had finished, Otis said only that he was relieved to receive the information. He did not seem at all surprised.

"When will we get Berger's report?" he asked.

"Soon as it's typed up. No later than tomorrow afternoon," Bob said.

Otis nodded, then closed the meeting. "I thank you for coming by so promptly, Robert."

Once Bob Niles had left his office, Otis Cruikshank sank back in his chair. Thank God! He thought for a moment, then picked up his phone and called home.

"Heather, my dear, the first results are back. And they are good. Very good."

Carole Evans had called again. Woolsey had called twice. The last time his secretary had left a nasty-sounding message. Dr. Niles was to call Mr. Woolsey, at once!

Bob Niles dialed the Administrator's number.

"Well?" Woolsey demanded. "You've been back for over an hour. What happened? I want a full report. And I want it now!"

"By phone?"

"By phone!"

Bob described the finding in detail. Except for the three rabbits from the Unlucky Seven, all animals treated with TF were responding positively. In some of the new scans, hot spots had completely disappeared. At the end of his report, Woolsey said, "Well, that sounds extremely promising!"

Bob could hear the excitement in his voice. "Remember, these are only our initial findings," he warned.

But Woolsey would not be discouraged. "Damn fine!" he said. "I'll talk to Otis at once."

Carole Evans' response was positive but guarded. She was a scientist, not an administrator. She said only, "I'm glad it sounds encouraging, for Otis' sake."

Bob's phone rang again. This time the operator informed him that while he was on his lengthy conversations, a call had come in for him. The woman had left no name, just a message. The message was: "Look outside."

It was snowing. Big, fat flakes.

Bob checked his animals, slipped out of his lab coat and grabbed his topcoat off the rack. By the time he reached Trask House, the snow was beginning to stick. It promised to be a good, heavy snowfall.

He dialed Heather's number.

"I looked outside."

She didn't respond, but asked instead, "How did it go today?"

"I'm delighted to say the results were as good as could be expected. But they're only preliminary. And very tentative," he cautioned.

"What happens now?"

"We continue the TF injections. We wait another two weeks. We do another set of scans. In the meantime, you and I take advantage of this beautiful snow." He hesitated, then asked, "Don't we?"

He waited. Finally she said, "I'd have to arrange things at school. . . ."

"Can you?"

"I'll try."

She called him the next afternoon. Bob was in the lab, supervising additional injections of transfer factor. She left a message:

I tried. And I'm delighted to say the results are as good as could be expected. But they are not preliminary or tentative. They are very positive.

160

CHAPTER

EIGHTEEN

They had been climbing through the foothills for two hours. The road ahead was clear. But the countryside that stretched on both sides of them was patchy—brown where it was bare, pure white where the recent snow had drifted into the lowlands and against the slopes. The farther they climbed, the deeper the snow became.

They had made little conversation while they drove. Bob was content just to have Heather at his side. And as for Heather, the first results of the experiment had temporarily freed her of her conflicts.

They stopped for a brief lunch and then pushed on, eager to reach their destination.

The sun, far ahead of them to the west, was huge, red-gold. It reflected off the endless white snow as they finally pulled in between the high gates of the ski lodge. Skiers, returning from their day on the slopes, exchanged greetings and invitations to drinks and dinner. And someone called out the latest weather forecast: more snow.

What a welcome change!

They registered and were assigned to a chalet. It was rustic, a two-story A-frame with a large redwood deck facing the mountain range. Inside was a large room with a fireplace already stacked with kindling and logs, ready to be lit. In the corner a huge bed of old pine had a hand-sewn quilt neatly folded across the foot. Bob set down Heather's bag.

She looked a little puzzled. To head off her question, Bob said, "I reserved *two* rooms. Just in case." Then he added, "But I'm right next door."

By the time they had unpacked, the sun was gone. They decided to head for the bar.

An eight-foot log blazed in the huge stone fireplace. The room was crowded with faces—young faces—red, ruddy, bright and loud with laughter and talk. As Bob made his way to the bar to get their drinks, Heather found a small corner table close to the picture window that looked across the huge front deck and out toward the night.

They raised glasses. He attempted to make a toast, but in the din she couldn't hear him. Finally they both shrugged, laughed and took their first sips. It was enough to be together, in the midst of the happy youthful crowd.

"You ski well?" Bob asked.

"I stay up."

"We'll try some of the lower slopes in the morning until you get your legs," he volunteered.

She nodded. "Look," she said, and pointed out the window at the snow, already starting to fall.

There was singing in the bar later. When one song was ended, another sprang up in a different part of the room. College songs. Rock songs. Ballads. Westerns. They sang gaily along, song after song. Finally Bob glanced at his watch.

"If we want to be out early, we'd better get some sleep," he said.

They left the main lodge and walked through the falling snow toward the chalet. The snow felt good on their faces, sounded dry and squeaky under their boots. They climbed the stairs of the chalet and walked along the deck to the far end. At her door he handed her her key. She hesitated,

162

took it and said, very softly, "If you don't mind too much . . ."

"I said I'd understand."

Bob rose early. The sun was just coming up. He drew back the curtains and looked out across the great white expanse. Fresh untracked snow was a foot high as far as he could see. In the distance, toward the west, the tops of the snowy mountains were reflecting the first golden light of the sun. This was a far different kind of ski country than he'd been used to in the East. More challenging. He looked forward to it.

It was not quite seven. He wondered if he dared to wake Heather. He realized he knew so little about her. For instance, was she an early riser or did she sleep until noon?

Just then there was a knock on the wall. Bob knocked back and went out to meet her. When he came to her door she was ready, in a ski suit of navy blue with a wide bright red stripe across her breasts.

"Sleep well?" he asked.

"Very," she said, smiling.

"Good. Let's get some breakfast."

They were high up on the lift, the fresh snow passing under them. The first few skiers were already making tracks in the virgin powder. They reached the top, slipped off the lift, adjusted their goggles and were ready. Heather dug in her poles and jumped off to a quick start. Before Bob knew it, she was below him, maneuvering expertly around the moguls. She had perfect control of her graceful body. And obviously much more experience than she had claimed. She was outdistancing him rapidly.

When he reached the bottom of the run she was waiting for him, her cheeks rosy, her blue eyes glistening with excitement.

"You lured me up here on the pretext that you barely

knew how to ski," he accused, smiling. "After this, I'm ready for the beginners' slope."

"I watched you," she said. "You're not bad. Just a little rusty." But it wasn't true. Bob had to admit to himself that he had never been as adept as she.

They rode back up and made a second descent. This time, whether she held back or he had gained confidence, they were more evenly matched and reached the bottom of the slope at almost the same time.

It was midafternoon. After a hearty, warming lunch, they were ready to ski for the rest of the day. When the lift reached the crest and they had slipped off the chairs, Heather didn't turn and poise herself to go down the slope as before. Instead, she moved gracefully along the top of the ridge and turned right toward another slope. Bob followed her. Below them was fresh untracked powder. Deep, deep powder, the kind that only very good skiers could manage with grace and skill.

"Game?" she asked.

"I didn't suspect you were a powder hound."

"Lots of things you don't know about me," she said, positioning herself to take off.

He couldn't deny her. "Game," he said.

She pushed off and started down. She made slow, graceful turns that could result in figure 8s if he made opposite and compensating turns. Bob pushed off. It took great effort to maintain control in the deep powder. But vanity and his competitive spirit allowed him to succeed. He forced his body and his legs to bend to his will. By the time he joined her at the bottom she was staring back up the mountainside.

"Perfect," she said.

He looked back. She was being generous. Her tracks were indeed perfect, while his were a bit too wide of hers at some points and too close at others. But at least he had completed the run.

They arrived back at the lodge by late afternoon in time to enjoy the sauna. He needed it, to relieve his legs and arms from the knots and pains created by the unaccustomed strain. Later they met in the steaming Jacuzzi pool and luxuriated in the streams of rushing hot water that massaged their arms and legs, relaxing and comforting their tired muscles. When they dived into the outdoor swimming pool, Bob discovered that Heather swam as gracefully as she skied. Drops of water glistening on her rosy windburned cheeks, matching the brightness in her eyes. He stretched out his arms as she came near, brought her close and kissed her.

The hot toddies had been drunk, the songs had been sung. It was growing late. They left the beamed bar and trudged across the crusty snow and up the stairs to the deck of their chalet. The night was clear and the stars shone bright. They breathed deeply of the pure cold air and exhaled with great delight and satisfaction.

When they reached her door, Heather handed her key to Bob. He looked into her eyes to see if she meant what he hoped. Yes. He unlocked the door.

Bob built the fire, and as it blazed they sat before it on the floor. He embraced her, kissed her. She yielded easily. Soon they were stretched before the fire, naked and unashamed. They pressed their bodies close. He enjoyed the fact that she wanted him. Hers was not the sudden passionate, aggressive hunger that Carole Evans had exhibited. In Heather it was love; it was wanting in a way far more tender.

He made love to her, deeply, satisfying. Then they both fell asleep.

In the morning, Heather woke before he did. She leaned on her side, admiring the way he looked asleep, his black hair tousled and curly. By now most of her apprehensions had disappeared. He had not noticed the slight scar on her side, where Slade had done the excision. It had healed nicely, leaving only a faint whitish line, hidden most of the time. And her father had distributed his injections of TF so prudently that not even a doctor would suspect.

She felt no guilt now about not telling him. One day she would. When the experiment was over and before Otis made public his own journal. But until then it would remain secret. The love she felt for him would more than compensate for the slight deception. She was sure he would feel that way when he finally knew. For now, she felt justified in sharing his love, as long as she gave him all her love. She had, and she would.

It was their final morning. They were packing. They had to leave early if they were to reach Trask Park by nightfall. It was a good day for driving—no snow, and just enough clouds in the sky to shield them from the bright rising sun as they drove east. They said little. Heather sat close to Bob. She leaned her head against his shoulder, and after a while she drifted off to sleep. She was tired from the long days on the slopes and the long nights when they were discovering each other. But she seemed peaceful and content.

He hadn't thought of it before, but now as he drove along, with her head resting on his shoulder and her breathing so even and comforting, he considered it. Marriage. Not immediately, but later, once the experiment had proved out. Then would be the time to discuss it.

He drove her to her house and helped her in with her skis and her bag. At the door she kissed him. He held her a long time. While he did, Otis came up the driveway on his usual evening walk home from the office. He greeted them. Bob felt suddenly self-conscious. But Otis said nothing more as he went into the house.

Bob stopped off at the lab before heading for Trask House. He went into the animal rooms, peering into cages and glancing at an occasional chart. Nothing of consequence had been noted in his four-day absence. The patients had been given their TF doses according to schedule. Now their bodies were reacting, and evidently in precisely the way they were supposed to. He'd know better in the morning once he talked to Rosa.

He returned to his apartment, which seemed unusually small and lonely. Discovering Heather and sharing her love made being apart from her far more difficult than it had been before.

Early the next morning, Rosa filled him in on what had happened while he was away. Two of the Unlucky Seven had died. She had had them autopsied in the necropsy room, and tissue samples of the tumors had been taken and preserved for Bob's examination.

As for the other patients, there were no changes of any kind. No evidence of any spread of the melanoma.

Bob checked his control groups, then went to report to Otis. Otis listened and nodded. He had no response or suggestion. None was demanded in the waiting stages of the experiment.

As Bob got up to leave, Otis called out to him.

Now it would come, Bob thought—some question about the weekend. He felt suddenly ill at ease.

But Otis said, "Soon as we can, we must assemble all the data. I've got to begin preparing my paper for the Carter Symposium."

"Yes, of course," Bob replied, greatly relieved.

As Niles softly closed the door, Otis Cruikshank also felt relieved. He had been concerned about that thin white scar on Heather's side, just under her right arm. He had wondered if Bob had noticed, and feared he would ask too many difficult questions.

NINETEEN

Berger leaned back from the lighted viewing boxes and joined Bob in the shadows. Very softly, as if distrusting his own eyes, Berger said, "Take a look. Take a good, long look."

Bob moved in to study two sets of plates. Taken four weeks apart, they served as a better basis for comparison than the usual biweekly body scans.

"Clean," Bob concluded. There were no noticeable hot spots. Those which had appeared in the old scan were now gone. "I would say this is evidence of complete remission."

"So would I," Berger said. "Congratulations!"

"Before we do any celebrating I'd like to try several things."

"Such as?"

"I'd like to scan these two patients, including brain scans. Immediately. While we're viewing the rest of the results. Two out of a group of fifty-two don't prove anything statistically. But at least I want to be absolutely sure about these two."

Berger and Bob Niles spent the afternoon and evening reading the scans of the fifty other patients, comparing them with the month-old scans. By the time they'd finished, the rescans of the first two were ready. Their earlier results were confirmed.

"There's no question now," Berger said. "These two are entirely free of melanoma." He was elated. "Niles, this could be the most important medical breakthrough in decades."

Bob was still hesitant to accept the results—and the implications—without further corroboration. "Let's rescan two others that seem to be in remission," he said.

Two animals were selected at random and submitted to the collimator. When the new scans were completed, Berger set them up, along with the plates of one month ago and this morning's plates.

"No mistake," he said. "There is no doubt. Those animals are clean!"

Bob nodded. He felt his legs begin to give way, and he dropped into a chair.

"God, man, you're trembling."

"Wouldn't you be?" Bob asked. "In the face of what those scans mean?"

"Who knows better than I?" Berger asked. "What this could mean for my patients!"

Berger too collapsed into a chair. They sat in silence until Rosa came in. The cages were all stowed in the truck and ready to return to Trask Park.

Bob shook hands with Berger. "Otis will want to integrate your findings into his paper. He'll need all your scans for his presentation."

"Of course. Anything I can do," Berger volunteered. Then he added modestly, "I wonder . . ."

"Yes?"

"Would you mind suggesting to Otis that I'd like to go along to New York? I don't want any credit. But I'd like to be there. It'll be a great moment."

"I'm sure he'd be delighted. I'll mention it."

"Thanks."

They shook hands. "Make a note in your diary," Berger said. "This could well be a historic day."

It was past midnight when Bob returned his patients to their cages. Too late to disturb Otis. Results of such magnitude had to be reserved for the cold light of day.

He called Cruikshank's secretary first thing in the morning and insisted on seeing Otis at once. He arrived to discover that Otis had assembled Edgar Woolsey and Carole Evans to hear his report.

Woolsey was the first to respond when Bob finished. "Fantastic! Amazing!"

But Otis Cruikshank interrupted. "I want those figures again, Robert."

"Of the fifty-two patients, twelve show complete remission. Thirty-two show marked regression of tumor. The remaining eight show a discernible regression."

"None show any tumor growth?"

"No. And none show a stabilized condition where the tumor has remained the same size. All of them responded positively to some degree."

"And the results of the patient controls? Those receiving tumor injection but no transfer factor?" Otis asked.

"All fifty show marked increases in tumor growth. Plus metastases. Eleven have already died. On autopsy, the cause of death is clearly manifest. Melanoma."

Edgar Woolsey couldn't contain himself. "Damn it, Otis! How much proof do you need?"

Cruikshank didn't answer. But after a long silence he said, "Carole, who would you say is our best pathologist?"

"Spangler."

"Of course," Otis said. "All right, Robert. I want half the animals that appear to show remission to be sacrificed and autopsied at once."

"Don't you trust the scans?" Woolsey demanded.

"With a result of this potential, I want us to be able to face our peers and show them the result, pathologically as well as on scans. I want that proof in tissue blocks!"

"I've got to report this to Marietta Carter," Woolsey said.

"Wait a few more days," Otis insisted.

"A few more days!" Woolsey exploded. "We're into December already. Your presentation is only six weeks away. Six weeks and four days, to be exact. I want to drum up some excitement—some publicity."

Otis said nothing.

"*We* need it," Woolsey continued, "and *you're* entitled to it! It's been a long time since . . ."

Woolsey didn't complete the sentence. A sudden silence filled the room. "I'm sorry, Otis," Woolsey apologized. "A very imprudent thing to say."

"Yes, but what makes it painful is that it's true," Otis said somberly. Then he added, "But that's an argument for the reverse of what you're urging. When I make the announcement, my findings must be sound—absolutely irrefutable. And I can't be absolutely sure until the scans are corroborated by the pathological findings."

"If I could call Marietta Carter and just *hint* at what we have," Edgar Woolsey suggested.

"We will proceed on the assumption that we don't have anything. *Yet!*"

"Then as soon as Spangler's autopsies corroborate the scans?"

"Yes," Otis finally agreed.

After Woolsey and Carole Evans left, Bob said, "Berger is absolutely convinced."

"Berger?" Otis said thoughtfully. "Yes."

"He asked if he could come along to New York when you make your presentation."

"I'd be delighted," Otis said. "He deserves to be acknowledged. I'll make the arrangements today."

"Then you know," Bob said. "Deep down, you know it's worked. Don't you?"

"Deep down? Robert, lad, deep down I *always* knew it would work."

As Bob started for the door, Otis remembered, "Oh, by the way, don't make any plans for Christmas Eve. Ellen'll be sending you an invitation. We're having open house. We'll want you to come by for some eggnog and a late supper."

"Oh, yes, fine. Thank you."

Bob didn't mention that he and Heather had talked about going off for another skiing weekend during the holiday.

The next morning the first four patients who had evidenced complete remission were sacrificed by one of the handlers and their bodies were presented to Dr. Hugh Spangler in the necropsy room of Bob Niles's laboratory.

In midmorning Edgar Woolsey dropped by to observe. He tried to make his visit seem coincidental to other business he had in the building, and he did not stay long. But neither Bob nor Spangler was fooled.

"He'll hover over us like a hawk."

"Don't I know it," Spangler said as he placed some tissue under the microscope. He put the specimen into focus and was silent for a time.

"Well?"

"Distinct evidence of fibrosis. Take a look."

The specimen was clearly scar tissue, a residuum of the melanoma that had once thrived there. Bob felt a surge of enthusiasm. "That's one confirmed cure at least!"

As he spoke, the door of the necropsy room opened and Edgar Woolsey poked his head in again. "Oh, sorry," he said. "I keep getting these labs mixed up. Sorry." He withdrew from the room and closed the door again. But he had distinctly heard Bob Niles say there was at least one confirmed cure. How much proof do I need? Woolsey asked himself. One cure is enough indication for me.

Late in the afternoon, Otis dropped into the necropsy room.

"Like to take a look?" Bob asked.

"If I'm not interrupting."

"Please," Spangler invited, slipping off his high stool and giving way to Otis.

Otis stared through the microscope. "Fibrosed tissue."

"Fourth case. All four show the same evidence of remission," Spangler said.

"Good, good." Otis left the room without saying another word.

As soon as the door closed, Spangler said, "Christ! you'd think he'd jump for joy with results like these. He must have been pretty convinced he'd succeed!" And he resumed dictating his findings into the tape recorder.

At quarter to five New York time, Edgar Woolsey picked up his private phone in order to bypass his secretary.

After several rings, an efficient male voice answered. "Mrs. Carter's office. May I help you?"

"This is Edgar Woolsey. I would like to talk to Mrs. Carter."

"I'm afraid Mrs. Carter's in a meeting."

"I feel sure that she won't mind being interrupted when she hears what I have to report," Woolsey said confidently.

Soon the condescending voice of Marietta Carter came to him over the phone.

"Edgar, how nice to hear from you. No bad news, I hope. Otis Cruikshank *will* be here in January, won't he?"

"He certainly will," Woolsey said. "I just wanted you to know—strictly *entre nous*, of course—the data are in."

"And the results?" she asked eagerly.

"*Couldn't be better*," Woolsey said. "Of course, I trust you not to breathe a word."

"Of course."

"Otis would be upset," Woolsey continued. "But I wanted you to know that this will be a presentation of major importance. You can go all out in your publicity."

"Excellent!" Marietta Carter said. "Thank you for calling me, Edgar. And when you come to New York I want you to bring your projected budget for next year and tell me the part you think the Carter Foundation might play in it."

When Edgar Woolsey hung up he felt justified. It had been necessary to make his call before Marietta Carter committed too much of her funds to other institutions. He was sure now Trask Institute stood at the top of her list.

TWENTY

For days after his call to Marietta Carter, Edgar Woolsey pressured Otis Cruikshank to send on to New York a new, more optimistic abstract, indicating the wide scope of the presentation he would make at the Carter Symposium. Otis refused. Instead, he selected a Peer Review Committee from among the staff to examine all the data and the findings.

Bob Niles outlined the experiment, detailing all the procedures. Berger explained his findings on the nuclear scans. Spangler followed with tissue blocks and enlarged photos of his findings on autopsy. Then the members of the committee studied all exhibits carefully, asked many questions and after days of intensive study, finally came to a unanimous conclusion.

The results justified the protocol. The number of complete remissions was extremely significant. Even if there had been only the same number of noticeable regressions, the Cruikshank experiment must be considered a tremendous success.

Otis Cruikshank could no longer resist Woolsey's pressure. He drafted a new abstract and dispatched it to Marietta Carter. He also asked Bob to consolidate all the data and rough out a paper reporting in detail on the entire experiment and all findings. Once Bob had prepared the draft, Otis took over.

In the lab, Bob continued his work on his remaining

patients. They received their periodic scans from Berger. And each week, a number were sacrificed and autopsied by Spangler. The percentage of complete remissions remained stable. Of the rest, all showed clear signs of marked regression of symptoms. Each set of new data was supplied to Otis so that he could update his figures, pointing toward the day when he would mark his charts final and approve them for inclusion into his paper.

Concurrently, a new air of optimism was being generated around the Institute.

Edgar Woolsey made several trips to Chicago to meet with the Board of Trustees. He was ebullient with promises and optimistic forecasts, and these extended to everyone connected with the Cruikshank protocol.

Young Niles would certainly be in for a promotion and a substantial increase. After all, the young man was also a board-certified physician. Spangler too deserved an increase. And Berger, that nuclearist at the University Hospital, he should receive more than just an honorarium. He had made a great contribution to the work. Then, of course, there was the lab team—Rosa Gregory, Ania Sokolov, Charlie Sanders.

In this prodigal mood, Edgar Woolsey dispensed praise and rewards for everyone. As for Otis Cruikshank, all his doubts about Otis' secret night work disappeared. Woolsey even considered burning the incriminating file he still had tucked away in his desk drawer.

He was suddenly proud of Otis' record for extreme caution. These days too many scientists went off half-cocked. Yes, Edgar Woolsey said to himself, it was a comfort to work with a man as cautious and reliable as Otis Cruikshank. Perhaps he should put on a strong campaign to secure a Nobel for Otis. For the Cruikshank Phenomenon. Woolsey liked the sound of it. The Cruikshank Phenomenon. It was an appropriate name for a technique that might well open the door to large-scale cures for human melanoma.

Otis Cruikshank was adding the latest data to his charts. He leaned back and admired the results. He could already imagine the impact they would have when presented at the Carter Symposium. Then it would start all over again—the flood of invitations to chair symposia all over the country and all over the world. But he would be selective, accepting only those few opportunities which would enhance the international reputation of Trask Institute. His discovery would give Trask a tremendous boost in momentum—enough to serve for the rest of his tenure.

His phone rang. "Cruikshank," he announced.

"Otis? Coffman!" a hearty voice announced.

For an instant the name Coffman baffled him. Then he remembered: Ward Coffman, Cal Tech.

"Ward?" Otis asked.

"Right! I know I'm disturbing you, so I won't keep you. But I had to call and congratulate you as soon as I heard."

"Heard what?"

"Why, the Cruikshank Phenomenon! If it's everything it promises to be, it's fantastic! We're all looking forward to it! I'll be sitting in the front row, cheering."

"Oh. Thanks, Ward. Thanks."

"Now go back to work. That's all you Scottish Calvinists are good for!" Coffman was laughing when he hung up.

Otis had great respect for Coffman, and his praise was meaningful, but he was furious that knowledge of his work was already circulating so widely in the scientific community. He called Edgar Woolsey at once.

"Edgar! What the hell is going on?"

"What do you mean?"

"Someone is leaking news about my protocol. I just got a call from California!"

"I don't know who could be doing it," Woolsey said blithely. "Certainly no one here at Trask."

"Are you sure you haven't talked to Marietta Carter lately?"

"Talked to her?" Woolsey replied. "I'm glad she hasn't been badgering me. You know how she is when her symposia are coming up. Frankly, I wouldn't put it past her to have someone nosing around here to pick up information. If she discovered anything, that's the way she got it." He said no more.

Nevertheless, Otis was convinced that Woolsey had leaked the news. Yet he didn't mind too much. His data were solid, his results even better than he had anticipated.

Early the next morning as Otis Cruikshank was setting out for his office, Bob Niles's sports car pulled up in the driveway. It had been a cold night. The moisture that had accumulated and frozen crackled under the weight of his tires. He got out of the car just as Otis opened the front door.

"Good morning, Robert," Otis called out, hoping that he was as casual as a father was required to be these days with a young man calling to take his daughter off for a weekend of skiing and, he had to face it, lovemaking. "What's the weather forecast?"

"Ski reports say five inches of new powder on a base of twenty-two inches."

"Good, good," Otis said, and he started off toward Trask Park.

Bob strapped Heather's skis to the roof of the car next to his own and put her bag into the trunk. As they pulled out of the driveway they noticed Ellen in the living-room window, waving good-bye.

"Poor Mom and Dad," Heather said. "They're trying so hard to be 'modern.' But I'd like to have a tape recorder under the dinner table tonight."

They laughed.

As the car turned onto the Interstate, Heather said, "I'll bet Mother will say, 'One thing you have to admit, Otis, he's a very nice young man.' Poor Dad. He's taking it harder than Mother."

"The question is, how are *you* taking it?" Bob asked suddenly.

"Me? Why?"

"Because pretty soon we're going to have to make up our minds."

"Yes," she said; "yes, I guess we will."

"Well?"

"Well what?"

"I've just asked you to marry me. Aren't you going to answer?"

"Is that what you were doing?" she evaded. "I thought occasions like this called for more romantic language."

"They do. But I'm not very good at it," he confessed. "Well?"

"May I have the rest of the weekend to think about it?"

The remainder of the drive was silent and thoughtful. It was one thing to fall in love, to be in love, even to make love, without disclosing her secret, but quite another to consider marriage and children. Especially children who might inherit a genetic weakness even science didn't yet understand.

Even if she dared take that risk for her children, what about Bob? He had a right to know and make that decision for his children, too.

Still, she thought, even Bob had said the experiment had succeeded. There was proof—scans, graphs, tests. And it was continuing to work as it had worked on her. Every three months she received additional proof. Every scan came up clean.

They arrived at the Lodge in the late afternoon. He checked them in and they went to their room. They had an early dinner, joined briefly in the songfest in the bar, then left early.

The maid had turned down the quilt on the big high bed and started the fire. The room was warm, though the windows facing the chill north wind were iced over. It

179

was a room that invited love. They wanted each other, equal in their desire.

Eventually they lay on their backs watching the pattern of reflected flames on the ceiling. Heather fell asleep, her head resting in the crook of his arm. Bob lay perfectly still so as not to disturb her. He looked down at her profile, which was highlighted by the glow from the fire.

She was a fine-looking girl—no, a fine-looking woman, he reminded himself again. She was a mature, solid human being. A perfect wife. If she decided to become his wife.

She moved in her sleep, turning to rest on her left side. Her arm moved slightly, revealing a faint white line which Bob recognized as scar tissue from some incision or wound. Probably an injury from childhood. He must ask her about it sometime.

The three days passed too quickly. They skied all day, and the nights were never long enough. Too soon they were packing again. Early the last morning, skis strapped to the rack on the roof of the car, they were on their way home.

He waited until they were back on the highway. "Well?"

"Well, what?"

"You've had all weekend to think about it."

"Oh, that."

He waited.

"I think it would be nice if we announced it at Mother's Christmas Eve reception."

"Nice? I think it would be terrific!"

She moved closer to him. He put his arm around her. He drove that way until they stopped for lunch.

Before they reached Trask Park, she said suddenly, "Let's not tell anyone at all until Christmas Eve."

"Why?" he asked.

"I don't know. Just a feeling. Please? Let's wait until Christmas Eve?"

"Of course. Sure. If you want it that way," he agreed.

Christmas was only days away. But Heather needed that time to think. Perhaps she could think of some way to tell him the truth without revealing her father's part in it.

In Bob Niles's laboratory at Trask Institute, two of the four surviving patients in the Cruikshank experiment were nibbling at little brown pellets of food. A third was sucking at the wick connected to the water bottle. The fourth crouched in the back of its cage, experiencing some discomfort related to a rash on its belly.

TWENTY-ONE

There had been a light snow during the day. But when night came the snow ended. The clouds broke up and moved out. The sky was deep blue and radiant with stars. A bright moon reflected off the fresh, gleaming snow.

Bob Niles walked along the freshly cleared pathway that led from the river across the campus of Trask Park toward the row of large houses that were decorated in many-colored Christmas lights. He looked forward to Ellen's Christmas Eve party with great anticipation. It marked the beginning of all good things. He had found someone he could love without reservation, and he had reached an important level in his professional life with the success of the Cruikshank protocol.

People were arriving at the Cruikshanks'. Bob could hear the excited voices. As he reached the driveway he was greeted by Dr. and Mrs. Wolfam, by Rosa Gregory, by Charlie Sanders with his young wife and a small, shy, flaxen-haired boy of five, who was Charles, Junior.

Inside the house there were laughter and a gaiety which exceeded that of all previous Christmases in the Cruikshank house. This year, with the impending publication of the Cruikshank Phenomenon, all things seemed brighter.

Bob took off his boots and hung his coat on the long rack

that had been set up for the occasion. He made his way slowly through the crowd into the living room, where he found the men bunched around the fireplace and the women in another group nearby.

Bob mingled with the men, but kept watching Heather as she distributed cookies to the children. She not only filled both their hands, but stuffed some into their pockets as well. She noticed him, smiled, waved with her free hand and turned back to the children. They had agreed to make their announcement at the end of the evening, when only Ellen and Otis and a few others were still there. Bob could hardly wait.

The men were discussing Institute matters—Edgar Woolsey in the center, extemporizing about the grandiose plans he was making now that it was certain Trask would be receiving all sorts of huge grants. Otis Cruikshank sipped his creamy, nutmeg-speckled eggnog and remained silent.

Suddenly Bob noticed Carole Evans, standing among all the men. Her shining black hair was carefully arranged around her head as usual, but she had braided in a strand of green velvet, and her low-cut dress showed a hint of her breasts. She acknowledged Bob with a small smile and nod of her head and turned back to Edgar Woolsey.

Someone handed Bob a cup of eggnog. He sipped it as he circulated around the room, greeting all his colleagues, meeting their wives and children.

Gradually the crowd began to thin. By ten o'clock, only the dozen who were expected for supper remained. Ellen opened the double doors into the dining room and revealed a huge turkey, a ham and a variety of colorful salads. On the server stood half a dozen bottles of pink champagne and frosted crystal glasses.

The guests filled their plates and their glasses, then returned to the living room to find places to sit.

Edgar Woolsey requested they remain standing. The evening would not be complete without a toast to Otis Cruikshank, to whom they all owed so much. In his toast

Woolsey called the coming Carter Symposium a milestone in the history of Trask Institute, an event of unprecedented importance.

The guests cheered Woolsey's words and drank their toasts. Bob looked to Heather, who then stepped forward and said proudly, "We have something to announce."

Everyone stopped eating and glanced up at her.

"Dr. Robert Niles and Ms. Heather Cruikshank announce their intention to marry. Very soon!"

There was a single instant of silence, then an outpouring of good wishes and congratulations. Ellen rushed to Heather and embraced her. More deliberately, Otis came across the room to shake Bob's hand and throw a comradely arm across his shoulder. As Ellen came to kiss Bob, Otis turned to embrace his daughter.

"I'm glad you decided," he whispered to her. "We've lived with this fear for too long—far too long."

"I'll tell him. One day soon. Before the wedding. I have to!" she whispered back.

"Once I make my presentation," Otis agreed.

It was past midnight when Bob crossed the campus again on his way to Trask House, his boots making a crunching sound on the crusty snow. The air was icy cold. He was happier than he had ever imagined he could be. His life was finally taking form. He was a man with goals that went beyond his career. He had always known life couldn't be all science. And he was happy now that it would be true. He wanted a family—a wife, sons, daughters, grandchildren . . . He did not want to be "married to his work," as one of his medical-school professors had termed it.

Perhaps for this reason, Bob did not stop off at the lab as he usually did on his way back to Trask House at night. He would wait until morning to check his patients and controls. Besides, with the data so close to completion, there remained little chance of catastrophe.

The next day was bright, made brighter by a glaring sun. As far as he could see, the campus was deserted. The men and women who usually converged on the various buildings were nowhere in evidence this Christmas morning.

Bob Niles let himself into the lab and walked down the corridors, flipping on light switches until he got to the first animal room. He poked his head in, listened. There was a stir occasioned by his appearance, but no suspicious sounds from the control animals, those who had received only pure transfer factor.

In the next animal room, there were obvious sounds and signs of distress. These were his unfortunates, his few surviving untreated cancer patients.

He stopped by to look in on his donors, hardy producers of billions upon billions of the strong melanoma-specific white cells, from which the TF was extracted. They seemed to be not only thriving but proud.

He came now to his patients. When these last four were sacrificed and autopsied, his final data would be complete. He snapped on the lights. The startled animals scurried in their cages and then were still. Bob checked their feed and water and observed each one for a moment.

One of the rabbits seemed to be acting strangely. It crouched back in its cage, its eyes wide and staring. He studied it, then reached in and gently lifted the animal out. Superficially, it looked like the others, until he turned it on its back and ran his fingers along its soft, pink, furry belly. Something trapped his fingertips. His fingers retraced their path. There was definitely something there.

Quickly, he took the animal out into the surgery, snapped on the switch over the stainless steel table and examined the belly of the animal in the strong white light. As he brushed back the soft white hairs he could see a mark of indistinct shape, deep brown, almost black, and at the center, a hard core. It seemed impossible, but it was there.

Very carefully he took up the clippers, affixed a No. 10 head and ran it over the animal's belly.

There was no need to use the No. 40 head. What he wanted to know was now apparent to his naked eye. He held the animal under the white light. There was indeed a small, uneven patch of dark skin on the pink belly. It had the hard, deep-core feeling of a developed melanoma.

For an instant Bob began to feel his own heart pumping as wildly as that of the animal. And his legs felt weak. He returned swiftly to the animal room and placed the patient back in its cage.

He took out a second one and examined it superficially. Nothing. Even under the sharp light in surgery, he could find no suspicious sign. He brushed through the hair on the rabbit's belly. Nothing.

Returning it to its cage, Bob felt considerably better. After all, one out of fifty-two was surely only a statistical aberration.

He took out the third patient and examined it. Nothing. He examined the last patient. The light revealed nothing, but as he felt the animal's body he noticed a tiny suspicious lump just under its breastbone. It seemed to have a hard core.

Bob consulted the charts, especially those of the first and last patients he had examined. Every dose of TF was listed as it had been on all the others. But it was always possible that in a routine procedure involving fifty-two animals someone might have made an error, noting down an injection that had been intended but not actually given.

He considered the possibility of thawing some of the transfer factor and immediately administering a huge dose to the first patient. But that would be a departure from the protocol. He could not.

He wanted to call Berger, but decided not to. He would tell no one, wait out the day, perhaps even the next day. He would tell no one, not even Otis, until he had verified the alarming facts.

He snapped off all the lights and was about to leave when he had a thought. If he did decide to consult Berger, he didn't want to waste the three days it took for the gallium to be absorbed. He unlocked the medication closet and injected each of his last four patients with the proper dosage of gallium 67.

The rest of the day was extremely difficult. He kept assuring himself that one patient with a definite recurrence of the disease could be a statistical freak. If it was only one patient. If.

CHAPTER
TWENTY-TWO

On the 29th of December, four days later, Bob Niles slipped into the lab extremely early so that he would not be observed by any staff member. He collected his four patients into one cage, placed it in the back of his car and drove directly to the University Hospital.

There he led Berger to believe that these four were from his untreated control group. He said he had noticed signs of spontaneous regression of symptoms which he wanted to check out. Berger processed the animals in pairs.

Within forty minutes the plate revealing the first two scans was available. Berger examined them closely.

Finally he turned to Bob. "Nothing to worry about. Your data can remain unchanged. There's clear evidence of positive uptake in both cases. There is absolutely no sign of any regression here, let alone a spontaneous remission."

Bob said nothing.

In a short time the nurse brought in the second double scan. Berger studied it carefully, shaking his head. "Marked hot spots. No regression. These animals are growing good-sized, clearly defined melanomas. You couldn't ask for better results in your control group."

All the way back to Trask Park Bob debated. There was no question he had to reveal his shocking discovery. The question was, how?

He returned his animals to their cages, went to his office and locked the door. It was half past twelve in Cleveland and half past nine in Los Angeles. He called the Cleveland Clinic first, repeating his request for information about the strain of melanoma cells it had supplied. This time he received a brusque, impatient reply. The Cleveland Clinic had no record of any shipment of cells to Trask Institute!

His call to the laboratory at UCLA produced the same response. No melanoma cells had ever been shipped to Trask.

Bob hesitated for a moment, then dialed Otis Cruikshank's office. Otis' secretary put him through.

"Yes?"

"Sir, I must talk to you at once."

"I'm proofing what I hope will be the final draft of my paper, Robert. Can't it wait a few hours?"

"No, sir," Bob said firmly.

Otis' tone changed markedly; he was now concerned. "Something personal?"

"No, sir. But it's urgent I talk to you immediately."

"Well," Otis Cruikshank equivocated, "if it's important to you, I guess I can stand an interruption. Come up in fifteen minutes."

"Yes, sir. Fifteen minutes." Bob looked at the clock on the wall. Fifteen minutes.

Otis Cruikshank looked up over his reading glasses.

"Now, lad, what's got you so worked up?" he asked pleasantly.

"Sir, we have begun to get an unexpected reaction in our last four patients."

"Unexpected?"

"They show evidence of marked retrogression."

"Retrogression? But that's impossible!"

"I thought so too. But the evidence is there. In one case a rampant melanoma of the skin."

"And the others?"

"I had them scanned. All of them react positively. Distinct hot spots. Berger says there's no doubt."

"Berger?"

"I didn't want to discuss this with anyone but you. So I told him they were controls."

Otis Cruikshank started away from his desk. He went to the window and stared out. He stood there for a while, his hands clasped behind his back. From time to time he shook his head in disbelief. Occasionally Bob could hear him say, "Impossible! Absolutely impossible!"

Finally he turned back. "It's a statistical freak!"

Cautiously, Bob suggested, "One of four could be a statistical freak. Even two of four. But four of four?"

"It's four of fifty-two. Less than ten percent!" Otis argued.

"One could say it's four of fifty-two and less than ten percent," Bob said respectfully. "But I think it's statistically significant that that ten percent constitutes *one hundred* percent of all patients who have been allowed to survive this long."

"Impossible," Otis Cruikshank murmured again.

"Come over to the lab and see for yourself."

Otis didn't respond. In a while he said in a strange, thoughtful voice, "I've no reason to doubt your findings. But it's impossible. It *must* work! It *has* to work."

"I know how you feel. But you're the man who always told me, 'Don't let your desire for proof warp your interpretation of results.' "

"You don't understand!" Otis exploded suddenly. "This isn't like any other experiment I've ever been involved in!"

Bob stared at Otis, who turned away to look out the window again.

"In every previous experiment I've started out seeking to discover something. This time I knew the result before I started!"

He had said more than he intended. He turned to face Bob. He was debating whether to tell him of Heather's illness and recovery. He could not do that. Not without Heather's approval.

"I'm not doubting your facts, Robert, just your interpretation. I've had a strong intuition about the outcome of this experiment. I've never wavered in my belief in its success. Forty-eight patients exhibit substantial regression or complete remission on both scans and autopsy. That's proof enough for me—for anyone!"

"But what about the four in my lab? Maybe if the others had lived as long, they too would have retrogressed," Bob suggested.

"It was a necessary part of the protocol!" Otis said sharply. "We had to do stage-by-stage autopsies to establish their cures beyond a doubt! We've done that. We have solid, hard evidence of how well it worked!"

"We have clearly established that using transfer factor early enough produces cures! Let's not overlook that just because of a less-than-ten-percent reversal of our findings from causes we don't understand!"

"Yes, sir." Bob paused; then he asked, "What shall I do with these latest findings?"

"What have you been doing with all your findings till now?" Otis asked.

"Reporting to you. Then reporting to Dr. Evans."

"Then you'll continue to do exactly that," Otis said firmly. "We're not to vary from our usual operating procedures. Is that clear?"

Bob nodded, then added, "Sir, I called the Cleveland Clinic again. They have no record of sending you any melanoma cells."

"Then it must have been UCLA." Otis returned to his work, thinking he had brought the subject to a close.

"I called. They have no record either."

Otis glanced up. "Strange," he said. "But there's no doubt about one thing. They are human melanoma cells. Any pathologist can attest to that. And in the end that's all that really matters, isn't it?"

Puzzled as he was, Bob had no choice but to agree. "Yes, sir. That's all that really matters."

The strong white light glared down on the pink belly of the rabbit. Bob handled it gently, pointing out to Carole Evans the menacing dark brownish spot in the center of it.

"All four?" she asked.

"All four. *All* retrogressing."

She thought for a moment. "The fault might lie in your preparation of the transfer factor."

"All patients received the same transfer factor from the same donors."

"You freeze it, then thaw only the required dosage each time?" she asked.

"Yes."

"You haven't produced any new transfer factor in how long?" she asked.

"Transfer factor isn't likely to lose its characteristics while in a frozen state."

"That's only your assumption, Doctor. We should make an attempt to prove it out."

"We can't restage the entire protocol; there's not enough time," Bob said.

"I wasn't suggesting that. I *am* suggesting the immediate production of fresh transfer factor and the injection of massive doses into these four, who may have been allowed to deteriorate too far as it is." Carole Evans had become extremely tense and officious.

"Of course."

"In the meantime we should keep this extremely confidential. Your findings may turn out to be totally misleading or highly irrelevant."

After Carole Evans left, Bob began injecting the five most productive donors with an additional stimulating dose of melanoma cells. He had just finished when Edgar Woolsey came storming into the lab. He wore a flower in his lapel, which meant important visitors were being received at Trask today. He had obviously interrupted a significant occasion to confront Bob.

"What's this I hear?" he demanded.

"If you heard it from Dr. Evans, it's true. We've had an unexpected development. A reversal of our results."

"I understand there's some question about your procedures," Woolsey said sternly.

"We've followed all the procedures outlined in the protocol. Dr. Evans' suggestion is merely a hypothesis."

"The experiment couldn't have worked so well till now and suddenly gone sour!" Woolsey insisted.

"I'm not drawing any conclusions. I am simply reporting what we've found. So that it can play a part in Dr. Cruikshank's final report."

Woolsey was silent, but his face was flushed with indignation and rage. Finally, he said, "Until we've had a chance to probe this further, I don't want any irresponsible talk around here. Dr. Cruikshank is facing one of the most important presentations of his entire career. I don't want him influenced or disturbed by hysterical conclusions. Is that understood?"

"Understood," Bob said, keeping his temper until Woolsey had left his lab.

Then he said fiercely, "Sonofabitch! How did I suddenly become everyone's enemy?"

To give his four retrogressing patients a chance, Bob operated on the new melanomas and injected the animals with large doses of fresh transfer factor. He watched them closely, examining them each day for a whole week. They did not improve.

Time was running out. It was the second week in January. Otis was due to deliver his paper in New York on the twenty-fifth.

Finally even Carole Evans was forced to admit the evidence was conclusive. The Cruikshank Phenomenon had suffered a serious, perhaps complete, reversal.

TWENTY-THREE

When Bob entered Otis' office he noticed that the papers usually sprawled across the desk were now in tidy stacks. In the center lay his own freshly typed draft of the report on the Cruikshank Phenomenon.

He handed Otis the copy of his latest procedures and results. Otis settled back in his chair and studied them carefully.

Bob waited anxiously, trying not to fix his eyes on Otis Cruikshank, to whom this latest series of findings must come as a great blow.

"And what do you interpret all this to mean?" Otis demanded when he had finished reading.

"An unexpected finding of significant importance has come up. It must be taken into account."

"I agree with you," Otis said. "But what's the meaning of it?"

"Perhaps the entire protocol should be rescheduled, to give it a longer time span. To see if time itself is a crucial element in the experiment. Or if, after a certain number of injections, the TF loses its effectiveness."

"Are you suggesting that I withdraw my abstract—cancel my presentation?" Otis asked.

Bob knew that other men had been forced to do that. But Otis Cruikshank had never had to undergo such public embarrassment during his long and distinguished career.

"I'm only suggesting that we be most conservative in our interpretation, because of this latest finding."

Within an hour, Otis Cruikshank called Dr. Cyril Berger, later than usual, staying in his laboratory, poring over all the nuclearist, and made a request. That night he worked the materials Berger had sent.

He placed a series of scans in the viewing box and snapped on the lights. They were all the nuclear scans of one patient. Heather Cruikshank.

Otis wished that he dared have Bob here with him now. He wished he could show him all this irrefutable evidence, from the first scan indicating the melanoma to those showing the hot spot in her brain, and finally the later ones—nine of them—all completely clear.

Heather's scans were undeniable proof that transfer factor administered early enough, in correct dosages at proper intervals, did work a remission!

And this was not an experiment of only a few months! If time were the factor, then Heather's more than two years of treatment had to be far more significant than the erratic results demonstrated by a mere four rabbits out of fifty-two.

In Otis' mind, these scans invalidated all of Bob Niles's contentions. He felt surer now than he had at any time before.

In the morning he sent for Bob.

"I've been weighing what you said about those four animals, Robert. And your theories as to what happened. I shall include them, but I'll not give them any great significance.

"If nothing else, our results should lead other men to new and more extensive research in transfer factor. It would be a pity if a misinterpretation of our data led to discouraging that. I trust you're satisfied now."

Bob nodded, relieved that the episode had passed without

bitterness. Not only was his relationship with Otis at stake, but there was Heather. He was sure of her love. Still, a conflict with her father could be more than unsettling. They were a close family. He didn't want her to have to make that choice.

"I'll get a copy of my draft to Woolsey by this afternoon," Otis said, "now that we've got this matter squared away."

"Niles! Come up to my office!" Woolsey commanded, and slammed down the phone.

Within three minutes Bob was in his doorway. He said, "Now, then, Niles, what the hell are you up to?"

"Nothing. I simply reported my findings to Dr. Cruikshank and Dr. Evans exactly as you ordered."

"I don't mean that!" Woolsey exploded. "I understand you've taken it upon yourself to tamper with the Cruikshank protocol. Is that correct?"

"Once the results began to turn questionable—"

Woolsey interrupted fiercely. "Who said they turned questionable? I didn't hear Dr. Cruikshank say that. You're the only one who used the word 'questionable'!"

Bob felt a flush of anger. He calmed himself. "Dr. Cruikshank thinks the new data are significant enough to include in his presentation. He and I differ only on the degree of their significance."

"Do I understand that you have the nerve to question the interpretation of a man like Otis Cruikshank? I won't have it! I am ordering you to finish up your work on the protocol and submit your findings to Dr. Cruikshank. He will make *all* the interpretations. Is that understood?"

"Yes, sir."

But as soon as Bob left the office, Woolsey dialed Carole Evans' private line.

"Carole?"

"Yes?"

196

"Did you know that Otis intends to include those last four patients in his presentation?"

"Yes."

"You never told me!" he shouted.

"I always assumed he'd include them. I thought you did too."

"I assumed no such thing!"

It was obvious now to Edgar Woolsey that additional steps would have to be taken. And swiftly.

CHAPTER

TWENTY-FOUR

Otis Cruikshank sat back in his desk chair and studied the memo that had just been delivered from the office of the Administrator: Plan for Reorganization and Retrenchment.

He turned the title page to discover a list of projects that might have to be canceled. Some were dear to Otis; some were part of the life work of men who had served under him for as many as a dozen years. After the list of projects came the names and salaries of men and women who would have to be terminated under retrenchment. Many devoted and highly capable researchers were listed. There were staff members on the long list for whom Otis Cruikshank was determined to fight. It was one thing to read unemployment statistics in the newspapers or hear them on the television news. But when each one was a person you knew and had worked with, it became a source of deep personal pain. Perhaps if he sat down with Woolsey they could figure out alternative economies that would create less human hardship.

Otis dropped the depressing document onto the desk. He cursed Edgar Woolsey for having sent it to him, of all times, when he was only seventy-two hours from leaving for New York to preside over the Carter Foundation Symposium. He shouldn't be bothered with administrative matters now. He should be reviewing his slides to make sure they were in the proper order. He should be rehearsing his figures and data to make his presentation smooth and easily understood. He should be familiarizing himself with the data on those last four patients which Bob was preparing. Otis was tempted to call Woolsey and have it out with him at once. No. First the slides and data. Then Woolsey.

The projector was set up and all the slides arranged in order. Bob darkened the room and snapped the first slide into place. There appeared on the screen a huge color close-up of the shaved area of the first of the last four patients. A large dark brown outbreak of melanoma was strikingly apparent. A second shot of the same rabbit, with white fluffy fur apparent around the shaved area, showed the melanoma from another angle.

Then Bob flashed on the screen the autopsied bodies of the three rabbits which had developed internal masses. There had been no way to present those findings except to sacrifice them, dissect them, lay bare the ugly melanomas within their bodies.

After the last photo, Otis said, "I'll want your memo to go with those, Robert."

"It's almost ready."

"That one last survivor—put the thing out of its misery. It's told us everything it has to tell."

"No need. It was dead this morning when I got here."

"Just as well," Otis said. "And now for Mr. Woolsey."

"Trouble?"

"Retrenchment," Otis said sadly.

Edgar Woolsey had prepared himself to give every outward evidence of compassion and concern. But he had set certain goals for this meeting. Time and Otis Cruikshank's temperament were on his side. With Otis' mind torn between retrenchment and what awaited him in New York, Woolsey felt he should be sufficiently tractable. "Otis, I must apologize," Woolsey said in his most charming manner. "I didn't choose this time. It was thrust on me. Willis Conroy called me yesterday."

This was a lie, but Woolsey could risk it. Otis didn't often deal directly with the Chairman of the Board of Trustees.

"As you know, Conroy is a close-to-the-vest banker type. He put it this way. He's not saying the cuts will be necessary. Certainly not if we get that Carter Foundation grant. But he did think the only fiscally responsible way was to have a plan ready to put into operation if we *didn't* get that money. I had no choice but to draft it and send it on to you."

Woolsey rose from his soft, luxurious leather chair and began to pace.

"We know what a personal wrench this is. And I want to assure you that Conroy stressed several times, 'Be sure to tell Dr. Cruikshank that this is no reflection on him. We don't mean to tell him how to run his research. We're willing to abide by his decisions as to who should be cut. Provided we get the necessary cuts.' That's what Conroy said."

Nothing personal? Otis Cruikshank asked himself. How could it be anything *but* personal? It was his responsibility to keep his staff provided for. His responsibility to see that Trask received its share of nationwide publicity, which was the basis of all grants. His responsibility to remain eternally fertile, producing results that would attract more and more money. Now he recalled all the projects he had turned down that would have ensured space in the public press. Instead he had chosen projects that made more enduring contributions to science.

Otis Cruikshank felt as painfully guilty as a father who had failed his own children.

"Of course," Edgar Woolsey was saying, "if things in New York go as well as we hope, we won't have to be concerned with all this. It's just a stopgap measure. In case anything goes wrong."

"Yes, I understand," Otis said absentmindedly.

Woolsey probed gently, "I suppose you've given a great deal of thought to these latest findings of Niles's?"

"We have to."

"I'm not a scientist, Otis, so perhaps I don't understand," Woolsey began, dissembling and pretending ignorance of all matters scientific, "but this protocol started out to treat rabbits in a lab just the same way patients are treated in a clinical situation. Right?"

"Right."

"Well, then, let's say that instead of fifty-two rabbits with melanoma we had fifty-two *human* patients. And they were treated with transfer factor and forty-eight showed either marked regression of symptoms or complete remission; wouldn't that be considered a fantastic success?"

Woolsey tried to seem ingenuous. "I mean, in real life the figures would probably be reversed. Four might survive for a short time and forty-eight would die quickly of melanoma. Isn't that right?"

"Yes," Otis granted. "So?"

"Well, then, why are we trying to deprecate our own results? Why are we trying to take all the glamour, all the sex appeal, out of an experiment that is not only daring but enormously successful?" Woolsey asked. "After all, Otis, everyone concedes that this is your most brilliant conception in years. *Years*, Otis!"

Woolsey thought he'd handled that aspect of his argument skillfully, pointing up the correlation between the budget cuts and Otis' long lapse between discoveries.

"Otis, you know I agree absolutely with your policy of not doing what they do at other research institutions. A man makes a discovery and does a paper on it and it appears in a journal. Then he rewrites it just the slightest bit and it appears a second and third time. That's highly unprofessional. I have nothing but contempt for those space-grabbers. But when there's a contribution, one that's entitled to the best space, I wonder if we aren't being a bit too cautious and, in the long run, foolish if we don't put our best foot forward."

"Meaning?" Otis challenged.

"Meaning . . ." Woolsey cleared his throat. "Meaning that those four animals at the end of the protocol shouldn't be allowed to overshadow the total result, which is fantastic!"

He paused. Otis looked thoughtful. Woolsey felt he was making headway.

"I mean, your protocol called for only fifty rabbits," Woolsey went on. "That would mean only two patients who showed a return of symptoms. And even if you just reported on the forty-eight patients who were completely or partially cured, the main purpose of the protocol would be fulfilled." He tried to make this sound like an afterthought, not a deliberate suggestion. "And then all this retrenchment would be unnecessary, wouldn't it?"

Woolsey did not expect a reply. He sighed as if to end the meeting.

Otis sat silent for a time. He didn't know why his outrage was not greater than his pain. Perhaps he was getting old, soft. In his earlier years he would have told off Edgar Woolsey and stormed out of his office. But now he was tired.

"Edgar," he began, "I've just come from viewing the photos of those last four patients. What I saw is undeniable, although I'm not yet sure precisely what it means."

"If you're not sure—"

"But that does not relieve me of the responsibility of reporting it!"

"Even if it invalidates your protocol?"

"What do you mean by invalidate?" Otis demanded. "Suppose what happened to those four is the only *valid* statistic in the entire experiment? Suppose it means that transfer factor isn't the cure that I hoped it would be? That is a scientific fact of importance and must be reported!"

Woolsey spoke very softly. "It is not the kind of scientific fact that will win a large grant from the Carter Foundation."

"I . . . I agree with that. But that's their standard. I have mine."

"Of course, Otis. Conroy asked that I present a final retrenchment schedule to him before we all leave for New York. Will I have your suggestions by the end of the day?"

"You'll have them!"

Back in his office, Otis Cruikshank applied himself to the memo. He went down the list of names of proposed candidates for termination. Many of those people were dear to him. Old friends and devoted scientists, like Abner Gottlieb, for example. His family had been killed in the war, and since then Abner had been totally dedicated to science.

Otis called Personnel to inquire, did Abner Gottlieb have sufficient tenure to entitle him to retire on a pension? When he was told Dr. Gottlieb would be eligible for a pension of three-quarters of his regular salary, Otis felt somewhat relieved. At least the old man wouldn't be cut adrift and in want as well. Perhaps if Otis could juggle the names a bit, to list only those who had earned pension rights, he would be able to make the cuts without inflicting unnecessary hardship. Pension money came out of a fund and would be no drain on the annual operating budget. Otis cursed himself for thinking like an accountant and a politician, but he had no choice.

Within an hour, Otis had checked out seventeen more the names. All were eligible for substantial pensions. Now he felt free to return to his data for the Carter Symposium.

He was deep into his material when his telephone buzzer interrupted him. It must be Robert with the new memo to go with those last slides. Without waiting to be informed, Otis lifted his phone and said, "Send him in."

He heard his door open, but he did not look up. "Just put it down on the desk, Robert," he said.

Instead of Bob Niles, Otis Cruikshank heard another voice—soft, apologetic.

"Otis?"

Cruikshank looked up. Abner Gottlieb.

"Abner? Something wrong?" Otis asked, startled.

"That's what I came to ask you, Otis."

Scuttlebutt about retrenchment had obviously got around quicker than usual.

"Sit down, Abner. Please."

Gottlieb slipped into a chair, but held himself erect and tense.

"You heard about my inquiry?"

"Yes," Gottlieb said, nodding sadly. "Was it something I did? Or failed to do?"

"No, no, no," Otis was quick to assure him. "If there were anything like that I'd speak to you directly. It was only an inquiry. Just in case they don't come up with our full budget for the year."

Otis picked up the memo Woolsey had sent him. "It's all in here. A contingency plan. It's terrible, Abner. But I'm forced to do it. I've got to consider everyone and make decisions that impose the least hardship."

"I understand, Otis," Gottlieb said softly. "But may I propose something? Retire me on my pension. I'll get along. I don't need much. But I would like the right to stay on and continue my work."

"God knows, you're one of our best virologists, but I don't know if that's possible."

"Why not?" Gottlieb asked. "There's nothing in the rules of Trask Institute that prevents you from accepting the services of a volunteer. Is there?"

"There may be something to do with liability insurance, things like that. I just don't know."

"Then find out, Otis. Please?" Gottlieb implored. "Because without Trask, without my work, what is there?

Nothing. I've never asked for any special privilege before. But I do now."

"Abner, I told you, it's only a stopgap proposal. After my presentation in New York, we may have all the funding we're going to need."

"I hope so," Gottlieb said fervently. "I hope so."

They shook hands, and Gottlieb left. Bob had been waiting outside to deliver the slides and his memo that explained them.

"Thanks, Robert," Otis said. "This will give me a chance to review the whole thing at home tonight."

After Bob had gone, Otis settled down to read the memo. But after a few sentences, his interest flagged. His mind kept going back to Abner Gottlieb.

Why, Otis demanded of himself, why did I ever have the ambition to become a Director of Research?

Something Woolsey had said suddenly nagged at him. He pulled out the copy of his revised abstract which had been sent to the Carter Foundation a few weeks ago. He had not mentioned any specific number of animals as patients, so that was where Woolsey had conceived his idea to report on only forty-eight. Woolsey *would* find a loophole like that. Otis Cruikshank sank deep into thought.

Within half an hour after Abner Gottlieb was seen leaving Otis Cruikshank's office, that fact was reported to Edgar Woolsey. He was secretly delighted. Everything was going according to plan.

CHAPTER
TWENTY-FIVE

Drs. Otis Cruikshank, Carole Evans, Robert Niles and Cyril Berger and the Director of Administration of Trask Institute, Edgar Woolsey, boarded the early-morning non-stop jet to New York. Although they usually traveled economy, today Woolsey had reserved first-class seats for everyone.

Woolsey felt confident and looked forward to four days of excitement and triumph, culminating in a sizable check signed by Marietta Carter. He was sure Otis could not resist the pressure he had applied. He also looked forward to making love to Carole Evans—without having to sneak back home. He intended to spend the whole night with her. Four whole nights.

Exuberant, he stood in the wide aisle, summoned the stewardess and ordered a king's breakfast for Dr. Cruikshank: scrambled eggs with sausage, croissants and plenty of fresh hot coffee.

Otis Cruikshank dug deeper and deeper into his seat, trying to escape Woolsey's flamboyant display. He picked unenthusiastically at the breakfast as he reviewed the notes for his presentation. Beside him on the empty seat was the box of slides, each numbered and correlated to his discourse. When he came to the last section of it, just preceding his comments and conclusions, he had to insert the memo Bob had drawn up to cover the unexpected results with the last four survivors. Exactly how would he introduce the subject?

Perhaps he'd say, "This experiment, like all experiments, is subject to unexpected results. In the latter stages the last four patients showed signs of retrogression due to factors which we do not yet understand. We would have repeated that part of the protocol if there had been enough time between that discovery and this symposium."

It was an honest statement. It satisfied his sense of integrity and at the same time did not destroy the impact of his remarkable results. As Edgar Woolsey had said, it would be unfair to invalidate all their findings by making too much of the bizarre results with the last four. Besides, Heather had shown no recurrence, and that was the one case completely under his control. No one could misinterpret that. These thoughts went through Otis Cruikshank's mind as he made one last review of his data and his notes.

When the plane landed at Kennedy Airport, Otis entrusted his slides to Bob Niles and carried his notes himself. With his reading glasses still high up on his head, he strode down the noisy corridor of the terminal building, flanked by Edgar Woolsey and Carole Evans. Bob and Cyril Berger brought up the rear.

As they passed through the barrier that blocked persons not cleared, a uniformed chauffeur was straining to identify them.

"Dr. Cruikshank?" the chauffeur kept calling out to any man who seemed a likely candidate.

"This is Dr. Cruikshank," Edgar Woolsey announced proudly.

"Mrs. Carter sent her car for you," the man said, and directed them toward the huge blue Bentley, fragrant with the smell of costly leather.

"You see, Otis," Edgar Woolsey commented, "you're being welcomed like a conquering hero. She's telling us she's already made up her mind. The grant is ours. All we have to do is follow through."

He said no more, but Otis Cruikshank was aware of his true message. He thought of the memo about retrenchment and of his own long hiatus between discoveries. Unconsciously, he reached down and felt for his briefcase at his feet.

Since this was a visit of special import and promise, Edgar Woolsey had arranged accommodations at the Plaza. A large suite for himself, with a discreetly convenient bedroom–sitting room for Carole on the same floor. A suite for Otis. And modest rooms overlooking Central Park for Cyril Berger and Bob Niles. Bob settled in, unpacked and went through the box of slides, making absolutely sure that they were arranged in order. From now on Otis would have little time to spend on the slides.

First there was the opening luncheon reception, to which all the scientists were invited to greet Marietta Carter and to renew old acquaintanceships. Men who had known each other for years but met only infrequently embraced each other, chatted, discussed each other's work.

Bob moved among the crowd and read name tags. In this one reception room were at least fifty of the most famous medical and scientific investigators in the world. Just being present here was exciting. But as he moved from group to group, he heard one subject referred to more than all others —the Cruikshank presentation; and this fact made the event even more significant for him.

He had heard Marietta Carter saying, "We feel this is a historic meeting. When I just hinted at what the Cruikshank Phenomenon could mean, *Newsweek* wanted an exclusive. And the *Today* show is clamoring for even five minutes with Dr. Cruikshank."

Edgar Woolsey beamed. But Otis Cruikshank's face was flushed and he appeared ill at ease. He wished Marietta Carter would stop making extravagant claims for his protocol. She was building up expectations that might not be justified, considering those four last survivors.

She introduced Otis to a young man whose name he forgot immediately.

"I've read your abstract, Dr. Cruikshank," the young man said. "If your presentation carries out the promise, I'd say you were standing on the brink of a breakthrough of importance."

Marietta Carter beamed. "Remember, Otis, you're speaking to *The Washington Post*."

Otis Cruikshank did not like discussing scientific matters with laymen—especially with newsmen, who were likely to distort the information and mislead the public.

Bob reached Otis' side just as the older man was responding to the question.

"I'm always suspicious of scientists who use adjectives. Science should deal in nouns. In facts. Phrases like 'tremendous importance' do not belong in discussions about scientific discovery," Otis said.

Marietta Carter's smile seemed to wane. She glanced at Edgar Woolsey to express her displeasure.

"Dr. Cruikshank is known to understate his achievements," Woolsey spoke up. "Most men in this room would give their eyeteeth to have made half the discoveries that Otis Cruikshank announces with little fanfare and no adjectives."

The interviewer from the *Post* made a small note on his pad. At that point Edgar Woolsey put his arm around the young man and steered him toward the bar, where they could have a drink and discuss the Cruikshank Phenomenon.

Otis excused himself and went off to greet some old friends he'd spotted across the room, leaving Bob Niles alone with Marietta Carter.

"You actually did all the work," she remarked. "It must have been fascinating—tremendously exciting."

"I agree with Otis. Adjectives do not belong in scientific discussions. If I discussed Dr. Cruikshank's work in terms other than those he uses, I'd be betraying his attitude toward science and himself."

"You're really very fond of him."

"He's a great man. What makes him great is his absolute adherence to truth. If people ever come to feel the same way about me, I'll consider that the highest honor I can achieve."

Marietta Carter looked into Bob's eyes and was greatly impressed.

"I think one day they will feel that way about you," she said.

Then she left him to join another group of distinguished men and women.

Alone, Bob Niles suddenly regretted that the protocol hadn't ended two weeks sooner. Then everything would have wound up neatly and they would have avoided all these problems.

The next two days passed in the usual fashion. Several meetings took place simultaneously, involving different specialties. Each man or woman chose to attend those most closely allied with his or her own field of research. Bob went from one seminar to another, listening a bit here, then going on to another. He became aware of his impatience. He was simply too tense and nervous to allow himself to become involved in any presentation except the crucial one Otis Cruikshank would make on the last day.

By afternoon of the third day, he gave up, went back to his room at the Plaza and put in a call to Heather.

Heather sounded breathless and delighted. The warmth and eagerness of her greeting made him feel at ease again.

"I miss you," he said.

"When will you be back?" she asked. "It's snowing again. It's going to be a great weekend for skiing."

"We're due to leave Friday. Unless the weather changes and we get socked in, we should be back by noon."

"If I can get Monday off, we could still get most of the weekend."

"Great," he said.

"Okay. See you Friday. Unless you're delayed." Then Heather said softly, "I wish you were here now."

He hung up. He wondered why he had called. Yes, he missed her. But it was more than that. Perhaps he needed reassurance of her love now, in the face of the doubt his new data had cast on her father's protocol.

Bob ate dinner alone, then went back to the hotel and turned on the television news. His phone rang. It was Otis with a favor to ask.

"Would you sit next to the projectionist tomorrow afternoon while I deliver my presentation? Just to make sure the slides are in order and nothing goes wrong?"

Bob agreed.

In his own suite Otis thanked him and hung up the phone, but before his hand had left the instrument it rang.

"Yes?"

"I have a long-distance call waiting for you," the operator said.

"I'll take it."

"Otis? Darling?" It was Ellen. "How are you?"

"I'm fine. Couldn't be better! Although I must say I'm damned annoyed with the fuss they're making over me."

"You deserve it!" she said firmly. "And it's about time you learned how to accept praise!"

"I wonder what they'd say if they knew how this really started."

"They will, darling. One day you'll have to tell them."

"Yes, I guess," he said thoughtfully. Then, "How is Heather?"

"Fine. Anxious for Bob to get back."

"Of course. It won't be long now. Good night, my darling."

CHAPTER

TWENTY-SIX

The auditorium fell silent with anticipation as Dr. Otis Cruikshank approached the podium to make the Symposium's concluding presentation on An Investigation of the Use of Transfer Factor in the Treatment of Melanoma. So much had been hinted about his startling findings that all other presentations made during the four days' sessions seemed only a prelude.

The hall was filled and still people crowded through the double doors. In front-row seats were Marietta Carter, Edgar Woolsey and Dr. Carole Evans. As Otis had requested, Robert Niles sat next to the projectionist in the rear.

Otis Cruikshank looked down at the first row and then out over the huge crowded room. It had been many years since he had stood before such a gathering. He shuffled through his notes once, then began:

"In this symposium we have heard ingenious and exciting results from which one unchallenged conclusion has emerged: the immune phenomenon in cancer is an observable fact. Although the concept is not new, the experimental evidence is, and it continues to mount.

"This leads to a strange dichotomy, not in the laboratory or in the patient, but in our own minds. We become so convinced that immunity must work that we embrace it, even

212

in the absence of present-day clinical application. Or we become so disenchanted by the difficulties of establishing proof that we forsake it.

"I suggest that the real answer may lie in a duplication of the clinical situation in the laboratory. To do this I have chosen from among the various forms of immuno-therapy not BCG or nonspecific immunotherapeutic agents but the use of transfer factor. Of course, the day we will be able to ward off cancer with an injection as we now prevent measles or polio is perhaps a century away. But the more immediate possibility of treating malignant tumors does deserve our attention.

"Unfortunately, until now researchers have dealt with the disease at a very early stage, while clinicians see patients only in advanced stages. Therefore, I decided to ask, Why not design an experiment in which laboratory 'patients' have been permitted to cultivate tumors that would compare to a tumor diagnosable in the ordinary routine of practice? And then, why not treat those patients in the precise manner in which human patients are being treated? With one critical difference: use transfer factor *before* we have another critical mass to contend with. Before the patient's immune system is overwhelmed by the disease. That would be the only true test of the efficacy of transfer factor. So I asked, Why not make that precise test?"

There was now intense concentration and curiosity in the auditorium. The usual shifting and coughing were nonexistent. Everyone's attention was focused on Otis Cruikshank and on the screen beside him, which would soon reveal in slides the evidence he had gathered.

Otis described the manner in which he had designed his protocol, how he had selected patients and donors, and he explained his various control groups. He described the method of diagnosis, Bob's surgical intervention, the preparation of transfer factor, its time and frequency of use.

Marietta Carter stared up at Otis Cruikshank with great concentration. Edgar Woolsey glanced at her from time to time. Occasionally he thought of those four miserable animals that stood between him and Marietta Carter's eternal appreciation.

In the back, Bob Niles listened intently to Otis' presentation. Even if the results were not perfect or incontrovertible, they were both startling and promising. They would inspire many other researchers to experiment further and perhaps discover the cause of the final aberration. Although he knew the presentation almost by heart, Otis' delivery was so strong and the experiment so challenging that Bob found he shared the audience's keen anticipation.

Otis Cruikshank himself was not unaware of the effect he was having on his audience—most particularly on Marietta Carter. He felt exhilarated. He was in complete command of the large and impressive symposium. All self-doubts were vanishing with the respect that was accorded him now. And he had not even begun to reveal the findings of most stunning impact.

As he proceeded with his presentation he grew stronger and more incisive. He abandoned his professional tone and became an advocate. He was a man in the full flush of an exciting idea, and he enjoyed it. He was a man no one could threaten. Gradually he began to speak not to the entire audience, but to two people. Marietta Carter and Edgar Woolsey.

Finally, he was ready to present his evidence. He pressed the hand signal for the first slide, a graph of the experiment in its initial phase. Then, as he described the work that Bob had done, he brought on color slides of representative melanomas which had been photographed before Bob's surgery and then after. He paused over the most significant slides and emphasized specific areas with a light-ray pointer. After he finished with the preliminary work he turned to the results, which were far more impressive.

The graphs indicated the progress of the patients, the startlingly few recurrences of the disease in the transfer-factor-treated animals, the recurrences in all those that had *not* been given transfer factor. The color photos of those animals showed large, deadly skin blemishes. When they did not, their scans showed marked nuclear hot spots. The contrasts were so startling that there were audible reactions from his audience, which watched with growing fascination, admiration and, finally, awe.

In the reflected light from the large screen Otis Cruikshank could see the face of Marietta Carter. Her gaze was fixed upon the screen, paying him the ultimate compliment, her total concentration and acceptance.

Otis Cruikshank moved on with assurance. The photos of the autopsied animals were shown. Each photograph was a new triumph, adding more proof. Like his audience, Otis Cruikshank was becoming intoxicated with the results. His pace accelerated.

Bob Niles watched the number of slides dwindle, his eyes always on the last dozen. What effect those last twelve slides would have on the audience he could not predict. Had Otis built up their expectations to such a degree that any letdown would invalidate the protocol completely? Or would they be able to appreciate the great hope which the bulk of the results provided?

Soon there were only six slides left before the final twelve.

Those six showed the autopsies and tissue specimens which Spangler, the pathologist, had prepared. The results were dramatic. Otis made them seem more so by his description. Bob began to hope that soon Otis would start to prepare the way for that last dozen slides.

Otis was now getting ready to deliver his conclusions. He stared down at Edgar Woolsey, Marietta Carter and Carole Evans in the front row. He was aware of Bob sitting alongside the projectionist. And he felt the enormous presence of his audience, silent and engrossed, waiting for his final remarks. Then he thought of the list of names, the cutbacks, his own role as Director of Research.

All these pressures weighed on him as he spoke, slowly

presenting his conclusion in a way that would leave an opening to report those last four patients.

Until he found that he chose not to.

Whatever those twelve slides might demonstrate, none of them measured up to the one unmentionable fact. Heather. She was alive and well and had passed scan after scan for more than two years with no trace of melanoma. She had a longer, clearer history of cure than any patient involved in the experiment!

Instead of discussing the final four patients, Otis closed with a note of caution. "We need not assume that these results will be maintained at the high level that was achieved in our experiment. But there is promise here for the use of transfer factor in clinical cases if applied early enough, with regularity and from strains with demonstrated effectiveness. It may not be correct to say we have found a cure for melanoma, but we have opened the door to a course of treatment that is extremely promising."

From one corner of the auditorium applause erupted, and it was picked up and carried throughout the huge hall. Scientific presentations usually received only polite applause. Otis Cruikshank received an ovation.

Edgar Woolsey, who had been tense and in a sweat through the last phases of Otis' presentation, slumped in his seat, exhausted but tremendously relieved. Evidently his strategy had worked.

Carole Evans sat silent and shocked.

Marietta Carter was already making her way to the rostrum to shake Otis Cruikshank's hand. A crowd of colleagues clambered up onto the stage to congratulate him.

The projectionist turned to Bob Niles and asked, "What about these last twelve slides?"

"I'll take them," Bob said, still stunned. He took the slides and slipped them into his pocket.

On the stage, Otis Cruikshank was surrounded by his colleagues. Two editors of professional journals were begging for his paper as well as the photographs that had accompanied it. Marietta Carter stood by Otis' side, his protector and benefactor, guarding him against the crowd that pressed in on him from all sides.

Finally she announced, "We have only a short time before the dinner. So please, give Dr. Cruikshank a chance to rest and change. Please!"

The crowd slowly disintegrated and drifted away. Edgar Woolsey seized Otis' hand and shook it vigorously. "You did it, Otis! You did it!"

Then Otis Cruikshank was escorted to Marietta Carter's Bentley, which waited to take him to the Plaza.

Bob still clutched the dozen slides that had not been seen. He was about to leave when he heard a voice behind him.

"Bob . . ."

It was Carole Evans. They stared at each other, neither willing to make the accusation. Carole attempted to say, "You can't blame him for not using data that can't be explained. . . ."

But she couldn't get the words out convincingly.

"They came up too late to be properly interpreted," she added.

"They came up" was all Bob said.

CHAPTER
TWENTY-SEVEN

The dinner that marked the closing of the Carter Symposium was held in the main ballroom of the Waldorf on Park Avenue. More than a thousand men and women from science, medicine, the media and industries allied with the sciences were present. Religious and political dignitaries held cherished places on the three-tiered dais. It was a gathering of the nation's brain power, a tribute to the influential Marietta Carter.

After dinner there were brief speeches, all of them lauding Mrs. Carter as exemplary of enlightened capitalism and the great public good that women could achieve. Then came the climax of the evening, the presentation of the Eamon Carter Award for the outstanding contribution to science during the past year.

This year there was no doubt the award would go to Otis Cruikshank. Marietta Carter polled the judges and presented the decision to the Secretary of Health, Education and Welfare, who concluded his address with the announcement. The Eamon Carter Award for this year belonged to Dr. Otis Cruikshank!

Marietta Carter was first to rise to her feet in the standing ovation. A thousand men and women at more than a hundred tables followed. The applause was thunderous and continuous as Otis Cruikshank made his way from his place on the dais to the podium.

Newsmen and cameras burst into action to cover the presentation of the medal and the prize of ten thousand dollars. Flashbulbs flared as the Secretary and Mrs. Carter handed the medal and check to Otis Cruikshank.

Marietta Carter stepped to the microphone. "After your tremendously significant presentation this afternoon," she said, "I'm more sure now than ever that this award honors the Carter Foundation more than it honors you."

There was loud applause as Otis Cruikshank stepped to the microphone and made an effort to speak. His lips were dry. The check and the medal in his hands were suddenly burdens, not honors. He stared out at the distinguished audience.

Quiet had spread across the huge ballroom as the audience waited. Just as silence was about to turn to restlessness and concern, Otis Cruikshank spoke.

"I . . . I am very grateful for this award. I am sure there are many in this audience tonight who are more deserving of it than I. So I accept this in the name of those who dedicate themselves to pure science. I dedicate this award to those men and women who labor all their lives and never achieve such honors. They are the real heroes of our profession."

Edgar Woolsey jumped to his feet, calling out, "Bravo! Bravo!" as he applauded. "Beautiful! Just beautiful!"

Bob Niles and Carole Evans sat still and silent, disillusioned.

Photographers were crowding around Otis, who tried to indulge them by remaining at the podium. It was too painful for him to smile, but when they insisted, he did hold up the gold medal. The check was becoming a piece of wilted paper in his sweaty hand. Finally, Mrs. Carter intervened and the room began to clear.

When almost everyone had gone, Otis discovered that Marietta Carter and her public relations chief had arranged a taped interview with a woman who presided over an early-morning show on one of the national television networks.

He refused. There was a moment of shocked silence. No one, not even the President of the United States, ever refused her an interview. The fact that the woman reporter had stayed up past her early bedtime made Otis' breach of media manners even more gauche. Marietta Carter turned to Edgar Woolsey for help. Gently, but with a firm grip on Otis Cruikshank's arm, Woolsey edged the scientist to a corner.

"Otis, you have to! That's what it's all about. We need the publicity! This is your chance to make up for all the opportunities you've let slip by in the past."

"I can't ... not after this afternoon ..." Otis said in a whisper.

"Otis! Chances like this don't come along often!"

"I almost gave back the award. I should have. I'll never know why I didn't," Otis confessed.

"It's too late for that. Now, come back and do as the lady says. Answer her questions. And be ..." He searched for the proper word. "... Be cooperative."

Across the room, the crew had finished setting up their lights and arranging two chairs for the interview. Because he felt he had no choice, Otis Cruikshank walked over. He apologized to the interviewer and dropped into the chair the director pointed out to him.

After a glowing tribute to the Carter Foundation, to Otis for winning the award and to her own program for securing the first national network television interview with this important scientist, the interviewer began to ask her questions. Within the first thirty seconds it became obvious to Otis she had hardly the slightest idea of his subject matter and its significance. Her first question was "With the discovery of the Cruikshank Phenomenon, how soon can we expect a cure for cancer?"

It was futile to try to answer such a broad question and

impossible to explore the problem in the few minutes allowed him under the pressure of TV timing. Otis contented himself with a general statement that his experiment pointed science in a hopeful direction. That other men would no doubt be coming forth with additional discoveries. And that that might bring the day of a cancer cure somewhat closer.

The interviewer was disappointed. She had obviously expected a news beat—certainly something more startling, newsworthy and specific than Otis' vague answer. She interrupted the interview abruptly.

"Cut! Cut! Forget it! There isn't thirty seconds of usable footage in the whole *shmeer!*"

Marietta Carter and Edgar Woolsey tried to prevail on her to try a second take. But she was adamant. She stalked out, dragging her mink coat along the floor.

Edgar Woolsey glared at Otis Cruikshank.

"It's impossible to answer such questions in just seconds," Otis defended.

"You could have said something newsworthy," Edgar Woolsey rebuked him in an angry whisper. "She wasn't asking you to cover the whole field. Just to give her something she could use, something with scientific sex appeal."

"Of course!" Otis said angrily. Then his mood turned grim. "I could have said something newsworthy. I could have told her about those last four patients. That would have made them sit up and listen!"

Otis Cruikshank got up and walked out of the empty ballroom. He felt weary, defeated. He walked all the way back to the Plaza. There was something he must do. He dialed Bob Niles's room. But there was no answer.

Bob Niles had left the Waldorf and walked across town from Park Avenue to Fifth, then up to Fifty-ninth. There was a bar in the hotel on the corner. But it was not called a bar. It was called a cocktail lounge. He went in, dropped onto a stool and ordered a double bourbon on the rocks. He stirred the mixture with his forefinger until the ice had melted just a bit, frosting the glass and chilling the bourbon. Then he downed the liquid in one long swallow.

He hadn't done anything like that since the first year of his residency when he had assisted the Chief of Surgery and seen him botch a case so badly that it was a foregone conclusion the patient would linger and then die.

He had the same feeling tonight.

He ordered another double bourbon. He sipped this one slowly; he had a lot of thinking to do. There was Otis, of course. But there was Heather, too. And there was a profession—that prostituted goddess, Science.

Perhaps Otis had been wiser than he knew when he insisted Bob go to medical school. Now Bob had something to fall back on. He could resign from Trask. There had been offers just before he left New York, from men he'd worked with, to come into medical groups they were organizing. There were plenty of advantages. You performed a service people needed and they rewarded you handsomely. You were an honored, well-paid professional. Not a highly educated beggar who had to go hat in hand seeking funds to continue his work through next year.

If the pressures of research could corrupt an honorable man like Otis Cruikshank, then no one was safe.

He dropped a ten-dollar bill on the bar and didn't wait for change. He walked across Fifth Avenue and sat on one of the benches that faced the Plaza Hotel. Which one of those lighted windows was Otis Cruikshank's? Or was Otis still at the Waldorf accepting congratulations and giving interviews?

At that moment Otis Cruikshank was trying to call him, but the operator reported again, "Sorry, Dr. Niles doesn't answer, sir." Otis would have liked to explain his actions. The young man was disappointed, disillusioned. But if he had a chance to talk to Bob, Otis felt sure he would understand.

Carole would understand, too. If he could talk to her. He had tried her room. But Dr. Evans had left a do-not-disturb on her line. Not even for emergencies.

Otis Cruikshank was alone. Alone with a solid-gold medal and a check for ten thousand dollars. Tax-free, he reminded himself bitterly. Tomorrow he would endorse the check to Trask Institute. He wanted no part of it.

Otis chose not to call Edgar Woolsey, but if he had he would have gotten no answer. Edgar Woolsey was in Dr. Carole Evans' suite. She was dressed in her orange chiffon robe, and she was unbraiding her long black hair. As soon as he removed her glasses, Woolsey would be aroused beyond control.

Suddenly Carole said, "Please, Edgar, please go. I'm tired of listening to you talk about today's great triumph, the greatest public relations coup by any research institute in the country. In fact, I am tired of *you*."

"Carole . . . sweetheart . . ." Edgar Woolsey protested. He tried to embrace her. She avoided him. He attempted to remove her glasses. She pushed aside his hand.

"I mean what I said, Edgar. I'll never forgive you for all the chicanery you used to make Otis do what he did. I detest you! Is that clear?"

"Carole . . . darling," Woolsey protested. "Give me a chance to explain."

"Explain what? The way you badgered him into agreeing to make his presentation at the Carter Symposium? Your constant pounding away at him, about what it would mean to Trask. And then your last stroke of genius. That list of people who would have to be laid off if we didn't get the Carter grant!"

"How did you know about that?"

"The way you intended everyone to know. The Institute grapevine. Edgar, you are a quite contemptible individual," Carole Evans said. "You've corrupted a good, decent honorable man, and I will always hate you for that."

She started to cry. He drew back from her and slipped down onto the couch.

"That's the game," he said. "I didn't make the rules. I only follow them. No one knows the conniving, the high-class deceptions, the multitude of disgraceful things I have to do to keep Trask going. I have to fawn and wheedle and lie. It's my profession. The only difference between me and the rest of you is that I stand alone. No one shares my burdens. No one understands them."

Carole Evans looked up. She felt a sudden compassion for Edgar Woolsey.

"Can't you understand what you mean to me? The only moments of enjoyment I have are spent with you. I scheme to make them possible. Sometimes when I pass you in the hallways I want to seize you, embrace you, make love to you then and there. I won't let you go. I can't."

"I'm sorry, Edgar. It's over," she said firmly.

"Carole . . . darling . . . tonight, in the flush of anger, I know how you feel. But there'll be tomorrow. You need this as much as I do."

He waited for her to deny it, but she didn't. She had made up her mind.

Finally Edgar Woolsey left her suite. He paused in the quiet carpeted hallway, hoping she would call him back. Instead he heard the bolt being shot into place.

Dr. Robert Niles, feeling his two double bourbons, rose from the park bench and started across deserted Fifty-ninth Street. He glanced at his watch. It was past midnight, and their plane would leave Kennedy at seven fifty-five. That meant he had to be packed and ready to leave the hotel at seven.

He decided to take a later plane. That would give him time to contact his colleague and ask about a place in that medical group. And it would also give him an excuse not to fly back on the same plane as Otis Cruikshank.

CHAPTER

TWENTY-EIGHT

The plane was preparing to make a landing. Dr. Robert Niles was far less eager than he'd been on his return many months ago. Instead of the exciting anticipation of a reunion with Otis Cruikshank, there was the impending confrontation.

During the three-hour flight he considered a plan of action, finally deciding the only thing to do was seek a meeting with Otis tomorrow. In that meeting he would resign. He would explain everything to Heather later. Then she would have to make her decision. At moments he felt she surely would go with him. At other moments he was sure she would not. The Cruikshanks shared great love and loyalty.

The plane touched down. When it taxied up to the gate, he rose, got his hat and coat, and entered the long terminal corridor, following the signs to claim his bag.

He had just pulled his bag from the luggage slide when he heard a voice call out.

"Bob!" It was Heather. The very tone of her voice indicated her alarm.

She rushed into his arms and held him tightly. Then he looked into her eyes.

"Darling?"

"Something terrible happened," she said. "I know it.

Dad came home with the medal, the award and the promise of a huge grant from the Carter Foundation. But it was all wrong. He didn't want to talk about it. Then when you didn't come back with him ... Bob?"

"Let's go where we can talk," he said. "My place."

They had said very little on the way. He put up some coffee, made a pretense at unpacking and finally had to face it.

"He didn't tell you what happened?"

"He said he was too tired to talk. He refused lunch, shut himself in his den and spent the afternoon alone. Mother and I are terribly worried."

"It would be easier for me if he had told you."

"Told me what?" Heather demanded.

"He copped out. Cheated!"

"My father? I don't believe you! He'd never do anything like that."

"Heather, darling, listen to me," he pleaded. "I was there. I saw and heard it happen. A great man betrayed himself and then had to go on with the charade of accepting their praise and their prizes."

Heather shook her head. She could not accept it.

"Before I go on, I have to know one thing." Bob hesitated, then said, "If I decide it's my duty to make it public, I want to know what it'll do to us."

"I know what I ought to say," she admitted softly. "But if he did what you said, he's going to need me now. I can't desert him."

"Darling, *I* didn't do anything wrong. Neither did you. I don't want this to separate us."

She was silent for a moment. Then she said, "If you want to resign, I'll go with you. But if you do anything to hurt my father, I'll never forgive you."

"You're asking me to do what he did—withhold the truth."

"I'm asking you not to destroy my father!"

226

"Don't you understand I can't remain silent and let a lie circulate in the scientific world? You might as well know. The experiment didn't quite work the way everyone was led to believe."

"What do you mean?" she asked, suddenly frightened.

"Everything seemed to go perfectly, until the last four animals—and then it reversed itself. The transfer factor did not completely succeed. The last four suffered retrogression. Fatal retrogression. Your father did not mention them in his presentation."

Heather sank slowly down into the chair. Whatever her father had done suddenly seemed less important than what she had to know about herself. "They only *seemed* to be cured? But then they developed melanoma again?" She had to be sure of what he was telling her.

"Yes," Bob admitted.

"But why? How could that happen?"

"Until someone performs another experiment, we have only theories to go on," Bob explained. "Time alone may be the vital element. Or else there may be a limit to how often we can stimulate a weak immune system."

Heather wondered about the factor of time. "How would the three months in a rabbit correlate to time in a human being? I mean, taking into account the difference in life span. I mean . . . I don't know what I mean," she said finally, and turned away.

"We don't know the answers to those questions yet," he said. "But the way to find out is not to withhold what we already know. And that's what Otis did."

"Perhaps he had a reason," she insisted, but with less conviction than before. Her own sudden vulnerability had undermined her defense of her father.

"There's no good reason to do something like that. None!" Bob insisted.

She shook her head and hid her face in her hands. He tried to hold her, kiss her. But she avoided him. "Let me go!" she pleaded. "Please, let me go!"

"Not until you tell me this won't destroy us."

"Maybe we're already destroyed," she said strangely.

She slipped from his arms and left him. He called to her. She never looked back.

Otis Cruikshank was alone in his den, surrounded by the work of a lifetime, which rested in leather-bound volumes on the bookshelves that lined the walls. He had spent more than a dozen hours without speaking to anyone, without food, without any but his own thoughts for company. He had argued with himself, reached different conclusions a hundred times, yet always returned to one single conviction. Whatever anyone else might believe of him, he had unassailable proof. Heather Cruikshank was alive and well. He had snatched his daughter from the deadly disease and kept her healthy for more than two years. No one could dispute that. No one!

A few minutes before midnight, there was a knock on his den door. "Dad . . . ?"

Heather—and from the sound of that single syllable, in great torment. He unlocked the door. Her eyes were red from weeping. He took her hand. It was icy cold.

"Where have you been?"

"Walking," she said vaguely. "Just walking. . . ."

He brought her to the fire, sat her down and rubbed her frozen hands to warm them.

"Dad . . ." she started to say, but couldn't continue.

"You've seen Bob."

She nodded.

"He told you?"

"Everything."

"What did you tell him?"

"Nothing."

"Perhaps you should have."

"Without your permission?" Suddenly she reached out to embrace Otis. "Dad, he said some terrible things about you."

"That's only because he doesn't know all the facts. Don't blame him."

"What if he tells everyone? He said he must."

"He may not," Otis said. "So don't worry about it. Let me get you some hot tea. Then you go up and get some sleep."

Otis started to rise, but she couldn't let him go.

"Dad? What Bob said about those last four patients . . . *Is that true?*" she asked slowly.

Otis hesitated, "Yes, my dear, it is true." Then he understood. "Is that why you were walking? Thinking about that?"

She nodded.

"It may not mean anything at all," he tried to reassure her. "We know you're fine. We get proof of it every three months."

"But for how long, Dad? For how long?"

Bob Niles arrived at his lab in the morning. It was empty and deserted. Rosa Gregory and Ania had been assigned to other duties now that the Cruikshank protocol had been completed. Sanders had gone on a long-overdue vacation. There were no more animals to tend, no handlers needed to tend them.

It was too early to call Otis Cruikshank's office. Bob wandered from room to room. The operating room, where he had done so much surgery during the experiment. The necropsy room, where the results had been carefully autopsied and recorded. He handled the instruments—hair clippers, ether jar, hypos, clamps and scalpels—used while the experiment had been in full swing. In the animal rooms now there was no stirring or rustling when he opened the doors.

He entered the animal room where his prize patients had been kept. Where his hopes had once been so high. It was lined with empty cages. No more patients. No temporary successes. No failures.

He went back to his office determined to call Otis. But before he could pick up the phone to dial, it rang.

"Niles speaking."

"Robert!" he heard Otis Cruikshank's crisp voice. "I would appreciate it if you would come to my office at once."

Otis Cruikshank stood with his back to the large window so that the strong morning light obscured his expression.

"Now, then, Robert, you chose not to fly back with us yesterday," Otis began.

Bob didn't answer.

"More precisely, you chose not to come back on the same plane with *me*. Isn't that so?"

"Yes."

"I don't blame you. I said I would mention those last four patients, and you had every right to expect that I would. But I didn't. You might want to know why."

"There's no reason good enough to justify withholding a truth discovered in the course of an experiment. You taught me that yourself."

"So I did. But there is one flaw in your statement. You said that I withheld a truth. You don't know that."

Bob was silent.

"If you really want the truth, go to my desk and open that green canvas lab book."

On the title page in the familiar handwriting of Otis Cruikshank, Bob saw inscribed, *Treatment and Results in the Case of Melanoma of the Patient H.*

"You will notice that each entry bears a date. The log was kept daily. There is no retrospective looking back, and no predictions. This is simply a record of each procedure carried out in a course of treatment I devised."

"You actually treated a *human* patient?" Bob asked.

"Yes. I should have consulted medical doctors, but they would have refused. I was determined not to be stopped. I was determined not to see this patient suffer the usual fate, in the usual slow and painful way. Today, that patient is alive. And free of the damned thing! So before you judge me, read that ledger. Then reconsider what I said. Which of us has the truth?"

Bob Niles locked the door of his office and settled down to read Otis Cruikshank's journal.

The purpose of this experiment is to determine the effectiveness of transfer factor on a human melanoma patient before the patient's immune system has been overwhelmed and rendered incapable of mounting a strong resistance to malignant tumor.

Otis had detailed every step in the course of the disease of the anonymous patient, from the first sign, to the surgeon's prognosis that the illness was treatable but not curable, to the subsequent surgery and recurrence.

It was decided to intervene with the use of transfer factor specially cultured in a donor who could mount a strong resistance to the patient's melanoma cells.
For this purpose, the investigator selected himself.

So Otis Cruikshank had been a donor of transfer factor. Bob was so startled that he paused before turning the page.

Fortunately, since patient and investigator were of the same blood type, many of the problems that might have been created otherwise were obviated.

There followed the day-by-day record of each step Otis had taken, beginning with his request for the melanoma cells from Dr. Slade.
So that was why the Cleveland Clinic and UCLA had no record of shipping such cells to Trask, Bob realized.
He read on, detail after detail. There were entries every two weeks detailing the amount and manner in which the

patient had been given a dosage of transfer factor. The results of every periodic set of nuclear scans were also noted. With quotes from Slade's reports and Berger's findings.

The last entry in the journal read:

> The most recent report on the patient's condition was attested to by Dr. Berger and confirmed in consultation with Dr. Robert Niles. The patient has made a complete recovery. Which the doctors ascribe to spontaneous remission, being unaware of the treatment involved. We await the next checkup with great confidence.

Bob Niles closed the green canvas-covered journal. He was stunned by what he had read.

It had taken a great deal of courage for Otis Cruikshank to show him this document. It amounted to a confession of two crimes of considerable gravity: practicing medicine without a license, and unauthorized human experimentation. But there was no denying what Otis had said; a live and healthy human patient was the most important truth. How to reconcile this with the last four animal patients?

Perhaps there had been a discrepancy between Otis' human experiment and his laboratory model. Bob began to reread the journal, slowly, painstakingly. When he was through, hours later, both procedures seemed to be exactly the same.

Bob Niles was still pondering the problem when his phone rang. Still engrossed, he answered vaguely. "Niles. Yes?"

"He told me he gave you his journal," Heather said tensely.

"Yes," Bob admitted, wondering why she sounded so concerned. Then it came to him, and he dared to ask, "Heather, the patient he called 'H' ...?"

"Yes," she admitted in a low, strained voice. "But I insisted I should be the one to tell you. I'm sorry ... sorry ..." Her last word was lost in a sob.

"Sorry? Heather, listen to me—"

He heard the click as she hung up. He took only a moment to lock Otis' journal in his desk drawer and then he ran down the corridor, out of the lab building and toward the Cruikshank house.

But when he reached the house, her little red sports car was not in the driveway. He rang the bell and pounded on the door at the same time. Ellen answered. "I've been expecting her any minute," she said. "She's hours late now."

Bob raced all the way back to Trask House and got into his car, determined to find her. There was no sign of her, no sign of her car. He started for the Interstate. The dark road was empty at this time of night. He headed his car west, along the road that he and Heather had driven on their weekends. He pressed down hard on the accelerator.

More than an hour later he spied a dark shape off on the shoulder of the road. From its contour he could make out that it was a sports car. As he pulled closer he could see the color. Red. And he could see Heather slumped over the steering wheel, in tears.

He embraced her, lifted her out of the car and carried her to his own. She pressed against his chest, sobbing and unable to talk. After a while she seemed to quiet, and finally she fell asleep. She slept all the way home. Just past midnight, they pulled into the Cruikshank driveway.

Otis and Ellen were relieved when they came in the door. They kissed Heather and hugged her. Then, because they knew that to be alone with Bob would be the best thing for her, they said good night.

Once they were alone, she told him everything. How she had known from the first time she saw him what the danger was to her. She had tried to discourage him, to avoid him. Because she knew the temptation.

"But it was useless. I fell in love telling myself, The Cruikshank protocol will work and in the end I'll be able to tell him everything. That I was cured, just as those rabbits were cured. And that it was all right for us to be in love. But it didn't work, did it?"

"What if I say it doesn't matter to me?" Bob asked.

"It has to matter!" she insisted. "Because a month from now what happened to them could happen to me. Then you would hate me for having let you fall in love with me. For having deceived you and for having left you so early in our lives. I couldn't bear the thought of your hating me for the rest of your time."

He rose to embrace her. She was unyielding.

"You're making a lot of assumptions you have no right to make," he said.

"You're giving assurances you have no right to give," she countered. "Those four . . . those four . . ."

In a way that Otis Cruikshank had never intended, the treatment of his daughter and the Cruikshank protocol had come to be inseparable.

TWENTY-NINE

Bob had tried to sleep the few remaining hours of that night, but it was useless. The cold winter dawn found him walking along the river, where the shallow water had turned to jagged edges of ice. The earth under his feet was hard and uneven, cresting in little pockets where snow from a previous fall had melted, then frozen. The ice cracked under his boots.

He walked for miles reviewing in his mind Otis' journal and the Cruikshank protocol. He tried to think calmly, to remove from his mind his love for Heather. He had to investigate every possibility not emotionally but scientifically. Perhaps the place to start was at the beginning, with Heather's original nuclear scans.

Back at Trask, he called Dr. Cyril Berger. Since it was Sunday, he tried Berger's home. But the nuclearist was at the hospital. "I've been asked to review the case," Bob told him. "Don't attach any significance to it at all."

"If you have any doubt, have her come in for another scan immediately," Berger insisted.

"Perhaps we will, after I've completed my review."

Berger realized that in his anxiety he had revealed a highly confidential fact. "I guess you know now, the patient is a woman," he said apologetically.

"Yes."

"Do you know who?"

"Yes, I do," Bob acknowledged.

"Then you know how I felt confirming such a diagnosis on a girl so young and so lovely," Berger said. "But also how great it felt confirming a spontaneous remission. God! I'll never forget that day! Come to my lab as soon as you wish."

Bob Niles wasted no time. He walked through the doors of University Hospital that same afternoon.

With great care Berger traced the development of the case—the first body scans, her operation and finally those distressing symptoms of a brain disorder. Then Berger presented the brain scan. He pointed out the small bulge lodged in the angular gyrus of her temporal lobe.

Bob recalled something from his classes in neurology but was not quite certain. He made a note to call Professor Ferretti in New York.

Berger was now coming to the later scans, showing the regression of Heather's tumor. The nine scans covering the last twenty-seven months clearly showed a complete remission.

"Is it possible there was a misdiagnosis?" Bob asked.

"You mean this area could have been a blood clot? Or a focal encephalitis?"

"Exactly."

"Well," Berger had to admit, "with nuclear scans it's not always possible to distinguish one from the other. Even an angiogram couldn't be definitive. But you have to remember this patient's history. The evidence was overwhelmingly in favor of a diagnosis of malignant brain tumor."

"But it is possible . . . " Bob insisted.

"Anything is possible," Berger granted. "In this case, short of going in and doing a biopsy, no one could state positively what was there. She refused surgery. So we only had our educated guess to work with. Then she began to recover."

"So there was never a need to make a confirmed diagnosis."

"Fortunately," Berger said.

What few questions Bob had left he would ask Ferretti, the neurosurgeon in New York. He tried Ferretti at home; no answer. He tried the hospital; Ferretti had left.

Bob woke very early the next morning. It was not yet eight o'clock in New York. He went to the lab to review the notes he had made during his session with Berger. Then he waited impatiently to call New York.

Ferretti was just leaving his office to go up to surgery and scrub. At first he was puzzled. "Niles? Oh, yes—Bob Niles. Didn't you decide to skip practice and go off to do research? Wise decision. I never heard of a guinea pig suing anyone for malpractice. What can I do for you?"

Gingerly, keeping always within the context of a hypothetical experiment, Bob explained the case.

"I see," Ferretti kept saying. "Metastatic tumor . . . corticomedullary junction . . . angular gyrus of the temporal lobe. Some men would go in and try to remove it. I'm pretty conservative. I'd say no."

"That isn't involved," Bob said. "The question is this: Since there's a barrier that keeps the ordinary blood circulation from reaching the brain, is it possible that antibodies in the bloodstream could affect a metastatic brain tumor?"

"The presence of a tumor could affect the blood brain barrier, breaking it down. So the tumor could pick up antibodies in the patient's bloodstream."

This confirmed Otis' plan and his experiment with Heather.

"Do you think it's possible that transfer factor could cause a remission in a small metastatic brain tumor?" Bob finally asked.

"Possible?" Ferretti repeated. "I've been a neurosurgeon too long to rule out any possibility. I've even seen one case of a spontaneous remission of a metastatic brain tumor, back when I was a resident. But if you ask me if it's *proba-ble*, I'd have to say no."

"I see."

After Bob had hung up the phone, he was still wondering what Ferretti would have said if he had been free to tell him all the facts in the case. Still, Ferretti had said the presence of Heather's tumor did make it possible for her blood supply to reach it. The transfer factor could have stimulated her immune system to produce lymphocytes which could have had an effect.

That much had been proved to his satisfaction, but it was not enough. He picked up the journal again and began to study it. Otis' work seemed unassailable.

He hauled out his own notes on the protocol. Perhaps Otis was right—something had been done in those last few weeks that departed from the model of the experiment.

As he reviewed the procedures, one fact struck him. Perhaps a small discrepancy between Otis' original experiment and his protocol.

The protocol called for testing the tumor specificity of the lymphocytes bred in the donor rabbits. Bob had carried out that test and proved the fact beyond any question. He went back to review Otis' journal. He could find no such entry. If Otis had made the test, he'd forgotten to record it. Not likely for a scientist as meticulous at Otis Cruikshank. For some reason, Otis had not found it necessary to make such a test.

He would have to ask him about that.

THIRTY

"Well, have you gone through my journal?" Otis Cruikshank asked—not the concerned father, but the scientist now.

"Three times."

"Did you correlate it with the model for the experiment?"

"Yes, sir."

"Your conclusions?" Otis demanded.

"The model for the experiment seems unassailable. But there *is* one point of difference."

"And that is?"

"In the protocol, we tested the donors' lymphocytes for melanoma specificity. You didn't do that when you processed your own transfer factor."

Otis was startled. "Are you sure?"

"It's not in here."

He dropped the journal onto Otis' desk. Otis seized it and hastily opened to the early pages. Very carefully, he read his detailed account of the first time he'd drawn off his blood, submitted samples of it to the Coulter counter and received a gratifyingly high white-cell count, and the step-by-step procedure thereafter through which he had extracted the transfer factor.

He reread those paragraphs. Robert Niles was right.

There was no record of his testing for melanoma specificity. Slowly he closed the journal.

He stared toward the window, trying to recall that anxious night in his lab almost three years ago, when he had secretly begun to carry out a procedure he knew to be illegal. He remembered all that vividly. Yet he had no clear recollection of having tested his lymphocytes on the melanoma cells. Still, he must have! Or had he intended to and been interrupted in his covert activity by someone? That cleaning woman, no doubt. And when he resumed, had he omitted that step in the process by error? It wouldn't have mattered. After all, he had exhibited a classic reaction to Heather's melanoma cells: big, red, splotchy erythema and a high titer level. All those facts he remembered quite clearly. Yet he had no recall of the specificity test.

"If I were called into a courtroom and put under oath, I couldn't swear I'd done it. But I couldn't say I hadn't. I simply do not remember."

"Would you mind if I did that test now?"

"What would it prove? We already know Heather is well."

The phone rang. It was Stanford University, inviting Otis to repeat his presentation there. He tried to say no, but the caller was persistent. Finally he promised to consider it and call back within the week.

"The ninth call in the last four days," Otis said. "A year ago there wasn't one call in four months."

Bob reiterated, "May I carry out that test?"

"Of course," Otis agreed.

At two-thirty in the afternoon, Otis Cruikshank arrived at Bob Niles's lab, where Bob drew some of his blood and submitted it to the Coulter counter. Otis' titer level proved very high indeed.

Bob sealed the blood bag and processed it in the centrifuge to extract the white cells. He prepared several petri dishes with a buffered nutrient and implanted several million white cells in each. Then he placed the dishes in a climate-controlled cabinet to keep them at normal human body temperature of 37 degrees centrigrade.

He prepared ten other petri dishes with nutrient. He deposited a layer of live melanoma cells in each and placed those dishes in a separate area of the controlled cabinet.

At the end of two days he examined them under his microscope. Both the melanoma cells and the lymphocytes were thriving.

Bob measured out six aliquots of cultured lymphocytes in dosages of one million cells, five million, fifty million, one hundred million, one billion and five billion cells. He placed the varying aliquots into six of the dishes containing melanoma cells. He did not treat the last four, which would serve as controls.

More than a scientific truth would be determined in the 37-degree atmosphere where the lymphocytes and the melanoma cells should begin interacting with each other.

The outcome would affect his career and his own life, as it would affect Otis Cruikshank's.

Perhaps even more.

By the end of the first day, Bob Niles could observe no changes in those petri dishes. Nor on the second day. The melanoma cells in the lymphocyte-treated dishes were still no less vital than those in the control dishes.

On the third day, Bob's anxiety began to dominate him. For there was still no change. One fact was becoming startlingly clear: There was no evidence of cytotoxicity. Otis Cruikshank's lymphocytes had no destructive effect on Heather's melanoma cells!

He debated giving the experiment another twenty-four hours, but knew it would be only an excuse to avoid confronting Otis with his result. He had to make the call.

"Sir, can you come down to my lab as soon as possible?"

He waited for almost an hour. When Otis came in, he said, "I never thought we'd be in this position. Woolsey

241

has just spent half the morning discussing the grants we've already been offered and the ones he thinks we will get by simply applying. All three of your protocols can be funded now, Robert."

When Bob did not respond, Otis became more sober. "Now, then?" he asked.

"Would you take a look at this?"

Otis slipped onto the stool and stared through the microscope at the brightly illuminated specimen. "What are the components?"

"Layer of cultured melanoma cells."

"Of course, and quite thriving," Otis said.

"An aliquot of a hundred million of your lymphocytes."

Otis was silent for a moment. "Perhaps it takes a stronger aliquot."

Bob substituted one specimen for another. "One billion lymphocytes added."

Otis stared at the evidence, magnified several thousand times.

"And this one," Bob said. "Five billion lymphocytes added."

Otis examined the last of the specimens. When he drew back from the microscope, his lean face was pale and concerned.

"How many days?"

"Three."

"Three days," Otis said grimly. "In three days there should have been some effect. I can't understand it."

"There's only one conclusion, sir," Bob said, with great consideration for Otis' feelings. "The assumption that your transfer factor accomplished Heather's cure must be incorrect."

"That's impossible!" Otis protested. "It worked, damn it! The cure worked!"

He turned on Bob. "You know as well as I do that things work clinically and no one can explain why. Aspirin? How does that work? Does anyone know? But it does

242

work. And who knows why children inoculated against tuberculosis have a lower incidence of leukemia? But it's a fact! There are phenomena in science that simply *are*. They *work*. Transfer factor is one of those. We *know* it works. We just don't know *how* or *why*."

Bob did not dispute the old man. Even a man as devoted to science and as self-critical as Otis Cruikshank had moments when he was a human being and a father before all else.

Finally Otis calmed. He said, "Are you accepting what Slade and Berger believe—that Heather had a spontaneous remission?"

"Maybe no remission was necessary. The diagnosis was never confirmed by surgery."

"She wouldn't let them," Otis said.

"The diagnosis could have been wrong. Berger admits it's possible it could have been a blood clot, which could have dissolved by itself."

"Melanomas do metastasize to the brain. And the position of the damned thing . . . !" Otis protested.

"It had all the indications of a metastatic tumor, true," Bob conceded. "But we know only one thing for sure. If it *was* melanoma, your transfer factor *didn't* cure her."

Otis felt compelled to take one last look through the microscope.

"Impossible . . . absolutely impossible. I exhibited such a strong reaction. Classical erythema. You should have seen it!"

He held out his arm. He pulled back the sleeve of his laboratory coat and turned to exhibit his bare arm.

"Right there! Large, red, angry. And then my white blood count! Damn it, don't tell me my white-cell production wasn't caused by that massive injection of her melanoma cells!"

"Could it have been due to some other incompatibility?"

"We're the same blood type."

"That accounts for the red cells. But your white cells

could have been incompatible. Did you test your leucocyte antigen types?"

"No need to," Otis explained. "I was able to accept her blood in a transfusion."

"When?" Bob asked, startled. He had never heard this before.

"Twelve, no, thirteen years ago. In Vienna. We were at a large international meeting—"

Bob interrupted, "Thirteen years ago? Heather wouldn't have been more than ten or eleven. They couldn't take enough blood from a child to make a transfusion worthwhile."

"I'm afraid in this instance it was done for the benefit of the donor. I'd developed a strep throat. Then the infection moved into my bloodstream, and they decided to transfuse me. Ellen and some of my colleagues who were type O were going to donate blood. Heather is type O and she wanted to help out too. She insisted. She was quite upset. It was shortly after Duncan had died. So to her being sick meant dying. She wanted to save me. When I began to recover, Heather felt she'd done it. Of course her blood didn't help, but obviously there was no white-cell incompatibility between us."

"I see," Bob said, nodding thoughtfully.

"I must get back to my office," Otis said. "Woolsey has been insisting on seeing me again."

Otis was gone. Bob sat in his lab pondering what had just happened. For some reason not scientific but emotional, the old man had completely blocked out Bob's findings. He refused to acknowledge that his injections of transfer factor had had no part in Heather's remission.

But the meeting had produced one fact which Bob Niles had to pursue to its end.

THIRTY-ONE

When he rang the bell at the Cruikshank home, Ellen answered. Tremendous concern was evident in her face.

"Heather won't see you. She feels too guilty. We aren't used to deception in this family. So we're not very good at it, I'm afraid."

"It's you I want to see," Bob said.

"Me? What about?"

"Vienna."

"Vienna?" She gestured Bob to the living room. "Now, then, what about Vienna?" she asked, quite puzzled.

"Did Heather really give her father a blood transfusion when she was only eleven years old?"

"It isn't at all what you think. The doctor refused, but she insisted. She grew quite hysterical. Fortunately, the doctor was an understanding man. When I explained about Duncan, he said he could do something about that. He would transfuse a small amount of her blood—enough to satisfy Heather and resolve her fears."

"Do you remember if anything happened to Otis immediately after Heather's transfusion?" Bob asked. "I don't mean days later; I mean minutes, an hour later."

"He'd been running such a fever for days that he was in and out of coma—"

"But did his temperature shoot up even higher after her transfusion?" Bob demanded.

Ellen paused, thinking back.

"Please try to remember. It could be highly significant," Bob insisted.

"Come to think of it, Heather wanted to see him right after, but the doctor said no because Otis' fever had grown worse."

"So there *was* a reaction. High fever. Chills?"

"Yes. What does—"

He interrupted her. "Now I do want to see Heather. I *have* to see her!"

He started from the room. Ellen called after him, "Please don't! She's still very upset!"

But Bob was already at the top of the stairs.

Heather was lying on her side, dozing. He moved to the bed and spoke softly. "Heather . . ."

She turned suddenly, looked up, then turned away.

"You don't have to talk to me," he said. "I just came to take a blood sample."

"Why?" she asked, without turning back. "You don't have to worry anymore. I won't marry. I won't have any children. Just leave me alone."

"Heather, please? What if I use it to help *us*?"

Slowly she turned back to look up at him.

"I must prove something to your father. And if I do, then it could change everything for us," he said gently.

She hesitated. Then finally she extended her arm to him.

Edgar Woolsey leaned back in his huge leather desk chair, smiling broadly. "The cover, Otis. Did you hear me? The cover of *Time* magazine!"

"You know how I feel about publicizing scientific work as if it were a cheap movie or a football star," Cruikshank protested.

"Otis, only the world's most important people and historic events get on the cover of *Time*. I'll bet you never thought, in your wildest dreams, you'd make it."

"I'm not so sure I'll make it now."

246

For the first time Woolsey's exuberance began to wilt and turn to impatience. He was growing tired of Otis' reluctance.

"Exactly what does that mean?"

"It means I'd like to consider it before I agree."

"But I've already promised *Time* an interview with you. They're waiting for my call. They've got an artist ready to come do your portrait for the cover. And a whole staff waiting to fly out and get your own personal version. The Science Editor himself is coming to supervise it all. You *can't* say *no!*"

Otis remained silent.

"Otis?"

"I said I'd like to think about it." He turned and started for the door.

"Otis!"

Otis Cruikshank turned to face Edgar Woolsey.

"This may not mean much to you, Otis. But it's the most important triumph of my career. For *my* sake, I would like you to give this favorable consideration." Then, with a note of warning in his voice, he added, "And of course, there are the benefits to be derived by Trask."

"Of course," Otis repeated ironically. "Benefits for Trask."

"Let me make that call. *Now!*" Woolsey insisted.

Otis glared at him, unrelenting. Woolsey pretended he had suddenly remembered something.

"Oh, by the way, Otis . . . I've been meaning to show you this."

He reached into his bottom desk drawer and took out a folder bulging with papers. He flipped through them slowly enough to allow Otis to identify them. They were reports from the Security Department of Trask Institute. Each contained the date and the time of one of his biweekly lab sessions when he had prepared the transfer factor for Heather's injections. One even bore reference to a white lab towel. Otis was shocked. He stared at the folder. He stared at Edgar Woolsey, who stared back, unrelenting.

"May I make that call, Otis? Now?"

Otis finally nodded—sadly, almost imperceptibly.

"Good," Woolsey said. Then he added, "Here, take this. Burn it."

He handed Otis Cruikshank the file.

Bob Niles hovered over the centrifuge until it stopped. He took the blood bag from the machine and pipetted the pure white-cell residue into a test tube. He added sufficient saline and stored it in the refrigerator.

He called Otis' office, but the scientist had asked not to be disturbed. It might be several hours, his secretary said.

"Tell him it's urgent," Bob added before he hung up.

He decided to get some coffee. The staff cafeteria was almost empty, but in the far corner, alone at a table, sat Carole Evans. He brought his steaming cup to her table.

"Mind if I join you?"

"No."

He sat down.

"Did you hear?" she asked.

"What?"

"*Time* is putting Otis on the cover. They're going to title it, 'The Big Breakthrough.' "

"I'm surprised Otis would involve himself in that sort of thing," Bob said.

"Why not?" Carole defended. "We need it. Not just Trask, but the whole scientific community. The public wants results for all those millions of dollars that go to cancer research. Well, this is a result! So what if he didn't mention those last four animals? Who knows what they mean? He did mimic the clinical situation and bring about some cures, some regressions of symptoms. . . ."

Determined as it had started out, her defense crumbled. Her eyes suddenly filled with tears. "Anyone but Otis. Anyone!" she said.

Bob looked at her sympathetically. "What are you going to do?" he asked.

"I have an offer in California to head up oncology research. I've decided to accept."

"You've always wanted to be a chief."

"Yes." Carole smiled through her tears. "Now I'll really be Mother Superior."

He reached across and took her hand to comfort her.

"I'll never forget you, Bob," she said softly. "But it wouldn't have come to anything."

"I know," he said.

"Are you going to leave? If you want to continue with research, I could find a place for you out there."

"I haven't decided yet what I'll do," Bob said.

"You'll *have* to leave. Woolsey won't want anyone around to trouble Otis' conscience." Suddenly she asked bitterly, "Why would Otis do it?"

"Because he truly believes those last four were a mistake, an aberration. And he thinks he had good reason for believing."

"What reason?"

"Good reason" was all Bob would say.

Bob had been in his lab an hour when he heard a knock at the door. Otis entered.

"I hear you've been trying to see me. 'Urgently,'" he said. "What is it, Robert?"

Bob went to the refrigerator and lifted the test tube out of the rack. He held it up. The milky solution filled half the tube. "White cells in solution. Heather's."

Otis stared at the test tube, then at Bob. "If you think it can prove anything, of course."

He slipped his arm out of his lab coat and rolled up his shirt sleeve. Bob prepared the hypodermic, washed Otis' forearm with alcohol and inserted the needle.

"I know what you're thinking," Otis said.

"It won't do any good to speculate now."

"No," Otis said grimly. "I guess we'll know soon enough."

That afternoon, Edgar Woolsey sat in Otis Cruikshank's office, suggesting ideas and phrases Otis might use in the interview that later would read well in *Time*. But while Woolsey talked, Otis concentrated on the spot on his arm where Bob Niles had injected that solution of Heather's white cells. There was no redness, no swelling, though it was still too early to expect any reaction.

Several times he examined it during the evening. Nothing. The next morning he had no need to look. There was an itching. By the time he reached Bob's lab, the spot surrounding the puncture was red and swollen as well.

Without a word, Otis pushed back his shirt sleeve and held out his arm for Bob to see. "I wasn't reacting to her melanoma but to her white cells," Otis admitted.

"It has all the characteristics of a melanoma reaction. You had good reason to assume it was."

"I must have been sensitized to her white cells years ago when I received that token transfusion from her."

"You reacted even then," Bob said.

"I did?" Otis asked, surprised. "I don't remember."

"How could you? You weren't fully conscious most of the time. But Ellen said you had chills and fever. A typical anaphylactic white-cell incompatibility."

Otis was silent until he finally admitted, "No, it couldn't have been my transfer factor that cured her."

"Not with the evidence we have now."

"And if I remove her 'cure' from my considerations, then those last four animals take on considerable significance; considerable. . . . I'll need some time alone, Robert. Yes, I'll need some time," he said.

As he turned to go, Bob thought that suddenly Otis looked old. Very old. Otis walked out slowly, weighed down by the burden of this shattering knowledge he had to ponder.

The cocktail party Woolsey had planned for the *Time* delegation had been in full swing for more than an hour. Edgar Woolsey was being his most charming self. The Science Editor was trying to interview Otis Cruikshank at the same time the artist was sketching him.

"He's the best there is, Dr. Cruikshank," the interviewer confided about the artist. "He's done De Gaulle, Muhammad Ali, Brezhnev, Jane Fonda . . ."

Otis held still for as long as he could, then said simply, "Please, could we stop now?"

The Science Editor gave a slight shake of the head to the artist, who backed away without concealing annoyance.

"Well, now," Woolsey took over like a master of ceremonies. "How shall we do this? One at a time or a free-for-all?"

"Why don't we just fire away and see what comes up?" the editor suggested.

"Good, good," Woolsey agreed. "Okay, Otis?"

"Of course, yes, let's just 'fire away,' " Otis said grimly.

Those on the Trask staff who had been invited to attend stepped back from the center of the room as the *Time* contingent gathered around Otis Cruikshank.

Bob Niles and Carole Evans glanced at each other, silently agreeing to slip out and leave as soon as a graceful opportunity arose.

The Science Editor opened the proceedings. "We're going to ask a lot of questions that may seem amateurish and even foolish to a man of your stature, Dr. Cruikshank. But after all, we're dealing with a readership which our demographic studies reveal contains as many housewives as executives. So we have to use terms and images that the average lay person can understand. I hope you'll forgive us some of our questions."

"May *I* suggest a question?" Otis asked.

"By all means!" the Science Editor agreed quickly.

"I should think the first question would be, Did the experiment succeed?"

"Of course," the Science Editor said, thinking it best to humor a brilliant man like Cruikshank. "Well, *did* it succeed?"

"*We honestly don't know,*" Otis said in a firm voice.

For a moment there was a sense of quiet amusement. The old scientist was having his little joke, no doubt, the editor thought. But Otis was not joking. The Science Editor's face lost its anticipatory smile. He turned to Edgar Woolsey, who had paled markedly. His eyes were fixed on Otis with a hostile glare.

"Otis, what is the meaning of this?"

Otis Cruikshank did not answer Edgar Woolsey. Instead, he turned to the group from *Time*. "Please get this down accurately," he said, "because I'm not sure I'm up to repeating it.

"Recently I presented a paper at the Carter Foundation Symposium dealing with the use of transfer factor in animals as a possible cure for one form of cancer. At that time I felt quite sure of my results.

"However, since that time I have good reason to believe that I failed to evaluate those results properly. So I am now forced to the conclusion that my interpretation of what has come to be known as the Cruikshank Phenomenon may well be totally in error.

"There were some encouraging results, but there is no cure yet. It is quite a long way off. Unintentionally, I have served to mislead the public. And my colleagues. I beg my friends in the scientific community to accept this statement of retraction with my sincere apologies.

"As to the Carter Foundation, I am returning the award and the prize which they were kind enough to bestow, but which I do not deserve."

Without another word, despite the avalanche of questions, Otis Cruikshank walked out of the room.

At the end of the day, Otis asked Bob to stop by his office. The room was growing dark in the early winter dusk.

"I've been thinking about everything that happened," he said. "About Heather. The protocol. The results. So close to the achievement of the dream, only to be frustrated by those last four animals. It isn't the first time I've had work go sour."

Bob asked, "Did it really go sour? If we discovered that transfer factor can at least help in the early clinical stages, that's important. And if we discovered that it may not work forever, that too is important. It was a landmark experiment. Yielding significant results. Not conclusive, but significant."

"Exactly!" Otis seized on it, "Then why, Robert? Why my need for the *conclusive* result, the *perfect* result? Why did I eliminate those four animals from my consideration?

"Vanity? The insecurity of a man moving from middle age into old age? Or the professional loneliness that comes when a man gradually finds himself uninvited by his colleagues? Isolated?

"Or should I absolve myself by saying, I did it not selfishly but for the benefit of Trask. For those men and women who depend on me. I rescued Abner Gottlieb a second time. Yes, I could have told myself all that. Except for one thing.

"I have resisted those pressures in the past. You might say, I have mounted my own immunity to them. Then why did I succumb this time?

"I've thought about that ever since that charade of an interview this afternoon. And now I know why. Because there was *one* pressure to which I was *not* immune.

"For years I've been pounding away at you young men,

253

Never desire the result so much that it warps your judgment. Still, I allowed that to happen to me."

Otis Cruikshank turned to face Bob Niles.

"The model for my experiment duplicated precisely what I did for Heather, didn't it?"

"Yes."

"Then suppose instead of white albino rabbits, those last four had been human beings. Suppose *one* of those last four were *Heather*. . . ."

Bob didn't answer.

"Don't you see, lad? To give them a place in my conclusions, to say that they proved the real truth would have meant that one day, perhaps one day soon, the same would happen to Heather. I couldn't accept that. I had to believe I'd found the cure for her. And I desperately had to prove it."

He sank into a nearby chair. "Now that we know her remission was spontaneous, I am relieved of that responsibility."

He was silent for a moment. Then he smiled ironically. "You know the real Cruikshank Phenomenon? What I discovered about myself. No matter the pressures, emotional or administrative: if I could refuse to acknowledge a scientific fact, then I am too old or too weak to fulfill the responsibility of this position any longer."

"You can't just quit," Bob protested.

"I *have* just quit," Otis said, his face lean and drawn, betraying his torment. "I leave all this to younger men. More aggressive men. To fight the institutional battles and the financial wars. To smile and fawn and get their pictures into the newspapers and on television, so they can attract huge grants and endowments.

"If I'm of any value, it is not in offices with large polished desks, but in laboratories—those stinking, messy places, where every once in a great while a little truth emerges. I never should have left there.

"You will find a letter on my desk, Robert."

Bob moved to the desk and turned on the lamp. There was a single sheet of stationery in the center of the otherwise clean desktop. It was Otis Cruikshank's resignation.

"Does Woolsey know?"

"It doesn't matter," Otis said. "Edgar Woolsey may be affected by this. But he is not involved in it. Administrators have their place. But it is not in the laboratory."

"Is there anything I can do?"

"Yes," Otis said thoughtfully.

"What?" Bob asked eagerly.

"Don't blame yourself. It would all have come out eventually. When some other investigator tried to duplicate the experiment. It's better they start out knowing the whole truth. Then I hope they'll carry on from there. So you've saved many men months of research, millions of dollars of grants. You've done your part, Robert. Done it well. Never blame yourself."

Then Otis added gently, "And never blame Heather. She wasn't intending to deceive you, only to protect me. I never should have imposed that conflict on her."

The meeting was over. Bob turned to stare across the dimly lit room.

"Don't leave us." Realizing he might have been misunderstood, Otis added, "The world of research, I mean. I know I was the one who insisted on your getting your medical degree to have something to fall back on. Well, now I'm asking, Don't fall back. We need young men who can resist the pressures and the temptations."

Dr. Robert Niles stepped out between the high bronze doors of the Administration Building of Trask Institute. The wind was penetratingly cold. The first flakes of a new snowfall were floating down. He reached out to catch some on his outstretched palm. They melted there. Snow would have special significance for him for the rest of his life.

He pulled up his coat collar and started swiftly across the campus toward the Cruikshank house.

When Heather refused to see him, he insisted. When she fought against listening to him, he explained. The results of the experiment had nothing to do with her. The fate of the last four did not forecast her fate. She could banish that concern from her mind forever. It was not certain she had had a recurrence of the melanoma. And if she had, then hers had been a complete spontaneous remission.

Heather finally turned toward him.

"And if it was?" she said. "I've read enough to know it's no guarantee. It could happen again, a year from now—five years, ten."

"Or never!"

"But it could, it could."

He embraced her, held her.

"Then I'll take the ten years. Or the five. Or even the one. As much time as we are given. I want you to marry me. But before you say yes, remember, it could be for a lifetime, too."

She pulled him closer. He could feel her warm tears against his cheek. But this time her tears were like a soft spring rain. Gentle and promising.